JENNIFER WILCK

The Perfect Deception

THE PERFECT MATCH BOOK 3

To all the smart girls out there

—especially my two—

always let your brilliance shine.

Other Books by Jennifer Wilck

Scarred Hearts Series
A Restless Heart
Unlock My Heart
A Heart Restrained

Stand Alone Romance Novels
In The Moment
A Heart of Little Faith

Harlequin Special Edition:
Holidays, Heart & Chutzpah
Home for the Challah Days
Matzah Ball Blues
Deadlines, Donuts & Dreidels

Harlequin The Fortunes of Texas:
Fortune's Secret Children Book 5
Fortune's Holiday Surprise

The Perfect Match Series
The Perfect Match
The Perfect Secret

CHAPTER ONE

After reading the email from his father, Adam dropped his head in his hands and massaged his temples. Freezing rain pattered against the window of his office, the sound of it making his head pound. Another deadline missed? This made the third time that a case he was working on was tanked due to misfiling a motion or missing a deadline. How the hell had this happened? His stomach turned at the tone of his father's email. He had to fix this. Now. As he walked the long hallway to his father's corner office, he glanced at his friends and co-workers out of the corner of his eye. None of them seemed to have this problem, or did they? Outside his father's office, he paused to draw a slow, steady breath. He hadn't missed the deadline. His paperwork was complete. It wasn't his fault. His father would have to believe him.

With a nod to his father's secretary, Diane, he knocked on the cherry wood door. He heard a muffled "come in," and he entered. His father didn't look up, so Adam sat in the black leather executive side chair across from his father's massive mahogany desk, crossed his arms, and waited to be acknowledged while staring at his father's shock of thick, white hair. He'd spent countless hours of his life staring at that proud head. The scratch of the fountain pen on the lined legal pad grated against his eardrums, but he refrained from interrupting him, even if he suspected the writing was a stalling tactic. It usually was. Noah Mandel was the best corporate lawyer in the state of New Jersey, and had forged his reputation carefully. Adam knew better than to mess with him.

From the time Adam was seven years old and his mother walked out, his father had made it clear that work came above all else. When Noah's wife left, she'd taken whatever affection he'd possessed. Adam learned early on that attachments to people, even those related to him, could be fleeting and only caused pain. Maintain control, protect your reputation and never let anyone get too close.

Finally, his father laid his pen on the desk and fixed his hawk-like gaze on his son. That stare still made Adam flinch, even at twenty-nine years old, but he resisted the urge and maintained his outwardly smooth façade. His father hated signs of weakness, perceived or otherwise. The two men remained silent, until his father spoke.

"We have a problem."

"We?" Adam asked.

"Don't get cocky."

"I didn't miss the deadline."

Another silence greeted that statement. "That's what you said last time, and the time before that." His father slid the letter from the court across his desk. "This letter says otherwise."

Adam frowned as he skimmed the letter. His gut tightened. The deadline to file the responsive pleading had been last Monday at midnight. He'd given his paralegal, Ashley, all the material she needed to file, had seen it in her possession and left the office. But this letter from the adversary stated the court had never received it. Therefore, their adversary was filing a default, requesting the court to issue an order that they won the case. In other words, Adam's client lost. "I have no idea what happened, Dad. I gave her the motion and told her to file it. Did anyone ask her about it?"

"Yes, Ashley says you never gave her the final documentation."

"That's insane. I gave her everything she needed in a manila envelope for her to mail."

"Did you see her mail it?"

"No, I left to go out with some people from work."

"So you were drinking." His father's eyebrows raised in disapproval.

"I had two beers. I wasn't drunk. I never have more than that when we go out. And that was after I gave her the materials." His reputation was too important to him, and too essential for his career, to ever lose control. Two beers with co-workers was his max.

"I'm not accusing you of drinking on the job. No one has ever smelled alcohol on your breath."

Adam refrained from cringing at the comment.

"But your eagerness to go out and party made you sloppy. Again."

One time. He'd rushed through an assignment for a case one time two years ago and his father never let him forget about it. He'd been meticulous since then, but his father didn't care. "No, Dad, I wasn't sloppy. I made sure everything was in order before I left."

"So what happened?" His father leaned forward, his gaze piercing.

Adam gripped the armrests until his fingers ached. "I have no idea." Why wasn't his father interrogating Ashley?

"So you don't remember? Now you're blacking out when you drink?" His father glared at him. "I thought you said you only had two beers."

"I did. Why isn't Ashley here being questioned?"

"Because I've already talked to her and she swears you never gave her anything to file. Between missing this deadline on the motion, messing up the deadline for filing that initial complaint on the Bradley case, and your sloppiness two years ago, you're proving that your head isn't in this game."

"Dad, the Hyde case was two years ago and the Bradley case was a misunderstanding." The excuse sounded lame to his ears, but he wasn't going to give away any more information. Not until he figured out why his cases were suddenly being called into question. "I've been on top of things since then, I swear. Maybe something is fishy with Ashley. She's been acting odd around me lately. We should be looking into her and why she's fabricating this story."

"I didn't raise a son to slough off blame to someone else. This firm has our name on it. That means the buck stops with me. And you. It's dishonorable to try to blame someone else for your mistakes. Do you have proof that you gave her the motion? You didn't have one with the Bradley case, didn't you learn your lesson this time? And why, if you were so concerned about doing your job correctly, would you have left before the filing was completed? You don't need me to answer that question for you, do you?"

Adam flexed his fingers as he waited for the barrage of questions to stop. "I'm sure there was someone around who saw me give her the file, Dad. As for leaving before she finished filing, since when do I have to micromanage a paralegal?"

His father held up a hand. "Adam, that's enough. Our name is on the door. This is my firm. You have a standard to live up to, one that you are failing at, at the moment. I'm not going to warn you again."

Adam's eyelid twitched, and he rose and walked toward the door.

"Oh, and Adam? I know you're working toward that promotion to junior partner, but with this lingering over your head..."

Adam gripped the doorknob, willing his tongue to listen to his brain and remain silent. No one who argued with his father ever won.

Dina pulled her car out onto the busy Morristown street, her latest pile of library books on the seat beside her. The best part of being a librarian was her access to books—thousands and thousands of vellum-smelling, page-crackling books. She smiled as she came to a traffic light. Shabbat services tonight followed by a weekend of reading. It was just what she wanted to do on the coldest weekend of the year.

As she left the town proper and headed into the outskirts, she drove over one of the many huge potholes the county had yet to fix. Her car continued to bump after she'd passed it and she pulled over onto the shoulder. A freezing drizzle was falling and she hugged her coat tighter around her. *Great, just what my frizzy hair needs*, she thought as she bent down to look at the tire. Flat.

She popped the trunk and rooted around for the jack. With her warning lights flashing, she positioned the jack behind the rear wheel and began pumping, watching the car rise. She rubbed her chilled hands together before trying to remove the spare from its compartment. Headlights lit her view of her trunk and she turned as a car pulled up behind her. A man got out of the car and she fingered her cellphone in her pocket. At rush hour, there were plenty of other cars on the road, but she backed up a little and reached for a crowbar, also in the trunk.

"You look like you could use some help," the man said as he approached. He wore a wool overcoat, which flapped open, revealing a dark suit and a pressed blue shirt. His hands were stuffed in his pockets. The icy drizzle speckled his shoulders and his tawny hair with a silver halo. Moss green eyes glowed in the dim light from the passing cars. He reminded her of a mountain lion.

"Nope, I'm fine, thanks."

"Are you sure? It's freezing out here. I can have you back on the road in a few minutes." He was a head taller than she was, and he smelled like cloves. Despite his unneeded assistance, Dina had to fight the warm feeling of home his smell suggested.

"Fifty percent of women know how to change their tires, and I'm one of them." Dina picked up the crow bar, preparing to change the tire herself.

He backed away, hands up, the vein in his neck pulsing. "I was just trying to help. Never mind. I seriously cannot win with women," he muttered.

She swallowed. Maybe she'd been too harsh. Before she could soften her tone, or ask him what he was talking about, a police car pulled up and rolled down the driver side window. "Ma'am, is everything okay? Sir, is there a problem?"

"I'm fine, but thanks. It's just a flat," she said to the officer.

"Sir?"

He grinned. "Nothing, officer, I was just offering to help her change her tire."

The officer nodded, but turned to Dina anyway. "Ma'am, do you need assistance?"

"I'm almost done." Why did no one believe she could do this?

"Are you sure?"

"Officer, I really am fine and he was just trying to help me."

The officer scanned the other man. "What's your name?"

"Adam Mandel." He stood up straighter, thrusting his shoulders back.

"Ma'am?"

"Dina Jacobs."

He exited his car and approached them. "Can I see some ID?"

The man named Adam tipped his head, before digging his ID out of an expensive-looking leather wallet and handing it to the officer. Dina gave hers as well. The officer scanned them both before returning them. "Okay, I'm just going to wait in my patrol car until you two get on your way." He pulled up past her car and waited.

Dina looked at the Good Samaritan and felt bad for him. Chances were he hadn't had any other motive than to help her, and now he was being eyed suspiciously by the cop. He strode back to his sports car, and she heaved a sigh. "Wait!" she called out.

She jogged toward him, trying not to slip on the icy pavement. "I didn't mean to get you in any trouble. I think I over-reacted. I appreciate your trying to help me."

His stance relaxed and he smiled, warming her despite the cold weather. "I didn't mean to come on too strong, honestly. Last chance if you want me to help you with the tire, though. You look cold."

She was, even if his green-eyed gaze acted like a heat ray. "That would be great."

He handed her his keys. "Sit in my car and get warm. You can turn on the music if you want. I'll be done in a jiffy."

She climbed into his BMW and turned the ignition key. The motor purred. Heat blasted from the vents and she sighed in delight as she sank into the butter-soft leather seat. The dashboard gleamed, looking like something you'd see in a fighter jet. She had no idea where the controls were even if she wanted to turn on the radio. Five minutes later, he began walking toward her, so she got out of the car.

"All fixed," he said.

"I really appreciate your helping me out. Can I buy you a cup of coffee?"

He hesitated. "Nah," he said, "I'm good."

"Are you sure? You look pretty cold...and wet. It's the least I can do."

He rolled his shoulders, the wool of his overcoat glistening from the moisture. "Follow me to the diner?"

She nodded and waved to the cop, who pulled out onto the road behind them. As she drove, she realized she'd never be home in time for Shabbat services. Oh well. She was thanking him for a *mitzvah*. There were worse reasons to miss temple.

He pulled his Beamer into an empty spot, leaving the one closest to the door and the light, for...dammit, he didn't remember her name. Unlike his lack of memory about Ashley, this memory lapse could be fixed. He shook his head, trying to dispel the thought. Well, whatever her name was, she seemed sweet enough and she shouldn't have to walk through a dark parking lot alone. He took the stairs two at a time and waited for her in the foyer, staring at the team pictures on the walls and the multicolored stacks of business cards in the rack. A moment later, her nondescript-looking car pulled into the spot he'd left for her and she joined him.

"Hey, I just realized, I don't remember your name," he said. He hid his embarrassment with a smile.

Her round face reddened, but she laughed. It was a beautiful laugh. "It's Dina Jacobs." She held her hand out and he clasped it, finding it softer and smaller than he'd expected.

"Hello, Dina Jacobs. I'm Adam Mandel."

She pulled her hand away and clasped both of them together in front of her. "I know. Shall we sit down?"

She was nervous, he thought, as he followed her and the hostess to their booth next to the window. His neck heated. Was she always like this or was it in reaction to him? Did his anger at his father spill over to his actions with her? As he slid into the booth, he made a concerted effort to relax his muscles and to forget about the accusation—at least for now.

Their booth overlooked the parking lot and the highway, so it didn't provide much of a view. The faux-leather menus were huge with page after vinyl page of everything you could imagine. It was an indecisive person's hell. Luckily he was just having coffee.

"You know what you're ordering already?" Her menu was open, and she was scanning each page, as if she'd never seen such a plethora of food before.

"You invited me for coffee."

She snorted, which he somehow found refreshing and adorable. "Oh, please. It's dinnertime. You can't possibly tell me you're not hungry."

Well, when she put it that way. He studied the burger section.

"So, other than rescuing women on the side of the road, and almost being arrested by a cop, what do you do?"

"I'm a corporate attorney, working in Morristown."

"I'm a librarian at the main library in town."

If anyone fit the stereotype, it was Dina. Matching pink sweater set, frizzy black hair pulled back with combs—all she needed were reading glasses hanging around her neck. But she wasn't old enough for those. She looked around his age.

"Did you always want to be a librarian?"

"I've always been more comfortable in the imaginary worlds created by books, so yes, I did. I suppose you don't get to read books much."

"Why would you assume that?" He worked hard to maintain his image. Between his designer suits, well-groomed appearance, and his JD degree, the last thing anyone would ever mistake him for was an idiot.

Her eyes widened. "Because corporate law practice requires tons of hours, and I'd assume a lot of reading of law materials. You probably don't want to spend what little down time you have reading for pleasure."

He leaned toward her, arms on the table. "You're around books all day, right?"

She nodded.

"Do you read when you go home?"

She nodded again.

"Then why would you think otherwise of me?"

She blinked. For the first time he noticed her eyes were violet.

"You're right. I made a snap judgment based on your car and your clothes, and I don't know what else."

She played with her water glass before continuing. "If I weren't already treating you to dinner, I would now."

He sat back in the booth. "There's always dessert." He winked. He couldn't tell who was more surprised, he or Dina. Because despite her incorrect assumptions about him, he was starting to enjoy himself.

She ran a hand through her hair, fingers getting caught in the tiny knots caused by the rain. "So, what do you like to read?"

Her hair intrigued him and he responded without thinking. "Actually, I love reading science fiction and comic books." Dammit, why had he just told her that? He'd never told anyone about his fondness for those subjects—the people he hung out with wouldn't understand. It didn't exactly fit his image, at least, not the one he projected. He should have said mysteries. Or thrillers. Maybe she'd drop the subject.

"Really? I never would have thought that about you. I've always found superheroes appealing, though."

He should let the subject drop. "My favorite is Captain America. His stories make me nostalgic." *So much for that idea.*

"I'll keep that in mind."

At his quizzical look, she continued. "If we get anything interesting in the library. Why does Captain America make you nostalgic?"

Damn. He played with his water glass. "My mom used to read them to me."

The server came with their burgers. As he set down the plates, Adam used the time to try to think of a different subject. Any subject to turn the conversation in a different direction. Before he could put together a coherent sentence, Dina spoke again.

"Do you like working at your firm?"

He swallowed. Talk about changing subjects. "It has its challenges. It's my dad's firm. I started there because it was expected of me, and a smaller firm provides great learning experiences. But it's hard being the son of the lead partner, because everyone watches you to see how you're treated." *If you screw up, it's even worse.* He shrugged, letting his mouth spread in a half-smile. He looked around. God, he wished they served alcohol.

Her tone was soothing. "I'll bet having people's eyes on you all the time must be difficult. Because even if they're not judging you, you sort of always think they are."

This complete stranger understood. He looked at her over his burger. Her eyes really were lovely. Her long lashes made shadows on her creamy skin. Her lips were pretty too.

"It's one of the reasons I want to move to a larger New York City firm. The hours are longer, but the separation would be worth it."

"Do they still make their lawyers work all night? I mean, you're not fresh out of law school anymore, right? My cousin is a lawyer and he never left the office when he worked for one of those big firms."

"I'm almost four years out and the hours will be a lot more than here, but no, I shouldn't need to work all night. Especially if I can leave where I am as a junior partner." *Which right now was a crapshoot, especially if I keep screwing up.*

"Do you think you'll make it?"

It had been a long time since he'd talked to a woman who showed genuine interest in him. Most of the ones he associated with wanted nothing more than a hookup or a rich boyfriend who could spend a lot of money on them. He found himself warming to her. "I'm not sure, but I'm hopeful."

The bill came and he whipped out his credit card. They reached for the check at the same time. Their hands touched. A jolt of something ran up his arm. Beneath his fingers, her hand fit perfectly. He wished he could sit longer like this.

"I said I was going to pay," she said.

Her voice broke whatever spell he'd fallen under. When she pulled her hand, and the bill, away, she broke the physical bond as well. His hand felt empty. He moved it to his lap, clenching it in a fist.

"It's not necessary, Dina. I was happy to help."

"I wasn't very nice and this is my way of apologizing."

He tipped his head in acknowledgement. "Next time, it's on me."

As they walked toward the cashier, she shrugged her shoulders. "Did you know about seventy-five percent of men aren't comfortable letting the woman pay the check?"

He looked at her askance. "Can I have your number?" What the hell was he doing?

She shook her head and he thought she would refuse, but she rattled off her number. "You'll probably be a successful New York attorney by the time you think of doing this again."

Her smile lightened her words, but as he watched her drive away, he couldn't help but wonder. Could there be a next time?

CHAPTER TWO

Dina walked into the library Monday carrying a stack of books. As planned, she'd spent the weekend reading, coming up for air occasionally to eat. It had been ages since she'd had the time to do that, and it had been just what she'd needed. Her smile was huge as she approached the circulation desk.

"Whoa, those are all yours, Dina?" Her friend, Tracy Batton, laughed as she reached out to steady the pile on the desk. "How in the world can you read so many?"

"Speed reading. And they were great. Well, most of them. This one," she pulled one from the middle of the pile and then jumped to prevent the pile from toppling, "wasn't fabulous."

"Not a bad ratio. Guess I know what you did this weekend."

"In its entirety." Well, except for Friday night.

"I envy you. Joe and I spent the whole weekend home with a sick baby."

Dina's smile faded. "Oh, poor thing. But I actually envy you, Tracy. Because you've got your life together and you have something to show for it." She'd give anything to have a life like Tracy's.

"Come on, Dina. You do too. You've got a job you love, great friends...what's wrong?"

"I'm probably just dreading my high school reunion. I just got the invitation to my tenth."

"So don't go."

"I'm tempted. I'm pretty sure I attended high school with every mean girl on the planet. And they all grew up into scary PTA moms, nasty soccer moms, and bitchy executives. But they all have someone to take with them and as usual, I'll be going alone."

"Want to borrow Joe?"

Dina burst out laughing. "That would be hilarious. But no. I'm probably not going, anyway. Only about twenty to thirty percent of alums actually go. Don't mind me, I'll figure it out."

She went to her cubicle in the office on the second floor and spent the rest of the morning updating files, and cataloguing. Usually she loved her job, but today she found her mind wandering. What was she going to do about her ten-year reunion? There was no point in going if she was going to be miserable, but a part of her wanted to see how people had turned out. It was kind of a big milestone, and probably the last one she'd go to.

Would her high school classmates resemble the women she often saw in the library perusing magazines—long straight hair, slip dresses, phones out? Would the guys she remembered still have their hair, or would they be like the man sitting at the computer this morning, sporting a bald spot and a ring of hair like a monk? How many of the women would already have children? She thought about the woman she passed in the children's section, pregnant, with four children attached to her like accessories, hanging from her arms and her skirt and grabbing her leg, dragging her toward the stuffed chairs, and wondered when it would be her turn. Would her classmates even remember her? Her shoulders slumped.

Jim from Inventory knocked on her cubicle and she jumped. "Just got a new shipment of books and I was told to ask if you had time to start on them?"

"Sure." She loved the new books. Getting them ready to be shelved and eventually borrowed was sure to improve her mood. Not to mention, give her a preview of what to add to her TBR list. She followed Jim to the acquisitions room and settled in among the boxes. The first box she opened was romances and as she assigned them their own Dewey decimal number, she made note of which ones she wanted to read. The next box was full of reference books. She was almost finished entering them into the computer when she came across one about the history of comic books. Her heart rate increased as she remembered what Adam had said about liking superheroes. He'd probably find this fascinating. Paging through it, she wondered if she should let him know about it. *He probably has no use for reference books. He's not a researcher.*

However, once Adam entered her mind, she had a hard time letting him go. She'd had a surprisingly good time with him at the diner. When she'd first seen him, after she got over the idea that he might be a serial killer, she'd pegged him for a playboy—fancy car, nice clothes, platinum credit card. Overall, not someone she'd choose to spend time with.

She wasn't usually attracted to good-looking men. Not as good looking as Adam, anyway. From her experience with them in high school and college, they tended to be shallow and looked for women as gorgeous as them. She'd examined herself too many times in the mirror to believe that a guy like Adam would fall for her. Reddish blond hair, green eyes, lanky, and as her mother would say, good bone structure. When he smiled, she'd spotted a dimple in his left cheek and he had an intriguing divot in his chin. His voice was like aged whiskey and even now, she could remember its timbre.

But something about Adam was different than how he appeared. Beyond his looks, he was smart. During their conversation in the diner, his intelligence had come through, turning her initial conclusion about him on its ear. That made him even more attractive to her. He'd obviously studied hard if he was a lawyer and he was interested in topics other than just law. And despite their reputation, superheroes were a fairly complex subject, tackling issues like race relations, women's rights and government, among others. Which brought her back to the box of books.

Should she contact him to tell him about the new book?

Shaking her head, she moved onto the next box. She was never going to see him again. And if he wanted to do research, he knew where to start. He didn't need her giving him useless information.

Her shoulders cramped. She stretched. Grabbing her lunch, she took it outside, and sat on a bench to watch passersby as she ate. A few moments later, Tracy joined her.

"Perfect day for this," her friend said.

Dina nodded. "After unpacking books all day, this is exactly what I need."

"Feeling better now?"

"Dina?" A husky bass voice vibrated through the air.

She looked up. Her stomach fluttered. "Adam? What are you doing here?"

He walked down the path toward where they were sitting, all pressed pants and shiny wingtips, and stopped in front of their bench. He stood with his back to the sun, making her squint.

"I needed to get out of the office for a little while," he said with a shrug, moving so he wasn't backlit. "I thought I'd stop by and say hello."

"I was thinking of you earlier." Why had she said that?

He smiled and his eyes lit up. "Is there a problem with your car?"

"My car? Oh, no, my car is fine. But we just got this book in that I thought you'd be interested in. Or not, since it's a research book. But it made me think of you." *Way to babble, Dina.*

His face tightened in wariness. "Oh?"

"*The History of Superheroes.*" She turned to her friend. "You know the book I'm talking about, right? He loves that stuff and it would be perfect for him, don't you think?"

He swallowed and stuffed his hands in his coat while eyeing Tracy. "Uh, okay. Most people think of me because of my charming personality." He winked and Tracy started to laugh.

Dina stiffened. "It's not on the shelves yet, but give it a week or so and it should be available if you want to take a look at it."

Adam shrugged. "I don't get to the library very often, and like you said, I probably won't have time to read for pleasure, especially such a childish subject." He flashed his perfect teeth in a wide grin at Tracy. "Hi, Adam Mandel."

"Tracy Batton. How do you two know each other?"

"Damsel in distress on the side of the road with a flat on Friday. No big deal."

Dina flinched. Something was off. She barely knew him, but the Adam talking to her friend was the guy she *thought* he was when she first met him—not the potential serial killer part, but the shallow guy she'd dismissed.

"Really? You didn't tell me about your knight in shining armor," Tracy said, turning to her.

Two could play this game. She shrugged.

He blinked. Before he looked away, she thought she saw remorse in his expression, but she couldn't be sure.

Tracy looked between the two of them and cleared her throat. "I guess I'll be going inside, now. Nice to meet you, Adam. See you later, Dina."

Dina rose. "No, I'll go inside with you. Bye, Adam."

With barely a backward glance, she followed Tracy inside. Once the door closed behind them, Tracy spun around. "What was that about?"

Boy, had she been wrong about him. Better to find out early though. Next time, she'd listen to her first thoughts. "No idea."

Adam adjusted the starched sleeve of his shirt beneath his wool suit jacket and pulled on his silk tie. Even he recognized he'd been an ass.

In what seemed to be becoming a regular occurrence, his morning had sucked. His father was giving him busy work, the paralegals in the office were whispering about him, and James, his main competition for a promotion was walking around like he'd just won the lottery.

Apparently, someone had spread the news and had implied he was trying to throw Ashley under the bus.

He'd needed a break, so he'd taken a walk, enjoying the early spring day. As his steps led him toward the library, he'd decided to stop by to see if Dina was there. Something about her had piqued his interest. In fact, her face popped into his head at the oddest times—once while he was at the gym, Saturday night at a bar with the guys, and today while he was driving to the office.

When he saw her sitting outside, he'd stopped to watch her for a few minutes, trying to figure out what about her intrigued him. She wasn't his type physically—she was short, rounder than he was used to and her clothes and hair would never be featured in a magazine, unless it was a "Tame Your Frizz," article. But her smile when she was talking to Tracy had warmed him. He'd wished the smile were directed at him. So he'd walked up to her.

And everything had fallen apart.

Because she'd talked about his love of superheroes. No one knew that about him. It was something he and his mom had shared. And then she'd left. He wasn't stupid enough to think she'd left because of his love for Captain America, but she'd known him better than anyone. She'd supposedly loved him. Yet she'd left anyway. His dad was an ass, so if he thought about it, he could understand why maybe she'd wanted to leave him, but her son? She must have seen something terrible in him if she'd left without taking him with her. Obviously there was nothing superhero-like in him. So he buried what was inside and worked hard to maintain his image—that of a fast-rising, über-successful lawyer. Nothing was going to get in the way of his making the right connections, climbing the ladder of success, and drawing the right people toward him. Those were the people who would ensure his happiness. If his image caused people to draw false conclusions about him, that was a risk he was willing to take.

Dina had acted like it wasn't weird. Maybe it wasn't, but it wouldn't help his image, any more than his love of science fiction or indie bands. Image was the only thing that kept people from walking away. Hearing Dina mention superheroes in front of Tracy had thrown him, so he'd reacted without thinking.

He owed her an apology for his attitude.

Which was why right now, at the end of the day, he was waiting outside the library for her. With flowers.

The door opened for what seemed like the hundredth time. It still wasn't her. He gave a vague smile, the kind that said, "I'm not waiting for you," and shifted from one foot to the other as his impatience grew. It was cold now that the sun was going down. Maybe she'd gotten off early. Maybe she'd left through a different entrance. Maybe she'd decided to stay after the building closed in order to avoid him.

Just as he was about to give up, she walked outside.

"Dina."

She stiffened. He'd swear she was thinking about going back inside. A sudden vision from his childhood of his mother walking away snaked into his head. He blinked to clear it. Like at lunch, her dark frizzy hair was pulled back in a ponytail, but it showed off her cheekbones and the shape of her face. Raising her chin, like she was gearing up for battle, she approached.

"Adam."

"These are for you." He held out the bouquet of flowers.

Her violet eyes softened to heather. She reached for the flowers and frowned. "Why?"

He tipped his head back. "I'm sorry about before."

She shrugged and started to walk past him. "Don't be."

Heat flushed through his body. He hurried to catch up with her, matching his stride to hers. "I was rude."

"It doesn't matter."

"Yes it does."

She spun around to face him. "The flowers are lovely, but there's nothing to apologize for. Give them to your girlfriend." She held them out to him, but he didn't take them.

"I don't have one at the moment."

She raised an eyebrow as if she didn't believe him. Frankly, he couldn't believe it either. After two months of being single, it was his longest dry spell since he could remember. But he wasn't going to tell her that. "Then give them to your mother."

He swallowed. "Don't have one of those either."

Now her eyes really did soften. He cursed himself for saying anything.

Dina stepped closer.

If she interrogated him about his mother, he was going to turn around and leave.

She held out a finger, ran it along the petal of one of the yellow roses. "They're pretty."

"Women like roses. I thought yellow suited you."

"Actually, my favorites are daisies."

He'd seen a bouquet of those, but he'd thought they looked cheap. Roses made a better impression. "Why?"

"Why what?"

"Why do you like daisies?" Why the hell did he care?

"They're cheerful and overlooked, usually, for more expensive, prettier smelling ones."

Her reaction tugged at his heart. "Seems like an odd reason to like them then."

She shrugged. "You asked."

"If I asked you out, would you say yes?" Whoa, where had that idea come from?

"You'd never ask me." She started walking again.

He followed. "I just did."

"No you didn't. You tested the waters, like what a political candidate does before announcing his candidacy."

"I'm pretty sure you're insulting me," he said, beginning to enjoy himself.

She stopped in front of her beat up car. When she didn't speak, he filled the silence. "Go out with me."

"No."

He stepped back. "Why not?"

"Because you don't really want me to go out with you. I'm not your type."

"How do you know what my type is?" He stilled.

She looked him up and down, like a piece of meat. "Pretty, wealthy, popular and not too smart. Not dumb, but average."

His face burned as he recognized the truth in her statement.

She laughed. "Go home, Adam. Thank you for the flowers."

He watched her drive away. He wasn't sure what just happened, but it wasn't what he'd intended.

The next day, she found him standing outside the library when it opened.

"Don't you have a job?" Dina asked.

He shifted from one foot to the other, an action she found endearing, even if he annoyed her. "For the moment."

"You'd probably have a better chance of keeping it if you were there, rather than here."

He chuckled. "Probably."

"Then why are you here?"

"I wanted to talk to you."

She sighed. "Give me a minute."

When he started to follow her she paused. "Wait here." She pointed to the lobby, and waited until he'd settled himself onto a bench before entering the employee area. She deposited her purse and sweater at her desk, waved to her boss and returned to the lobby. Adam was still there. Her stomach lurched. She shook her head. He was an annoyance, like indigestion, nothing more.

"Yes?" For some reason, she didn't know what to do with her hands. When they started fluttering at her sides, she folded them across her middle. Better to look the stern librarian than like a bird about to take flight.

He rose and shifted from one foot to the other. "I'm sorry about the other day."

"You already said that."

"I know, but I want to make it up to you."

"Why?"

"I have no idea."

"Is this normally how you woo women? If so, does it actually work?"

He blew out a breath, reminding her of a racehorse. "I'm usually a lot smoother than this."

Her inward smile was getting harder and harder to hide. He reminded her of Dorothy in the Wizard of

Oz, when she discovers she's not in Kansas anymore. She kept that to herself, however—he didn't seem like the type of man who would appreciate being compared to a girl, even if that girl was a character in a literary classic.

"Threatened by the smart girl?" She held her breath as the words escaped her mouth. She meant it as a joke, but some jokes weren't funny. Then again, he'd been dismissive of her the other day.

"If I say yes, will you take pity and go out with me?" A smile played about his mouth.

He was persistent, she had to give him that. The last time a "pretty boy" had pursued her this hard was when she was a freshman in high school, taking a senior-level chemistry class. One of the senior boys wanted to cheat off her lab report. She hadn't let him cheat then, because she was morally opposed to it. He'd continued to bother her about it for the rest of the year, as if the nagging would change her mind. It hadn't worked back then, but it was starting to work now. And that would never do. Maybe the best way to get rid of Adam was to agree to go out with him.

"Fine."

She'd expected him to grin some plastic, car salesman-y grin. Instead, his eyes lightened to emerald, backlit with a warm glow. Her heart lurched.

"How's Friday night?"

Blinking, she tried to focus on his words. "Um, actually, I go to temple on Friday nights."

He nodded. "Okay, how about Thursday night? There's a bar in Newark that has live bands Thursdays. They're usually pretty good."

A bar? He wanted to take her to a bar? In Newark? Visions of a quiet dinner or a show popped her bubble. She resigned herself to another night where she didn't fit in. High school all over again. It was too late to back out now. "Okay."

He confirmed her phone number and gave her his, promising to call later in the week to arrange specifics. He'd probably change his mind. But she wouldn't tell him that. Finally, he left and she returned to her desk.

"You have a date, how wonderful!" Rose, an older woman who worked with Dina, clapped her hands in glee.

"I wouldn't get too excited. He's totally not my type."

Rose winked. "Sometimes, those are the best kind, sweetie. Shave your legs and bring protection."

"What?" Dina couldn't believe Rose was saying this to her. In a library of all places. "I would never sleep with him on the first date."

The salt-and-pepper-haired woman gave a knowing smile. "You do know you don't need protection for sleeping, right?"

"You mean you weren't talking about ear plugs for noise?" Dina asked, eyebrow raised.

"He's handsome and likes you. Just be prepared."

As Dina returned to her desk and thought seriously about bleaching her ears, she discounted Rose's assessment. Adam didn't "like" her. He felt guilty, sure. He was concerned about what she thought of him, okay. But like her? Please.

CHAPTER THREE

On Monday, Adam walked straight to the paralegals. "Hey, Kim, I brought in my old study guides for the bar." He'd spent all day Sunday putting them in order for her. A single mom whose husband had walked out on her and her two children, she'd told him about her desire to become a lawyer, and he'd encouraged her, helping her out the last two years, entertaining her kids, and smoothing the way for her to leave early to study. She was in the home stretch and he was proud of his friend.

She jumped, looked around and gave him an awkward smile. "Thanks, Adam."

Others in the area stopped what they were doing and watched the exchange. It was weird. He held out a binder and after swallowing, Kim reached for it.

"Everything okay?" he asked. "I know the exam can be stressful, but with all the real-world experience you're getting here, and how hard you're studying, you're going to do great."

Her cheeks colored. "Yeah."

She was usually a lot more talkative. "If you want, I can give up my lunch hour today and help you study. I still remember the tricks and techniques I used."

"No, that's okay. But thanks." She got up from her desk, skirted around him and walked over to one of the other paralegals, who shot him a glance before whispering to Kim.

He stood there, feeling awkward, before returning to his office.

On Tuesday, he passed Kim at the copy machine. "Did you take a look at the stuff I gave you yesterday? If you need anything—"

"Adam, really, I'm fine. Thanks. I've got this on my own now."

"Are you sure? I can take Oliver and Jared out for ice cream again, or a movie, like last time, if you need time alone to study."

"I'm sure. Look, when you accuse one paralegal, you accuse all of us, and I don't think it's a good idea..." She looked around before returning her focus to him. "for us to be together, at least not right now. I need to work with these people, at least until I become a law-yer..."

He stiffened, gave her a nod and walked back to his office. Sinking into his chair, he buried his face in his hand. Kim and he were friends. Did she really believe Ashley over him? They had spent hours together and never once had he ever blamed anyone else for his screw ups. She knew him. Or she should.

By Wednesday, any doubts about whether or not Kim believed him disappeared. His history with her was irrelevant, because Ashley had convinced all the paralegals he had it out for her, and if they weren't careful, he'd go after them too. He'd tried to talk to her, but she wouldn't budge. Most worrisome of all was that he couldn't find the paper trail on his computer he'd left himself for just such a thing as this happening. He'd searched everywhere for it and it was gone.

This was three marks against him. One of which had lost them the case and unless something happened quickly, might result in losing the client. His father was pissed. Ashley was unshakeable. The other paralegals were avoiding him. Not only was it going to be impossible for him to work if he had to do everything himself, he was never going to make junior partner if this kept up.

He wracked his brain, trying to figure out why Ashley would do something like this. Other than one time where he'd given her an assignment and she'd messed it up, their interactions had been fine. Professional. Sure, she didn't like having to stay late, but that came with the job. He was always friendly and respectful to her. He'd greet her in the morning, just like he did everyone else. He asked her about her weekend, just like he did everyone else. He couldn't think of anything out of the ordinary. Could he have possibly said something that angered her? And if so, why hadn't she said something to him, either at the time, or now? He would have apologized immediately.

In the meantime, the paralegals gave him wary looks, Kim no longer wanted his help, and his father gave him grunt work. Putting aside the abandonment by his friends and father, how the hell was he supposed to prove himself ready for the promotion to junior partner if he'd been relegated to handling things even a first year could do with their eyes closed? He started to sweat. Why did everyone assume the worst of him?

He stared out the window down to the street below. A woman with curly hair walked by, reminding him of Dina and he smiled for the first time in days.

Dina was sweet. She was funny. Images of Dina smiling at him, leaning forward to ask questions, flitted through is head. Her face was round, with clear, pale skin, long lashes and full lips. Her eyes—he still couldn't believe they were violet—were beautiful. Maybe she wore contacts? Her hair fascinated him. It was different from the smooth, straight tresses he was used to seeing everywhere. Hers was a deep brown, almost black, with thick, frizzy waves. He wondered what it would feel like against his cheek. Would it be soft or springy or something he hadn't considered?

There was something about having all those curves to himself—to explore, admire and discover—that made him think about her more than he'd like. She was curvier than the women he typically dated, but then those women were model thin and complained about every calorie they put in their mouth. Half of his dinner conversations with them involved food, and not in any way he found fascinating. His conversations with Dina, on the other hand. They made him think.

He expelled a breath. It didn't matter. No matter how much he might have enjoyed dinner with her, he couldn't date a woman like her, a woman who could see through him as easily as Dina. A woman who would leave him if she discovered the real him—just like his mother, and now, apparently, Kim.

He shook his head. Dina was more religiously observant than he was if she went to temple every Friday night. Except last Friday night they'd had dinner at the diner. Was temple just an excuse to avoid him?

No, somehow, he thought Dina would be more direct than that. And now, despite his concerns, he was taking Dina out to a bar tomorrow night. He didn't do commitment, and his dating record showed that. Dina, on the other hand, was probably focused on commitment, which should make him nervous. Except she didn't seem to want to go out with him in the first place.

So why the hell was he taking her out?

Adam was picking her up in forty-five minutes. She'd already been standing in front of her closet for close to fifteen. Who did that? She had work clothes. She had weekend clothes. She had temple clothes. She even had clothes to go on a date. But this was Adam, *Mr. Flashypants.*

He was probably used to women showing lots of cleavage and leg. Her boobs were too big for her to be comfortable showing cleavage. She wasn't a mini-skirt kind of person. Which left...not too many options.

Ten minutes later, she settled on black boot-cut jeans and a drape-necked green cashmere sweater that accentuated her eyes. Black boots, chunky silver ear-rings, her silver Jewish star necklace, minimal makeup and she was done. Why she was trying to impress him, she had no idea.

When her apartment intercom buzzed, she grabbed her purse and jacket and met Adam on the porch of her converted Victorian.

Once again, he greeted her with his slow, small smile. A frisson of excitement went through her. He wore a black button-down, open at the neck and grey slacks. The dark colors set off his lighter hair and made his green eyes pop. He leaned over and kissed her cheek, surprising her. His lips were soft against her skin. She inhaled his spicy clean scent.

"You look pretty. I like what you did to your hair."

All she'd done was pull it back off her face in a low half-knot. He probably said this to all his dates. She fisted her hand at her side to keep from touching it. "Thanks."

She was not going to think about her cheek that he'd kissed.

He led her down the walkway and held open the car door for her. Up close, and in the daylight, she realized his car was a convertible. Of course it was. Luckily for her hair, the top was up.

"Nice car. Did you know Germany started making BMWs because after the Treaty of Versailles they were prohibited from making warplanes or warplane engines?" She gulped after the fact slipped out. She really needed to stop doing that.

He looked at her, chuckled, and eased onto the street. Jazz played through the car's sound system. Dina stared out the window as they drove down the highway and eventually onto the streets of Newark. She had no idea what to say, but the silence didn't seem to bother him. Adam pulled into a parking garage.

He opened the door for her, pocketing the ticket. "Come on, the bar's this way."

The area near the bar was busy with young professionals unwinding after a long day at work and older people grabbing a quick bite before the show at the performing arts center down the street. As they walked, Adam chatted about the types of bands he liked. Most of the names were unknown to her—her musical tastes ran more to classic rock. Once there, he gave his name and they were seated downstairs in a cozy booth in sight of the stage, but not too close. The room was dark, with silver up-lighting and multi-colored wall sconces that provided flair.

Everything about this place screamed, "What are you doing here?"

Sitting across the silvery speckled-granite topped table from each other, Dina studied Adam's face while he opened the wine menu. He was even more handsome than she'd remembered. Her stomach knotted.

"What's wrong?" Adam put the wine menu down.

"This is all just foreign to me."

"What do you mean?"

"Nothing. Never mind."

He fixed his attention on her, as if waiting for her to continue, but she wasn't about to pour out her discomfort to someone she was never going to see again. So she nodded toward the menu. "Is there a particular wine you were thinking of?"

"I was going to ask what you like."

"Anything but Manischewitz."

He laughed. "Hey, we have the same taste in wine!"

Dina couldn't help the laugh that escaped. Maybe he recognized how incongruous they were too. "Good to know. Because that might have been a deal breaker."

"You really have no preference for red or white even?"

"I'm open to trying something new."

The slow smile spread. Motioning for the waitress, he gave their wine order. Turning his attention back to her, he leaned forward. "So, do you get first dibs on the books that come in?"

She laughed again. "Not exactly. I mean, I get to see what's in stock so I know what to add to my list, but we usually have a waiting list of people who want the books, and I don't get to jump ahead in line."

"The people seem pretty nice. What's your friend like, the one you were talking to the other day?"

Wait. Why was he asking about Tracy? "What do you want to know about her?"

"How'd you two meet?"

That was innocuous. The knot in her stomach loosened. "We work together. She started a few years before I did. She took me under her wing. I filled in for her when she took maternity leave."

"Are there a lot of people our age working there or just you and Tracy?"

It was a good question, and an easy one. "There's a pretty decent mix, actually."

They paused to study their menus and order, and when the waiter left, Adam continued with his questions. "Do you two socialize outside of work much?"

Dina relaxed as she thought about her friend. "She's pretty busy with her family, but we go to lunch. Occasionally we'll go shopping or see a movie on a weekend."

"Oh, the Morristown movie theater is great—their seats are really comfortable."

"Yeah, although I wish they'd get more classic movies, but I guess those don't appeal to as many people."

"The black and white ones? There are a few I've seen that are really great. *Citizen Kane* was one of my favorites. What's yours?"

"Orson Welles was terrific in that," she said.

"'I don't think there's one word that can describe a man's life.' I love that line."

"Why?"

Just then, the waiter brought their dinners, a steak for Adam and filet of sole for Dina. The meat sizzled. Its garlicky scent mixed with the smell of the fish and the fruity salsa, making Dina's stomach growl. Once they'd each tasted their food, she prompted him. "The movie line?"

"Oh. I like how it's such a simple way to describe the complexity of a person. It's not dramatic, it doesn't exaggerate things, but it shows there can be more to someone or some situation than meets the eye."

Her heart thudded. Mr. Flashypants had a soul. A fairly deep one at that. "Discovering those hidden facets can be the most rewarding part of getting to know someone."

A flicker of uncertainty passed over his face. He sat back in his chair, adjusting his napkin on his lap. "Unless there's nothing there."

"What do you mean?" The sole was melt-in-your-mouth delicious. She hadn't stopped eating since the waiter set the plate in front of her. Now, however, she put down her fork.

His gaze shifted from the food in front of him, to the wall behind her ear, to the center of the room and he shrugged. "Some of us are exactly what we seem."

"I don't believe that. I think we all hide pieces of ourselves. No one walks around with a sign around their neck proclaiming this is the real me."

He sliced another piece of steak, finished chewing before he spoke again. "And you? Who are you?"

Like she would tell him. "I'm a vampire," she whispered.

"Ah, I guess seeing you out in the daylight and sharing this garlic bread with you really fooled me," he said with a wink. His shoulders loosened and once again, he relaxed.

They finished their meal together just as the band took the stage. Intrigued, Dina watched as they tuned their instruments before beginning their set. The music was a mix of new age rock with a little jazz and funk thrown in. She was surprised at how much she enjoyed it. Before she knew it, she was tapping her hands on the table to the beat. The other surprising thing? Adam knew the music, even singing along at times. She never would have pegged him as someone who liked this music style—it wasn't flashy or trendy enough. At least, she didn't think it was.

Her nostrils filled with his spicy clean aftershave. Something about his scent made her want to move closer to him, which was insane. She barely knew him, they were in public and there was a table of food separating them.

"How do you like the band?" he asked.

She nodded her head. "They're great. I've never heard of them before." Of course, she wasn't up on music, so that didn't mean anything.

"They're indie and fairly new. They're originally from Chicago. Glad you're enjoying yourself." He shifted his chair closer and placed his hand on the table close to hers. Their fingers brushed against each other. The contact sent jolts of electricity up Dina's arm.

He twined his fingers through hers and she stilled. Did he feel it too? Or was this how he acted with everyone? When the set ended and the lights came back on, she expected him and his supple fingers to move back to his side of the table. But he stayed where he was and took a dessert menu from the waiter. "We can share," he said. The waiter walked away. "See anything you like?"

She had an insane desire to say, "Yes, you." But he was talking about dessert. Her face heated as her mind wandered down a path it really shouldn't go on a first-slash-second-date-that-didn't-mean-anything-and-would-never-go-anywhere. She shook her head to clear it and tried to distract herself with thoughts of food.

Glancing over at him, she realized he was still waiting for an answer. Despite the fact she'd been staring at the menu, she had no idea what was written there. "I'll just have some ice cream."

He nodded, ordered for the two of them and fiddled with the silverware on the table.

"I never would have pegged you for someone who liked indie bands," she said.

He gave a wry grin. "Me neither. It showed up on my Pandora one day while I was running."

"You run?"

Nodding, he flipped the fork first one way then the other.

The motion of his hands mesmerized her—watching the play of the tendons as he spun the fork, seeing his fingers stretch as he strove not to drop the fork on the table, catching the light glinting off the silverware and the gold chain around his wrist.

"Five miles a day," he said.

She started. Five miles...oh, yeah. Running. "Great exercise."

"Do you run?"

"Only if someone's chasing me. Even then, I'd probably surrender. I prefer walking, preferably in the woods."

"Have you walked any of the county trails?"

She started to nod, but the lights dimmed. The band returned for their final set. This time, his nearness distracted her—the touch of his shoulder as he rocked in his seat in time to the beat, the thrum of his voice as he sang a private concert just for her. She remembered the first set for the music, but this second set was all about Adam. Spotlights from the stage glinted off his hair, creating streaks of white gold and copper. His silhouette reminded her of Greek sculptures in the museum—proud nose, firm chin, prominent cheekbones, wide forehead. Muscles in his forearms flexed beneath his black sleeve as he played air guitar or imitated the drummer.

When it was over, a breathless feeling constricted the breath in her chest. She took a hasty sip of water.

"Ready to go?" he asked.

When she nodded, he held out her chair and walked with her toward the door, his hand against the small of her back.

"Adam Mandel?"

He dropped his hand from her back. "Hey, Seth, how ya doin'?"

Like a flick of a switch, Mr. Flashypants was back.

"I didn't know you were into this band," Seth said.

The sound of Adam's laugh sent a chill down her spine. "You know me, always willing to try something new." But the tone of his voice indicated otherwise. "See you around, Seth."

Whereas before, Adam's hand on her back had warmed her, this time, when he put it there again, she felt as if he were steering her away from public view. She stayed silent on their walk back to the car, Adam's nonchalant whistle grating on her ears.

Once inside his car, she looked out the window at the city lights. There was nothing to see, but she didn't want to look at Adam.

"I'm glad we did this," he said, as he pulled onto the highway.

Her mother had taught her manners. No matter how uncomfortable she felt, she would live up to them. "The band was great. The food was delicious."

"Sorry about back there," he said. "I should have introduced you."

"It can be shocking to run into people in odd places." Except that didn't fully explain his change in demeanor.

She half listened to his small talk in the car as they drove the rest of the way home, trying to figure out why he demonstrated two such different sides of his personality.

He walked her to her door, paused outside of it, looking around as if to see if anyone was watching. "I had a lot of fun with you tonight," he said. "Thanks for giving me another chance."

"You're welcome."

He reached a hand out and traced a line down the side of her face. Prickles of goose bumps followed his finger. She shivered. Did she want him to kiss her? Before they ran into Seth, she would have said yes. Now she wasn't sure. Laughter from another building intruded.

He dropped his hand to his side. "I'll call you tomorrow?"

Nodding, she fished her keys out of her purse. He waited for her to get inside before raising his hand in a wave and jogging back to his car.

Adam let himself into his high-rise apartment after dropping off Dina at hers. She was a surprise he was enjoying discovering. When their hands had touched over dinner, he'd felt...something. "Sparks" was stupid, but he didn't know what else to call it. From the way she'd jumped, he'd bet she'd felt something too, especially when she didn't pull her hand away as he wound his fingers around hers. Standing at her door, he hadn't wanted to let her go so quickly.

He'd wanted to taste her lips. Her skin had been soft. If only Seth hadn't intruded and those people's laughter hadn't interrupted them. Next time. He'd have to make sure there was a next time, even if he was supposed to be cooling off his social life for the time being.

The red light of his answering machine glowed. His body tensed. Only one person called him on his home phone—his father. Tossing his keys onto the black granite counter, he hit play.

"Adam, it's Dad. Where the hell are you? It's a Thursday night. Please tell me you're not out partying. You're supposed to be improving your work ethic, not abandoning it. Call me."

Jabbing the Erase button, he stalked out onto his balcony. He gripped the railing as he stared into the night, no longer picturing Dina's face. His apartment complex was next to the train station, but if he looked out instead of down, he could see silhouettes of the trees on the Green in the distance.

When had his life turned to shit? Out of all the conclusions his father jumped to, he immediately leapt to partying? Maybe he was working. Or at the library. Or helping Kim study for the bar exam. He shook his head. With the types of assignments his father had foisted on him, there was no need to work late. The library? Hadn't been there since law school—stopping outside to talk to Dina the other day probably didn't count. Helping Kim? His father didn't know about that.

He shifted from one foot to the other. No wonder his father was suspicious. Although would it kill him to have a little faith in his son? He laughed to himself. His father's faith in anyone had disappeared when his wife left twenty-two years ago. Adam pushed away from the railing.

Heading back inside, he looked around. He wasn't in the mood to go to bed. He didn't feel like being alone. But there weren't any friends he could call. His gaze fell onto his law school graduation photo perched on the marble-topped coffee table. He stood next to his best law school friend, Jacob Black. They hadn't talked in a few months. Jacob knew his father. He knew Adam. Maybe he'd be able to give him career advice.

Pulling the name from his contacts, he dialed.

"Jacob! It's Adam."

"Hey, it's been a while."

Just the sound of his buddy's voice made him feel better. "Yeah, how are you?"

"Great. Busy with work, as I'm sure you are."

Adam swallowed. "Any chance you're free to catch up?"

"Absolutely. Tomorrow night?"

Dina might go to temple every Friday, but he didn't. "Sure."

CHAPTER FOUR

The next evening, Adam rode the train to Hoboken and fidgeted with his phone. Should he call Dina? She'd probably know some obscure fact about trains. He started to smile. He had a feeling she wouldn't ever understand his rules. Rule number one being no strings. Rule number two being if you start getting attached, reread rule number one. He'd had a nice time with her last night, hell, more than a nice time. Despite her sense of humor, which was subtle like her, she had depth. He couldn't afford that and he didn't want to hurt her. Frustrated, he shoved his phone back in his pocket and as the train stopped, disembarked with the other passengers. A short walk later, he entered the commuter bar where he'd arranged to meet Jacob.

His friend was seated at a table halfway back and raised his arm to flag Adam down.

"Hey, good to see you," Jacob said, shaking his hand. "It's been too long."

"You too. Tell me what's happening with you." Adam listened as Jacob filled him in on married life to Aviva and his job with a boutique law firm in Jersey City. Adam's stomach clenched. The beer he'd been drinking turned sour. Another one with a perfect life.

"You're usually a lot more talkative, Adz. What's going on?"

Adam opened his mouth, about to brush him off with his usual flip answer. But this was Jake, the one person he opened up to, even if only a little bit. He gripped the neck of his beer tighter and rubbed the condensation away. "My life's a mess." He gave him a quick rundown about the debacle at work.

Jacob winced. "Oh man, that's rough. Has your dad forgiven you yet?"

"Nope, and in the meantime, I'm doing scut work at the office. I'm also benched socially. Sort of."

"What's 'sort of' mean?"

"It means that normally I'd drown my sorrows with some gorgeous babe, but I can't since that only fuels my dad's fire. I need to keep my nose clean. Which, for the most part, I am."

"For the most part?"

"There's a woman but she's totally not my type."

Jacob raised his brows. Adam banged the back of his head against the wall. "She isn't. She's everything I don't look for in a woman. Seriously, my father needs to forgive me so I can get back to my social life and forget about this."

"Isn't that what landed you in this mess to begin with?"

Adam shook his head. He took another swig of beer. "I was sure Ashley would take care of it, and Dina? I don't see it happening." He blocked out images of her creamy skin, shaking his head and staring off into the distance.

"Why not?"

He shrugged. "She's not a 'no-strings' kind of woman."

"You're positive you're still a 'no-strings' kind of guy?"

Didn't matter what he wanted. She wouldn't want him when she found out about him. His mom, the one woman who was supposed to love him no matter what, hadn't given him a second thought when she'd left and cut off all contact. "Please. Not all of us are boring like you."

Jacob laughed. "Don't knock it 'til you try it. You know if you want, I can have my mother set you up."

Adam pulled away from the table in horror, his chair legs scraping against the floor. "*Yenta* Karen? You'd sic her on me? Are you kidding?"

"Yep. Just wanted to see you sweat."

"I love your mother, but there's no way I want her meddling in my life."

"I think you're missing out on a great opportunity," Jacob said with a wink. "I think you should reconsider Dina. Something in the tone of your voice when you talk about her makes me think your feelings for her are different."

"There's no point."

Dina walked into temple Friday night and let her worries fade away. The peacefulness of the sanctuary, with its stained glass windows depicting biblical scenes from the Torah, the ornately carved mahogany doors of the Ark where the Torah scrolls were kept, and the dim lighting calmed her. It was just the place she needed to be after a week filled with such uncertainty about Adam and her feelings toward him.

She sat in the pew toward the front and waited for the rabbi to begin her service. A rustling next to her brought her attention to Rebecca, her husband, Aaron, and their three children sliding into her row. Scooting over, she made room for them and handed prayer books down to them as they settled.

After the service, she followed Rebecca and her family into the Social Hall for the *Oneg*, where everyone socialized and ate dessert after reciting brief prayers over the wine and the *challah*.

"I love showing my children how many people come to services on Friday nights," Rebecca said to Dina, as she watched them run over to the dessert table for cookies and juice.

"And I love coming here Friday nights," Dina said. "It helps me settle after a week of stress."

Rebecca nodded. "We missed you last week."

"I was out to dinner and it ran late."

Rebecca's face lit up. "With anyone special?"

Dina sighed. She loved Rebecca. About ten years older than she was, Dina enjoyed having a friend at temple to keep her company and to talk to, but Rebecca was always trying to fix her up. "I got a flat tire and this guy stopped to help me. I was a little rude to him and to apologize, I took him to the diner."

"You invited a random stranger to the diner?" She covered her mouth with one hand and gripped Dina's shoulder with the other. "Are you crazy?" When Dina rolled her eyes, Rebecca shook her head. "What's he like?"

Dina pulled Rebecca off to the side, away from the other congregants. "Completely different from anyone I've ever dated, but that's not saying much."

"Different how? You're dating him?"

"No, he's flashy and seems concerned about his image and what other people think." But he's got depth. She'd heard it when they talked, usually when he wasn't aware he was revealing it. Rebecca's look of concern made Dina hold out her hand. "Don't worry, he's not my type at all."

Rebecca put her arm around her. "Well, I think I have someone perfect for you, so let me know and I can set you up with him."

Did she want to be set up again? Maybe. "Who are you thinking of?"

"He's a really sweet guy, a few years older than you. He's a researcher in Aaron's lab. Very smart. I think you two would be perfect together. He lives in Madison."

He didn't sound bad at all. "Okay, sure. Why not?"

"Great! I'll give him your phone number. His name is Zach Epstein."

When Dina left fifteen minutes later, she promised to let Rebecca know about her plans with Zach. If he called.

The large envelope embossed with her high school logo made Dina's palms sweat. As she pulled out the invitation to her tenth high school reunion, visions of the popular girls whispering as she walked in the hallways clicked through her brain. She'd been too smart in high school to fit in with anyone. Even the nerdy kids hadn't wanted to hang out with her—they'd giggled when she'd wanted to discuss the themes in *The Scarlet Letter* and looked at her like she was a bug when she'd proved she could recite the Constitution from memory. The only thing that had gotten her through those years were her teachers and books. Now she was invited to go back and reunite with them? No way.

Morbid curiosity made her read the invitation, rather than throwing it in the trash unopened like she had the five-year one. She frowned. It was a dinner dance on a Saturday night two months from now at a fancy hotel about an hour away in Princeton. The organizers had gone all out. Shaking her head, she started to slide the invitation back inside the envelope when her phone rang. Tossing the invitation on the table by her front door, she answered her phone as she walked further inside her apartment.

"Hello, Dina? This is Zach Epstein. Rebecca and Aaron Kopf gave me your name."

"Hi, Zach. Rebecca told me you might call."

"Oh. Good. I was wondering if you'd like to go out for a drink one night this week?"

She swallowed. No harm in seeing what happened. "Sure."

"Oh. Good. How's tomorrow? There's this neat place in Madison called The Game Set. It has board games. Do you like board games?"

Board games? "Sure, that sounds fun."

After getting the address, she hung up. She'd never heard of the place, but it would be different. And he sounded much more her type than Adam, who hadn't called despite telling her he would. Even if in her head, Adam was the one she pictured on the date.

CHAPTER FIVE

Dina stood in the doorway of The Game Set. The place was rustic looking, with a wooden floor and yellow walls. To the left was the bar. The rest of the place was taken up by game tables, shelves with board games stacked on them, and groupings of comfy-looking chairs and mismatched sofas. Toward the back was a room with a doorway marked Billiards. The place was filled with people of all ages and she walked through, looking for a guy on his own.

Movement from the bar drew her attention and a man with wire-rimmed glasses and dark, wavy hair waved to her.

"Zach?"

"Hi, Dina. Nice to meet you. You look just like Rebecca said you would." He shook her hand. His grasp was cool and firm and when he made eye contact with her, she noticed his warm, brown eyes. "Would you like a drink?"

He placed their orders and once their craft beers arrived, he directed her to a vacant table with two high stools. She climbed up, grateful she had taken his advice and worn jeans. He had too, with a button-down blue Oxford. He was tall and rangy with a mellow voice and a piercing stare.

"So tell me how you know Rebecca and Aaron," he said, when they'd settled, turning his stare on her.

Such intensity made her self-conscious and she could feel her cheeks heating. *Great, I probably match my pink sweater.* "We belong to the same temple. I've known her for years. And you work with Aaron?"

"Yes, I'm a research director in the lab next to his. How's your beer?" He jiggled his knee.

She took a sip of the dark brew. "A little bitter, but not bad, thanks. I've never heard of this place. Do you come here often?"

"Some of us in the lab come here for their game tournaments. It's a fun way to let off some steam." His face lit up. "Would you like to play one of the games?"

She would much prefer to talk and get to know him, but he didn't seem like much of a conversationalist. "Sure, why don't you pick one?"

He walked away for a few minutes and Dina checked her watch. Thirty minutes. She'd never checked her watch when she was with Adam.

When Zach returned, he brought Battleship. "I love this game," he said as he set up the board.

It had never been one of her favorites. "That's a great one. Did you know it used to be known as Salvo?"

"I had no idea. That's fascinating!"

As they played the game and talked, Dina tried hard not to compare him to Adam.

Zach wasn't flashy. He wore a smart watch, but it didn't cost more than her entire paycheck. His shirt was wrinkled in the back and his jeans were functional, rather than designer.

Zach wasn't smooth. His hair wasn't slicked back and he didn't seem to have a set of responses he took out and used.

Zach wasn't popular. Despite his claim that he and his friends came here often, there was no line of groupies waiting to talk to him while sizing her up.

Zach was...normal. He was smart, average-looking...and boring.

She sighed. "You sunk my battleship."

He smiled at the commercial reference as he added points to his side. He was smiling at the reference, right?

"I remember those commercials," he said, and relief trickled through her.

He pulled out the pegs in his board. "Want to play another one?"

Goodness, no. "I really enjoyed this one, but it's getting late and I think I need to get going." Okay, it was nine o'clock, but some people might consider that late. If you were seventy.

"Ah, sure. Can I walk you to your car?"

Think of Rebecca. "Sure."

She followed Zach out the door and walked with him down the main street of Madison. Lit store windows and bright street lamps offered a kaleidoscope of black, yellow and shades of grey for them to walk through, and at times it seemed to Dina as if they were walking through an old movie. Zach pointed out restaurants he and his colleagues had eaten at, stores he'd stopped in and interesting facts about the town, such as its nickname of The Rose City. "In the 1800s it had a flourishing rose-growing industry. In fact, the Morris and Essex rail line enabled that industry to flourish and for farmers to sell their produce in Manhattan."

"How interesting." And it was. As a lover of obscure facts, she could appreciate his knowledge. She looked up at him. He looked proud of knowing that information. And he'd thought her information about Battleship was fascinating. His intelligence sat well on him, truly becoming a part of who he was, unlike Adam, who hid his intelligence behind a veneer. Would Adam have known something like this? Would he have told her? And how would he have acted if he did?

"Oh wait, I see a colleague of mine up ahead," Zach said. "Come on, I'll introduce you."

Taking her arm, he led her half a block to a group of people standing outside a restaurant. "Steve, Ann, how are you?"

"Zach, funny running into you here."

"Let me introduce you to Dina. She and I were just at The Game Set." He made the introductions and everyone smiled and chatted with one another. Dina made small talk for a few minutes until Zach made eye contact with her, indicating it was time to leave.

Dina pulled up short. Unlike Adam, Zach had made a special effort to introduce her to his friends. He hadn't acted ashamed of her. Her intelligence didn't embarrass him.

As they left the group and Zach walked her to her car, she wondered what she should do. Was she being too hasty in her judgment of Zach? She had no idea if she'd see Adam again anyway. Maybe she shouldn't write Zach off just yet. He was kind and solicitous. His friends were welcoming. She could tell by the way he looked at her that he liked her. He was exactly the kind of guy she could picture herself with.

"It was great meeting you, Dina," Zach said. He leaned down and kissed her cheek. "I hope you had as much fun as I did."

"I enjoyed getting to know you, too, Zach." She smiled at him, and the relief on his face pushed her to make her decision. "I hope we can get together again."

Nodding, Zach opened her car door for her and held it while she got herself settled. "I'd like that," he said. "I'll call you."

As she pulled away, she wondered if he would. Because she wasn't planning to wait around on the off chance Adam decided to call.

Monday morning, Adam looked at his phone, scrolled through his contacts, and dialed Dina's number. The sound of her voice rolled over him, enveloping him like a warm blanket, but when he realized it was just her voice mail, he rolled his eyes. "Hey, Dina, it's Adam. Give me a call." He left his number and went back to the brief he was editing. When it was finished, he emailed it to the managing partner before stopping at the threshold of her office.

"Hi, Florence, I just emailed you the brief on the Hatchet case. Are we still set for court next week?"

"Oh, Adam, I was just going to call you. James is going to come with me instead."

Adam frowned at the grey-suited woman. He walked into her office. "What's going on? I've been working on that case with you. I thought everything was all set."

She moved behind her desk and peered over her reading glasses. "It was, but your father suggested it might be better to have James work on the case. We really need this case to succeed, and well, to be honest, I can't afford any careless mistakes. I hope you can understand that."

He masked his facial features and gave her a bland smile as his pulse pounded in his head. "Sure, of course. I'll send all my files over to James."

"Thanks, I appreciate it. I'm sorry about all of this, Adam. You're one of the smartest lawyers I've worked with—and I'm not just saying that because your father is my boss."

He left her office, hands in fists at his sides, lungs constricted. Yeah, right. Of course he was smart. But intelligence hadn't prevented Ashley from accusing him of throwing her under the bus, or lying—because he was convinced she was lying—about giving her the motion to file. It wasn't convincing his father or anyone else in this office to believe in him. He couldn't even count on Kim to believe in him. His mother had known he was smart. But it hadn't kept her from leaving. His head hurt. "Smart" wasn't getting him anywhere.

Shaking his head to banish the memories, he returned to his office and put together the files for James. It took him twice as long as it should have, because his hands shook. By the time he was finished, the day was almost over. He had a raging headache. He needed to get away, to forget about everything happening at work. Dina. Before he could think about why she was the first person to pop into his head, he grabbed his phone. He checked his messages, but she hadn't called him back. He'd stop by the library and pick her up to go somewhere. Anywhere. She'd take his mind off of here. Maybe they'd go into the city to a club.

Ten minutes later, he was in his car, screeching into a spot in the library lot. The woman who was friends with Dina—what was her name?—was walking toward her car. Tracy. That was it.

"Hey Tracy, is Dina around?"

She shielded her eyes from the sun. "Adam? No, she's home today. Everything okay?"

"Sure is," he said with a grin. Pulling out of the lot, he drove to Dina's apartment.

He pulled up to the old Victorian building and shook his head. It suited her perfectly. The converted house was well kept, but old fashioned. As pretty as it was, with colorful shutters and a shaded front porch, it wasn't his style. He preferred his modern apartment complex with a gym and underground garage. He found an empty spot on the street, locked his car, and tried the front door. It was locked, so he buzzed #2.

"Hello?"

Dina's voice made him smile, his first genuine smile all day. Some of the tension left his neck. "Hey Dina, it's Adam."

"Adam. Um, come on up."

She buzzed him in. He took the stairs two at a time. The hallway had that musty smell of ancient buildings, the staircase was protected by an antique-looking railing. She was waiting for him in the doorway of her apartment, her thick hair pulled back in a ponytail, dressed in a long sleeved T-shirt and sweatpants. Most women he dated would have been mortified to be seen so underdressed. Yet Dina looked perfect. She smiled. His gaze focused on her pink lips. What would they taste like?

"Get changed, we're going out."

Her smile faltered. "Did we have plans I forgot about?"

"No, I just thought it would be fun to go some-where. We could go into the city to a club, drive along the waterfront, whatever you want." He jingled his keys against his leg. He peered over her shoulder, trying to get a view of the inside of her apartment. He saw a glimpse of a kitchen counter, some overstuffed furni-ture, and a mix of colors.

"Adam, I can't just pick up and do that. I have plans. I was just about to start getting ready."

"Cancel them. Come out with me."

She stared at him. He fought the urge to squirm.

"Come on in."

From her bedroom, she called Zach. "I'm sorry, I need to postpone tonight. Can we reschedule? I have a semi-emergency that I need to take care of. I'm so sorry. I don't usually do things like this." She never cancelled plans, but something about Adam, a look in his eye, made her do it.

"Oh gosh, is there anything I can do?"

She thought about Adam currently sitting in her living room, jittery, upset, needing her. "No, it's some-thing I have to take care of on my own. I'm so sorry to do this last minute though."

"No problem. I'll call you later in the week and we can reschedule. I'm busy the next few days with an ex-periment I'm running, so I can tell you all about it when I see you next."

"Terrific. Thanks so much for understanding."

She hung up, glanced in the mirror, and shuddered. Well, Adam would have to deal with her looking like a schlump—that's what happens when you show up unannounced. Returning to her living room, she watched him pace, filled with a frenetic energy she didn't understand.

His eyes reflected hurt and sadness. She wanted to fold him into a hug, but he wouldn't stop moving. He probably wouldn't want her hug anyway. "What's going on, Adam?"

"Nothing. I just was in the mood for a good time and thought of you."

She cringed at the implication. He threw his hands up as if in surrender.

"No, wait, I didn't mean it like that."

"Then what did you mean?"

"Let's go somewhere, do something, drive fast."

He raked his hands through his short blond hair. A part of her wanted to feel its texture between her fingers while another part of her wanted to run and hide under her covers.

"Adam, I don't do spontaneity."

"Why the hell not?" He spun toward her and took her by the shoulders. Despite his quick movements, his hands were gentle. The hurt in his eyes had lessened. But it was still there. His hands were warm, his breath minty. While part of her wanted to run away, another part of her wanted to melt into him. "Because I'm a planner."

"And you have plans."

His gaze raked her from top to bottom, leaving a trail of heat in their wake. Only the heat wasn't desire, it was embarrassment. Because she knew very well what she looked like. She folded her arms across her chest. "I did, which I cancelled when you showed up."

"You were going to the gym?" He raised one side of his mouth into a lopsided smile.

She would have laughed if she had found his comment the least bit funny. "No, I was relaxing before getting ready to go out with someone who doesn't care what I look like." She inhaled as soon as the words left her mouth. "I...I didn't mean..."

Adam gave a bitter laugh. He shuttered the last of the emotion she'd thought she'd seen. "Of course you did. I should have considered you might be seeing someone else. My bad."

He edged toward the door. "Go 'uncancel' them. See you around."

Before she could say anything else, he strode down the stairs. The click of the door as it closed gently reverberated through her head. He was gone.

CHAPTER SIX

Hours later, Adam returned home from aimless driving, bleary eyed. Every muscle in his body ached from the tight control he'd maintained, and hadn't been able to release. Parking in the underground garage, he stumbled his way up to his apartment. When the elevator doors opened into the gold-carpeted lobby, he stopped short.

Dina was curled up in one of the red leather chairs. What the hell?

Bending down, he smelled coconuts in her hair. He inhaled, closing his eyes and imagining her wrapped naked around him, lying on a beach with the waves lapping at their toes. But they weren't at the beach and she wasn't naked. She also wasn't supposed to be here.

Anger, embarrassment, and desire combined as he looked at her, trying to figure out what the hell he was supposed to do with her. He couldn't leave her here—

it was two in the morning. He wasn't an ass, even if others might think so. It was rude. She'd be embarrassed. He wasn't that guy.

He knelt down and gently shook her shoulder. She was warm beneath his hand. "Dina?"

Her eyes opened. She blinked, her eyes almost eggplant in the dim light of the lobby. They were slightly unfocused. Extending her legs out from their curled-in-a-ball position, he heard the faintest of squeals as she stretched. His heart thumped. She reminded him of a cat stretching in the sun. His imagination went into overdrive as he pictured her naked in his bed, waking up after a night of making love. He fought the urge to pull her against his chest and nuzzle her hair. As if slammed by recognition, she started and sat up straight.

"Adam! What are you doing here?"

He raised an eyebrow. "I live here. The question is, what are you doing here?"

She looked around. The color of her creamy skin deepened like an overripe peach. "I must have fallen asleep."

Holding out a hand to her, he helped her up. "Come on upstairs."

"No, I need to go home."

"You haven't told me why you're here." He steered her toward the elevator.

"I came to apologize. But you weren't home, so I waited. Now you're back. I shouldn't have said what I did."

Adam pressed the button on the elevator and held the door while waving her inside. "I'm not sure exactly what you're sorry for. If anyone should apologize, it's me."

She leaned against the wall and angled her head until she could make eye contact with him. "You were upset. I should have tried to help you."

He froze, key poised to unlock his door. How the hell did this woman read him so clearly? And more importantly, how could he stop it? "It was no big deal."

"Yes it was."

He folded his arms across his chest and turned to her, nostrils flaring as all of his previous fears came rushing back. "How the hell would you know?"

"Anyone who knows you could tell."

What the hell was she talking about?

"I can tell you're still upset, even now."

"No, I'm just annoyed by a woman who was camping out in my lobby." He should have left her there.

"Right." She didn't look convinced. After a few moments of silence, she sighed and stayed in the elevator. "It's late, I need to go. Goodnight."

It was two o'clock in the morning. She was barely awake. "Please," he said. He ushered her to his door. "Come inside."

"Your apartment?"

"Yeah."

"Now?"

He looked around. "Yeah."

"Why?"

He rubbed a hand down his face. "Because it's too late for you to go home alone and I'm in no shape to drive you." Not waiting for her to argue, he put an arm around her shoulders and steered her inside. She fit well in the crook of his arm, all soft and warm. He searched his brain for a reason to keep his arm there. But apparently his brain was even more tired than usual, because he couldn't come up with a single one. And he called himself a red-blooded male. "Sit down," he said and pointed to the black leather sofa in his living room.

She sat, back straight, perched on the edge, as if she were afraid of...he didn't know what. Not him, right? She didn't know about the harassment claims, so there was no reason for her to be afraid of him. But she looked uncomfortable.

He left her sitting in his living room and went to the linen closet. Grabbing an extra blanket and pillow, he returned to her and pointed toward the hallway.

"My bedroom is down there. You can sleep in my bed."

She frowned. His finger itched to trace the crease in between her eyebrows. Hell, his whole body itched to touch any of her. Instead, he squeezed the linens in his arms.

"With you?"

God he wished he could say yes. "No, I'll sleep here."

"Why?"

"So you can get some sleep."

She jumped up. "You want me to sleep in your bed?"

Heat flooded his groin at the mental picture his mind painted. He gritted his teeth. "Yes."

"I can't do that. I have to go home."

He threw his head back and withheld a scream. "It's late. You're tired. Stay here."

"But I'll have to leave in the morning."

"That's usually what's required to get to work."

She shook her head. "No, in the morning it will be light. People will see me."

*Oh my God, she's talking about the walk of shame. She thinks people will see her and assume...*desire mixed with sympathy. He doubted anyone would think anything of it. But the thought of waking up in the same apartment as her made him hard, and he wasn't even planning on touching her.

"It will be fine," he said, when he could get the words past his strangled throat.

"Then give me those and I'll sleep out here." Before he could protest, she pulled the blanket and pillow from him.

He hadn't meant for her to sleep on the couch. He hadn't meant for her to use...His arm froze as he reached out for the blanket, but she pulled it onto her lap, sat cross-legged on the couch, and turned to him. "If you're going to make me stay, then you have to talk to me."

He liked talking to her. So this wasn't a problem. As long as he didn't reveal too much. And as long as she didn't notice the pattern on the blanket. "Let me just get changed." And maybe find something else for her to cover up in. When he returned to the living room in sweats, he carried another blanket. But she was already wrapped up in the first one, and he would draw too much attention if he made her change blankets. Instead, he held onto it and eased onto the recliner next to the sofa.

"What's wrong?" she asked.

He didn't know he'd been so obvious. "Muscles are sore."

She nodded. "What's making them sore?"

He shrugged and then winced. "No idea." She didn't need to know why he was tense.

"What happened today to make you so upset?"

This is what she wanted to talk about? He would much rather talk about other things. Like her. "So tell me about the guy you were seeing tonight."

"There's nothing to tell," she said. "You showed up and I cancelled my plans."

His hands clenched at the thought of her going out on a date. "Must not have been a great guy if you were so eager to cancel on him."

"He's nice."

"That's it? Nice?"

"And isn't embarrassed to be seen with me in public."

What the hell was she talking about? Oh. Right. Dammit. "I..." What was he supposed to say to her? That he was so concerned about what others thought of him that he raced to establish his reputation, forgetting about who he might already be with and how they would feel? "I'm sorry. My behavior was inexcusable, but you don't embarrass me."

She picked at the blanket. "Cute," she said.

Damn. She noticed. His stomach knotted. She was wrapped in his Star Wars blanket. The one Kim's kids had given him as a thank you for spending time with them. "Except when you make fun of my blanket."

She wrapped it tighter around herself. His embarrassment disappeared, replaced once again by desire. Even tired, he couldn't stop looking at her. Her face was clear, open, and she had such warmth emanating from her. He wanted to soak some of it up for himself.

"So why are your muscles sore?"

She was also stubborn. He shrugged.

"Okay, what was freaking you out at my apartment earlier?"

He needed to change the subject, fast. He thought back to his brief time in her apartment. He hadn't had time to notice much of it from the doorway, except that it was homey and sweet, like her. There'd been a big fancy envelope on the table by the front door.

"What was that fancy invitation for back at your place?"

Her face blanched. For a moment he thought she was going to faint. Who fainted these days? Maybe the same women who were concerned about the walk of shame? She didn't seem like the fainting type. But her cheeks regained their color, and more. She looked down at her lap. Mission accomplished, although his distraction came at her expense.

"It's nothing, just my high school reunion."

"Which one?"

"Tenth."

"Are you going?"

She shook her head. "Absolutely not."

"Why?"

"Because I don't feel like either being ignored or talked about. High school was not a fun time for me."

High school reunions were the time to show up all the people who thought little of you. "Of course you're going. We'll go together."

"What?"

Yeah, what? Had he really just offered to take her? "You and me. Your high school reunion." Apparently he had.

She shook her head. Her ponytail whipped back and forth like some over-zealous spectator at a tennis match. "That's crazy."

"You need a little crazy in your life. It'll be fun."

"You have no idea what it will be like. Popular girls who looked at me like I wasn't fit to wipe gum off their shoe. People who only talked to me to beg me to give them my homework to copy. People who hid their intelligence in order to have friends, and ignored me. Trust me, there's no one I want to see."

Adam stretched his shoulders at her description of people who sounded a lot like him.

Dina stared him down, as if daring him to do his worst. Ha, she obviously didn't know him. His worst had chased his mother away. His worst was turning his father into a slave driver. He couldn't allow himself to give her his worst. So he'd give her his best.

"I'm sure they've changed. Or at least grown older and fatter. You shouldn't miss it, especially if it scares you."

She yawned. "You're crazy, but I'm too tired to argue right now."

She snuggled down into the blanket. Adam had an overpowering desire to join her. He reached his hand out to hover over her leg. When she moved it as she got settled, his hand skimmed the blanket. A jolt of electricity zinged up his arm. He frowned. How was he attracted to her? She wasn't the sexiest woman he'd seen, she wasn't the prettiest even. But she had a quality about her that made all his other dates seem shallow. Somehow, he couldn't get enough of her. That scared the hell out of him.

Dina woke a couple hours later, the room still dark, her mind whirling, her body completely still. She didn't want to take the chance he'd come out and see her wide awake. She didn't want him to come out here at all, wearing whatever he wore to sleep—did he even wear clothes when he slept? Possibilities danced through her head, but unlike sheep, counting them would not help her sleep.

She turned carefully onto her side, brought her knee up toward her chest. She rested her hand on her ankle, the same ankle Adam had touched earlier. Even now, she felt shooting streaks of warmth up and down her calf from his touch. She wondered what it would feel like for him to touch her in other places. She buried her head in her pillow.

No, this couldn't happen. He wasn't attracted to her—she didn't fit his profile. She wasn't tall enough, skinny enough, or sexy enough to claim him for herself. She definitely wasn't experienced enough. Oh, how he'd laugh at her if he knew how a simple touch on her ankle through a blanket had affected her. The men she was used to, the even fewer she'd slept with, had never woken her out of a deep sleep—achy and twitchy, wanting more of...something. She was completely out of her depth with Adam.

She needed to fall back asleep in order to handle tomorrow. Because tomorrow, she had to leave here with her dignity intact.

The aroma of ground coffee and the whistling of steam brought her to the surface of consciousness. She blinked at the darkness that confronted her. As her sight adjusted to the lack of light, outlines of masculine geometric furniture in the room appeared. She glanced toward the large window on the opposite wall. Streetlights glowed from outside. How early was it?

Wrapping the Star Wars blanket around her shoulders, she walked into the galley kitchen. The clock set in the stainless-steel oven said five-thirty. She should leave, now, before too many people woke up and saw her. But oh, coffee. Dina inhaled. The toe-curling smell filled her nostrils, waking her up even without the benefits of the caffeine.

"Smells good, doesn't it?"

She shrieked, glaring at Adam as he let out a low, throaty laugh from the doorway behind her. He was wearing a white T-shirt and pajama pants. She swallowed. "You scared me on purpose."

"No, I didn't. But I will not deny finding it amusing."

Shaking her head, she drew the blanket closer around her shoulders. "I should go."

"And miss my coffee? If I say so myself, you'd be depriving yourself of something amazing."

His green eyes glowed in the dim under-cabinet lighting. For a moment, Dina wasn't positive he was referring to coffee. "Okay, I'll try your coffee," she said, making sure to be crystal clear in her answer, regardless of what he was referencing, "but then I really need to leave."

Adam walked toward her. He reached around her to open the cherry cabinet next to her head. This close to him, she was overwhelmed by his nearness. Warmth radiated from him, his cotton T-shirt brushed her cheek as he stretched his arm beyond her. His particular scent—spice and soap and, for the moment, sleep—battled with the smell of the brewing coffee, making her dizzy.

He grabbed two mugs and handed her one. Their fingers touched. She swallowed. "You're less likely to run into people if you wait until later, after most people have left for work."

"Work! Oy, I forgot. I have an eight-o'clock meeting." She took a sip of the coffee, moaned as she savored the nutty flavor. He was right, it was amazing.

"Good, isn't it?"

Her eyes flew open. Her cheeks warmed. His smile indicated he'd heard her moan. She wondered when he was going to call her out.

"Why don't you skip work and we can have an adventure," he said.

She raised an eyebrow over the rim of her mug. "Your dad would be okay with you playing hooky?"

Adam's face lost all expression. "He probably wouldn't care," he said.

He leaned against the black granite counter drinking his coffee, but Dina wasn't fooled. His shoulders were set, and his fingers gripped the mug so hard his knuckles were white. This was the Adam she remembered from her apartment, back before he'd distracted her with other things.

Taking a last sip of her drink, she rested the mug on the counter, walked over to him, and removed his mug from his hand. His look of surprise quickly shuttered.

"What are you doing?" he asked.

"What's going on with you and work?"

"Nothing."

"You and your dad?"

"You're very nosy for someone so short."

"Don't think you're going to distract me by turning this conversation toward me. Talk to me, Adam. There's no one else around."

Standing this close to him, she could see a vein pulse in his throat. His eyelid twitched. He avoided her gaze. It wasn't hard, she had to admit. She only came to his shoulder. But he'd never avoided looking at her before.

"Adam."

He sighed.

She watched his chest swell. Clenching her hands at her sides, she resisted the urge to run her hands over the muscles beneath his shirt. She needed him to talk to her, but she also needed to get to work. She didn't think touching him would speed up the process.

"My dad is giving me a hard time about something and limiting the amount and type of work he's giving me. He's making it harder for me to make junior partner."

She could see by his tortured expression it was a big deal. She could also see there was more to it than that.

"It must be really hard working for your father. Don't give up though. Talk to him about it. Let him know how you feel."

He looked at her as if she'd said he could fly. She waited for him to say something, but he remained silent. Then, taking her by the shoulders, he pushed her gently away, grabbed his coffee cup, and walked out of the kitchen. As he left, he called over his shoulder, "Don't forget to text me the information about your high school reunion."

Crap.

CHAPTER SEVEN

Dina returned to her apartment that evening, yawning. She kicked a yellow petal on the front sidewalk before she dragged herself up the stairs and into the front hall of her Victorian building. More petals intermingled with leaves lay scattered on the carpeted hallway. She frowned as she opened her mailbox. Some flower delivery service had made a mess.

After a mostly sleepless night at Adam's and a full day of work, all she wanted to do was draw a bath in her claw foot tub and go to bed. Immediately. She followed the trail of petals and leaves upstairs to her front door. Taped to it was a kelly-green envelope. She yanked it off and opened it.

Tracy said it was okay.

Her mind was too sluggish to process the meaning of the note, so she unlocked her door and gasped. Yellow flowers of every variety covered all the visible surfaces in her apartment. Centered on the occasional table in her front hallway was a vase of yellow sunflowers. Tossing her keys next to them, she moved into her living room, where vases of blanket flowers and daffodils littered her coffee table. Walking over to the windowsill, she sneezed at the goldenrod.

Kicking off her shoes, she walked barefoot into the kitchen and saw roses on the counters, ligularia in the sink and black eyed Susans on the stove. Stunned, she peeked into her bedroom. Snapdragons sat on her dresser, tickseeds were on her night table and coneflowers were tied in bunches on her bed. It was as if the pages of *The Encyclopedia of Plants and Flowers* had come to life. Another kelly-green note lay on her pillow and she sank to the floor to read it.

Please go to your high school reunion with me.
Adam

It was only when she saw each word alternating between green and gold that she realized Adam had chosen the flowers to coordinate with her school colors. She leaned against the side of her bed. Mr. Flashypants had struck again and he was a romantic. Apparently with her friend Tracy's help.

Taking her time, she stopped to examine all of the flowers, except for the goldenrod, which she carried at arm's length out to her balcony—allergies. Her lips twitched. He was the one who left the petals and leaves trailing from her front porch to her apartment door. It was...sweet and romantic and over the top. Pulling her phone out of her purse, she dialed Adam's number. He answered right away.

"So will you go with me?"

Had he been waiting for her call? "Thank you for the flowers." She tried to keep her voice modulated and steady, even though her heart was beating fast.

"Did you like them?"

"Everything except the goldenrod. They make me sneeze."

"I'm sorry!"

"It's okay. I put them out on the balcony where I can see them anyway."

"I'll remember that for next time."

He was going to do this again? "Mm hm."

"So, will you go with me?"

"It's *my* reunion. Shouldn't it be, 'can I go with you?'?"

"Details."

She laughed. "Yes."

The smile on Adam's face lasted the rest of the night as he watched TV and lay in bed. Dina invaded his dreams, which featured a silhouette he'd swear was her. He woke up the next morning with a smile that didn't dim as he walked from Starbucks into his office. Only his father's voice coming through the intercom, ordering him into his office at his "earliest convenience" made it disappear.

The man sure knew how to ruin the mood.

Plastering a neutral expression on his face, Adam sat across from his father at his massive desk.

"What's up?"

His father frowned. "Is that how you speak to me?"

Neutrality was difficult to maintain. Kudos to Switzerland. "I apologize."

With a nod, his father leaned forward, tenting his hands and resting his elbows on his mahogany desk. "Bradley & Company is threatening to take their business elsewhere, thanks to your carelessness."

His stomach plummeted to his toes.

His father's look of distaste matched Adam's feelings at having his father think so poorly of him.

"It's all bullshit!" Adam hurled himself out of the chair and paced his father's office.

"Sit down."

Shooting pain ringed his scalp as a tension headache began to form, but he sat.

"And the paralegals are unhappy working with you," his father said

"Even if you think I was careless with the account, which I wasn't, you know I didn't throw Ashley under the bus, Dad. My concerns are legitimate."

"Are you sure?"

Adam cradled his head in his hands before looking at his father. The man was in his fifties and had that ageless white-male privileged look about him—a full head of white hair, skin tanned and leathery from endless tennis matches at the club, and a powerful stance that made him look as formidable in court as his winning record implied.

"Yes."

His father focused his famous prosecutor stare at him. Adam felt as if he was turned the wrong way in a wind tunnel.

"Then you're going to need to fix your relationship with the paralegals. As for your carelessness, I can't afford any more of your screw-ups. Until further notice, you're taking time off."

Was there really no one in the paralegal department who would vouch for him? He might be the boss's son, but he always thought he had genuine relationships with them. Maybe he could talk to Kim in private.

The logical side of his brain knew his father had no choice but to take away his caseload. Bradley & Company was an important client with far-reaching influence. If they left, it would be significant loss to the law firm. But the rest of him knew making him hide away was the equivalent of announcing his guilt to the world. He'd never make junior partner this way. He wouldn't be able to move anywhere else without a good reference or current cases. He was screwed.

"You're not going to back me on this?"

His father stared past Adam's left ear. "The firm can't suffer, Adam. You know that."

He'd heard that phrase all his life. He'd just never heard it directed at him.

Dina stepped off the elevator into the waiting area of Mandel & Ryan, Attorneys at Law, and looked around wide-eyed. Between adjusting to the idea that Adam seemed to want to be more than just friends, and taking the leap to surprise him at his office, she didn't think she had any more nerves left.

She was wrong.

The smell of money—amounts of which she could never hope to have—practically assaulted her nostrils as she looked around the space. Everything she'd ever read about corporate law offices was true. The carpet beneath her feet was so soft, she wanted to roll around on it. The furniture was expensive wood and she thought the door into the inner sanctum might actually be zebrawood. A woman in a suit that looked like it was straight out of a fashion magazine looked at her over platinum-rimmed glasses. Her hair was perfect. Dina ran a hand over hers in discomfort.

"May I help you?"

Unlike some accents that identified the speaker's geography, hers identified her amount of money—lots. *Wow, even the office receptionist makes more money than I do.*

She shifted from one foot to the other. "Um, I'm here to see Adam Mandel."

"Is he expecting you?"

"No...not really." The idea of taking Adam out to lunch to thank him for the flowers had been a spur-of-the moment thing. It had sounded great in the security of the library stacks. Here, not so much.

The receptionist frowned. At least, Dina thought she frowned. Her face didn't move, but somehow managed to look more disapproving than she had before. "I'll see if he's available."

Dina perched on the supple black leather sofa and studied the magazines on the marble table in front of her—*Islands, Yachts International, Saveur, Unique Homes, Upscale Living, Architectural Digest* and the *Robb Report*. As if she hadn't already known the second she walked in here, she was way out of her league.

"I'm sorry, but—"

Whatever Little Miss Botox was about to say was interrupted by the zebrawood door opening.

He looked awful. Tension lines bisected his brow and a thin white line outlined his lips. He stopped dead when he saw her, and she thought maybe she'd made the biggest mistake of her life. A wash of red passed across his face and he looked around.

"Uh, Dina. What are you doing here?"

That was not the "Hey, I'm so glad to see you, Dina!" reaction she was looking for.

"I thought I'd take you to lunch."

A variety of emotions played across his face, but whatever he was going to say was halted by the zebrawood door opening a second time. A thirty-years older version of Adam stepped through and Dina didn't know whether to be impressed or frightened. Like Adam, he was tall with broad shoulders. His full head of white hair was slicked back. His piercing blue eyes were sharp, and he stood as if surrounded by a bubble of impenetrability. He scanned the room, looking down his aquiline nose.

"Adam, your key."

Adam stiffened and Dina reached a hand out and placed it on his upper arm. His muscle was rock hard—too hard to be caused by anything but tension. The muscles in his jaw bulged and his teeth ground together.

Why would he have to turn in his key?

Adam's father turned his stare to her. "May I help you?" His stare almost made Dina cringe. Instead she stepped forward.

"I'm Dina Jacobs." She held out her hand. "It's a pleasure to meet you." The words almost got stuck in her throat.

Little Miss Botox was practically falling over the reception desk eavesdropping, and Mr. Mandel must have noticed, because he stepped forward and took Dina's outstretched hand. His handshake was firm. Hers was too and surprise flashed across his face before he banked it down.

"Noah Mandel. How do you know my son?"

"Dad!"

She put a calming hand on Adam's chest. "We've been seeing each other for about a week now."

She didn't know whose face was more comical, Mr. Mandel's or Little Miss Botox's. Both mirrored each other—open fish mouth, raised eyebrows, flared nostrils—which was quite a feat for the receptionist, and a little reassuring somehow for Dina.

Adam's father, on the other hand, was alarming. Had Adam not mentioned her at all?

He cleared his throat, looked at Adam, and cleared it again. "Is this true?"

Finally finding his voice, Adam spoke. "Yes, Dad, it is."

"Do you think it's wise?"

"Yes, I do."

Suddenly, Adam put his arm around her shoulder and pulled her against him. He'd never shown her affection publicly. Pleasure, similar to the feeling she'd had when she saw the flowers, flowed through her. Remembering how similar to a gasping fish the other two had looked, she did her best not to let her jaw drop.

But she couldn't do anything about the warmth that spread throughout her body, or the lightheadedness she got from standing this close to him, or the zings of pleasure that were traveling up and down her body and pooling below her stomach.

She might not fit in with his lifestyle, but she knew how to make someone comfortable and her parents had taught her manners. Looking up at him, she said, "Thank you again for the flowers." Turning her focus to his father, she added, "He gave me the most beautiful flowers I've ever seen. You taught him well."

A hint of a frown crossed Noah's features before he inclined his head. Without another word, he turned and headed back into the office. When the door closed, silence stretched. Dina stayed in Adam's embrace, afraid to break the spell. Finally, when even Little Miss Botox had gone back to work, Dina glanced up at Adam.

He was smiling.

He pulled her out of the reception area, into the building's hallway outside his father's office. "You're a genius."

She was, but it wasn't something she mentioned during the first week of a relationship, so she doubted he was referring to her IQ. "What are you talking about?"

"My dad's been on my case about being more responsible, improving my image, etc. When he saw you with me, he backed down. This is the solution to all our problems."

This time she stiffened. He couldn't be…

"You need me to take you to the reunion. I need you to help my dad see I'm mature enough, attentive enough, for the promotion."

He was. Had she misread his intentions so badly after he sent her those flowers?

"We were already going to the reunion together," she said. "And shouldn't your performance at work determine whether or not you get a promotion?"

"I need a hidden weapon outside of work. And you, my dear," he planted a kiss on her forehead, "are it."

No, no, no. "You don't need a weapon. You need to have a conversation with your dad to fix things."

"My dad doesn't work that way."

The sinking feeling in her stomach increased. Because while she had started to feel something for Adam, he'd just turned her into a career asset for his own ambition.

"You'll help me convince my father, right?"

His green-eyed gaze sent shards of heat into her soul, and she did all she could to hide them. He might not care for her in a romantic way, but even she could see he cared for her as a friend. And she didn't have a lot of those. Certainly not male ones who were willing to take her to a reunion and save her the embarrassment of dealing with her old high school enemies by herself.

She could help him with this ruse until after the reunion. By then, she'd have gotten through seeing her old classmates, and his father would see how deserving he finally was. It was less than two months.

"Yes," she said.

It was the only thing she could do.

CHAPTER EIGHT

T his was the dumbest idea on the planet. No, in the galaxy. Maybe even the entire universe. *Yay, aliens, I've just let you all off the hook!* And now, not only was she talking to herself, she was talking to imaginary aliens. Obviously, she should call Adam and tell him she was sick, too sick to go to his father's house for dinner, too sick to participate in this charade.

Instead, she stood in her bathroom, trying to force her frizzy, gravity-defying hair into something chic and sophisticated, to go along with her black slacks and pale pink V-neck top. No matter what she did, her hair resembled a Brillo pad. Today was the one day it mattered, because in ten minutes Adam was picking her up.

Observing the futility of her endeavor, she pulled her hair back from her face with two combs, added pale pink lipstick and hoped it would be enough. She walked to her window and stared down at the street below. In the distance, she heard a motor racing and a moment later, Adam's fancy-schmancy sports car pulled up. It was black, expensive, and noisy. When her buzzer rang, she grabbed her purse, whispered *beh-hahts-lah-khah*, Hebrew for good luck, and jogged down the steps.

Adam exited the driver's side and opened the passenger door for her. As she started to slide in, he pulled her toward him and brushed her lips with his. He tasted minty and before she could analyze how his kiss made her feel, he pulled away.

"You look great."

She smiled and slid into the buttery leather seat as he sauntered around and started the car.

"Thanks."

He gripped the steering wheel and Dina watched him, wishing for easy camaraderie, but at a loss for how to get it. The tendons in his hands were taut and the muscles in his jaw bulged. When they stopped at the next traffic light, Dina rested her hand on his. Adam let out a breath and flexed his fingers beneath her hand. His jaw unclenched and he turned to her. "It's not you. I'm just not looking forward to this dinner."

"Because of me?"

"No. You're the only good thing about it. Because of my father." He pulled her hand toward his mouth and kissed her fingers. "I like your hair."

She laughed. "Seriously? I mean, I guess I should say, 'thank you,' but my hair does not deserve a compliment."

Reaching across the center console, he grabbed a hank of her hair and squeezed and released it. It bounced, like the spring in a pogo stick. "I like it. I will not stop complimenting something I like. And I like you. So get used to it."

"Yes, sir."

His cheek twitched and Dina saw the hint of a smile cross his face before he stifled it. But the mood in the car lightened, at least until they turned into a drive between two posts topped by massive lions. As Adam steered the car around the curve, a huge brick federal style mansion with beige stone pillars came into view.

Dina swallowed and peered out the window, half expecting a line of servants to stand outside in greeting. This is where Adam's father lived, and all she'd been worried about was her hair?

Parking in front of the broad stone steps leading up to an elaborately carved double door, Adam hopped out of the car and came around to Dina's side.

"Ready?" he asked, as he led her up the stairs.

"Sure." Fake it 'til you make it, baby.

He rang the bell and as the musical chimes echoed inside, Dina turned to him in puzzlement.

"Wouldn't it be easier to just walk in?"

Before Adam could answer, an older woman in black dress slacks and a white cotton blouse answered the door.

"Mr. Mandel. Your father is waiting for you in the living room."

Dina walked with Adam behind the woman, her feet sinking into the plush Aubusson carpet, and resisted the urge to reach for his hand. She could do this.

Outside the doorway of the living room, he reached for hers. His warm skin against hers and the press of his fingers was reassuring. Whether he needed the support, or whether he was doing it for show, didn't matter. They were together for the moment.

His father rose as they entered, Adam gave her hand a last squeeze but held on, and walked up to his father. They nodded to each other, and his father turned his attention to her.

She held out her hand and he grasped it. While Adam might be Mr. Flashypants, his father was The General, complete with military posture. It was a good thing her hand was in Adam's or she might be tempted to salute.

"It's a pleasure to see you again, Mr. Mandel. You have an impressive home."

He released her grasp and nodded. "You're quite different from Adam's usual dates."

Oof. She heard Adam's intake of breath and from the glint in his father's eye, Dina wondered if he was looking for a reaction. Her first impression of him hadn't been great, and he sure wasn't helping his cause now. But she was here for Adam, and she'd live up to her side of the bargain.

"I'm sure I am," she said, a wide grin on her face. Looping her arm through Adam's, she looked up at him, hoping his father could read her expression of adoration.

"May I offer you a drink?" The General asked.

When she nodded and Adam's father reached for the whiskey decanter, Dina blurted, "Did you know that if the 99 million cases of Scotch exported each year were laid end-to-end, they would run the distance between Edinburgh and New York six times?"

Dina froze as the words left her mouth, for the expressions on the men's faces were...odd. The General's hand was suspended midair above her tumbler, his mouth slightly open, his white brows furrowed. Adam looked between her and his father and seemed to be suppressing laughter.

"No, I did not know that. How...interesting," The General said. "Adam, would you like one?"

He nodded, eyes sparkling.

They sat in front of the fireplace, glasses in hand and Dina listened to The General and Adam make small talk. Or attempt to. They were really bad at it. The General mentioned the weather and Adam answered with a word or two. Dina launched into a description of cloud formations. Adam mentioned baseball and The General nodded. Just as the awkward exchange was becoming unbearable and Dina was about to break in with baseball stats, the woman who'd opened the front door for them entered the room after a soft knock.

"Dinner is served."

The General nodded his head, reminding Dina of an emperor surveying his subjects. He led them out of the living room, across the expansive foyer and into the dining room. If Adam hadn't held her by the hand, she would have stopped dead in the entryway.

The dining room—to call it a room was probably an insult—was awe-inspiring. From at least a twelve-foot ceiling dangled a crystal chandelier with enough lights to power a small country. Mirrors on either end of the room gave it the illusion of extending far further than its thirty feet. Decorated in taupe, mauve and cream, it exuded elegance. Dina wasn't sure she was dressed well enough for the room.

However, no one stopped her and no one offered her a change of clothing, so she sat in the Louis XVI chair Adam held out for her, stared at the bone china and silver laid out on the mahogany table, and pretended she fit in.

"This room is lovely," she said to The General, who inclined his head. "Did you know Louis XVI hated cats?"

It was as if her mouth had a mind of its own, which would be great if it involved kissing Adam, but in this instance, she didn't think obscure facts about furniture, or the kings after whom that furniture was named, was endearing her to Adam's father.

But this time, he laughed. "Cats? Really?"

Spreading her cream linen napkin on her lap, she nodded.

"Well, I'll be damned. I guess the dandy might have had some good qualities."

A raised eyebrow from Adam prevented her from contradicting The General on his use of dandy. Instead, she cleared her throat, tasted the butternut squash soup and listened as the two men talked about law. The subject didn't particularly interest her; but, their interaction did. Adam asked questions, as if to draw his father out. The General initially gave one or two word answers, but Adam persisted. Dina's heart broke listening to him trying to get his father to talk to him. She slid her foot forward beneath the table until it bumped into his. His gaze shot toward her and he paused mid-sentence.

His father noticed. "See, Adam, this is what I'm talking about. You lack focus. Careless mistakes are inevitable if you don't pay attention."

Dina's gasp was lost in the quiet clatter of her meal being served. "I'm sorry," she said, "but that was my fault. My foot hit Adam's and distracted him."

The General raised an eyebrow, reminding her of his son. "My son could do with fewer distractions."

Adam's hands had clasped into fists and he was poised to rise from the table. She was supposed to be helping him. Now was not the time for him to get into a fight with his father.

Instead, she smiled. "Well, if we eliminated all distractions, neither of us would be here tonight," she said, and The General's jaw dropped.

With a tip of her head, Dina switched her attention to the meal in front of her—according to the person who'd served her, it was grilled filet mignon with a brandy peppercorn sauce, roasted fingerling potatoes, and fresh spinach. It was delicious and she was glad of the break to focus on her food.

"Would you like more wine?" Adam held up the bottle and she shook her head.

"No, thank you. I'm good."

"Temperance," The General said. "Another good quality. Adam, you could learn a lot from her."

Adam's jaw clenched and Dina had had enough. "Actually, I've learned a lot from Adam as well."

Adam lowered the wine bottle to the table, but kept his hand clenched around it. She wanted to reach out, cover his hand and soothe him, but the table was too wide and climbing across it? Well, she wasn't that type of woman. Hoping he'd take her running her foot up his calf as a sign of comfort rather than foreplay, she continued her conversation with The General.

"His knowledge of heroes and mythology is fascinating. In fact," she turned back toward Adam, "I put aside some new reference materials and magazines that you might be interested in."

His hand relaxed and rested on the table. "Thanks. I'll stop by to look at them."

"Since when are you interested in that?" The General didn't bother looking up from his plate.

"I've always been interested in it. Don't you remember that class I took in college?"

"At Emory? No, I don't."

Dina came from a family that paid attention to every detail of her life. A particular class in college? Her parents could recall the day and time of the class, as well as the professor and her final grade.

She wiped her mouth and put down her fork. "What class was it?"

"Mythology and superheroes."

"I'll bet that was fascinating."

"Almost made me want to get a PhD."

His father snorted.

Dina turned to The General. "Have you always loved the law, or was there something else that piqued your interest?"

A look passed over his face with a dreamy quality that had she not seen, she would never have believed.

"I took a theater class once."

Adam paused mid bite. "Really? What kind?"

"Musical. I was told it was helpful for public speaking." He smiled as if lost in a memory. "That was a lot of fun."

"I didn't know you could sing," Adam said.

"I'm more of the shower variety." He hummed a few bars and after a couple of seconds, The General turned to his son. "I like this one. I don't know how you found her or what she sees in you, but if you're as smart as someone with my DNA is supposed to be, you'll keep her."

CHAPTER NINE

"Adam, before you go, can I speak with you a moment?"

They'd been just about to leave this mausoleum filled to the brim with memories of his mother, and Adam stepped away from Dina with a sigh. She smelled so good. Turning his back on his father, he brought Dina into the living room and made sure she was comfortably ensconced in a chair by the window. He placed a hand on her shoulder. Beneath the pale pink cashmere sweater, he could feel her delicate bones. The contrast between soft and sharp almost made him groan. He wanted to let himself be overwhelmed by her textures, not by his father's commands or by whispers of his mother's unhappiness. "I won't be long," he whispered, before returning to the foyer and his father. "Sure, Dad." He followed his father down the hall.

Clicking the heavy door shut behind him, he stood in his father's home office, the man's inner sanctum. He waited for the other shoe to drop. Because there was always another shoe.

"I've convinced Bradley to stay with us, but you're not allowed to work with them."

"Ever? They're on retainer."

"Doesn't matter. And you'll have to work without a paralegal for now."

"How about I contact the president of Bradley and apologize?"

His father squared off the papers on his desk. Adam stared. His father liked orderliness more than anything else. He didn't want to think where that left him.

"I can't have you anywhere near them right now. The agreement I made with him is tenuous at best. I have only our best people working with the company. And if you say or do anything that hits them the wrong way, they're gone. I won't risk it."

"I swear it wasn't me, Dad."

"I wish I could believe you, but you've screwed up twice before this. If you were anyone else, I would have fired you."

Adam ran a hand through his hair and tried to ignore the sudden nausea that made the food they'd just eaten threaten to come right back up. There was nothing left to say. He rose from the chair, his body leaden. As he turned to leave, his father stopped him.

"That promotion you want? I need to see a complete change in how you conduct your professional life, Adam. Because there's no way I can justify promoting you without significant changes in your behavior. That means you need to put your work first and your personal life second. Too many people have seen how you rush through things, and it causes doubt and distrust. You have my last name, and with that name comes responsibility. You, more than anyone, have to be above reproach. That applies to your personal life as well. No more stories around the office of how you're rushing out early to hit a club or staggering in late in the same clothes you wore the day before because you were with some random woman. This Dina of yours seems like a good start. Let's see if you can keep her."

Keep her, like a coveted toy? Or maybe a grade point average? Or possibly a wild animal needing to be tamed? What the hell did his father think of him? The irony of his father pushing him to commit to one woman, when he couldn't even keep Adam's mother from leaving, wasn't lost on him. The issue begged for a much longer discussion than he had the time for right now. Dina was waiting for him in the living room. Instead of rising to the bait, he nodded.

"Thanks for dinner."

His father followed him out of the office and back to the living room, where Dina was waiting.

"It was a pleasure to meet you, Dina."

Dina smiled, looked between Adam and his father. "It was an enlightening evening. Your house is beautiful and dinner was lovely. Thank you."

Between memories of his mother leaving and admonitions from his father, Adam couldn't get away from the house fast enough. He ushered Dina out the door. Swinging his car around, he drove down the long driveway. When he could no longer see the house in the rearview mirror, but had not yet reached the street, he put the car into park.

"What are you doing?" Dina asked. "Is everything alright?"

He gripped the wheel with both hands at ten and two, as instructed years ago by his driving teacher. His thumbs rapped out a beat on the wheel only he could hear. He bowed his head. He just needed a moment to regroup...

"Adam?"

He breathed in through his nose and out through his mouth, inhaling her coconut scent that perfumed his car. Unlike the other women he'd been with, her fragrance didn't make his eyes water. It reminded him of the beach. Turning toward her, he reached out and cupped her cheek. She stared at him, a quizzical look on her face. He ran his thumb over her cheekbones before burying his hand in her hair. His life was turning to shit, and all he could think of was her.

"I...You...." He groaned and pulled her toward him, brushing his lips against hers. They were soft, giving, like everything about her. After the intractability of his father, he welcomed the change.

He needed the change. But he needed Dina more.

She gripped his shoulders as he kissed her. She tasted like wine and chocolate. His hands drifted down her back, memorizing the outline of her body beneath her sweater. In a corner of his mind he wondered if his hands were as distracting as hers were for him. Because hers were currently playing with the hair on the back of his neck and sending chills down his spine.

The thought came to him in a rush of panic. She was going to leave him, just like everyone he'd ever cared about deeply.

He leaned forward, determined to make her stay. The gearshift dug into his rib, but he ignored the jab, needing to get closer to her. Pulling her against him, he traced kisses along her jaw. He nuzzled the skin behind her ear, smiling as she gasped. His hands roved her body, slipping under her sweater, sliding up her sides and stroking her breasts. Heat shot through him straight to his groin. He groaned. When her mouth opened, he plunged his tongue inside. She stilled before her tongue meet his.

He was moving too fast, he knew it. He shouldn't rush her. She was the only woman who made him feel good about himself. He needed her to like him, to care about him, to not leave. How was he supposed to achieve that?

She raised her hands to his face and pulled away so their noses touched. He wanted her mouth on his. He reached, but she stilled him with her hands.

"Shh," she said. "What's the rush?"

He tilted his head and rested his forehead against hers as his breathing slowed. He was afraid if he didn't rush, she'd find a reason to leave. But she was right, he was moving too fast. He pulled away. She really was going to leave him.

Turning back to the wheel, he swallowed. "Sorry. I'm sorry about that. It won't happen ag—."

Now it was she who leaned over and pulled his face toward her. She kissed him long and deep before pulling away. Again.

"I didn't say stop. I said slow down." She placed her hand over his on the steering wheel.

Flipping his hand, he grasped hers and kissed it.

"Sorry, I got carried away."

"And you were avoiding something?"

How the hell could she know that? "My father said some things..." He stopped.

"…that upset you." She finished his sentence and he smiled.

"That obvious?"

She nodded. "Do you want to talk about it?"

He shook his head. Never. "Maybe some other time."

She ran her hand through his hair. The touch of her fingers against his scalp was sending shards of electricity down to his toes.

With a sigh, he put the car into drive.

Outside of her apartment, he turned to her.

"Thanks for coming with me tonight."

"If you want to talk, just call."

He leaned over and gave her a chaste kiss on the mouth. He wanted more than "talk," much more, but he'd already moved too fast. With Dina, he needed to move slowly.

Three days later, and Dina could still feel the imprint of Adam's kiss on her lips. She shivered at the little jolts of electricity running through her body at the memory of his touch. When she closed her eyes, she could smell his scent.

This was ridiculous.

Adam didn't date women like her. His father had said as much. She suspected he dated tall, thin, and gorgeous. No matter how kind and considerate he was to her, the only reason he was dating her was to help him with his father. Even if his kisses made her toes curl.

As she sat at her computer, she had to stop thinking about the way the sound of his voice made her stomach vibrate and focus on the "little-boy-lost" look caused by whatever his father had said to him.

"Are you ready?"

Dina jumped as Tracy's voice sounded behind her and she swung her chair around. "Ready for what?"

Tracy rolled her eyes. "OMG, you can't possibly have forgotten we're going shopping for your reunion dress now, can you?"

Crap. "No, of course not. I was just preoccupied."

Tracy grabbed Dina's arm and practically dragged her out of the office and out into the sunshine, where Dina simultaneously squinted and rubbed her arm.

A dull throbbing started behind her eyes. "You know, I have perfectly fine dresses at home."

Tracy shook her head and kept walking. "How old are they?"

With a shrug, Dina trotted after Tracy, who personified a heat-seeking missile as she race-walked down the crowded midday sidewalk. She watched, mortified, as three random businessmen and two mothers with strollers rushed out of the way and glared at Tracy's back as she plowed through them.

Mouthing "I'm sorry," Dina caught up with her friend outside a small dress boutique. After seeing the scantily clad window mannequins, she opened her mouth to suggest they try a different store, but Tracy had already disappeared inside.

The bell hanging over the door jingled, drowning out the saleswoman's words to Tracy.

Tracy gave a broad smile and turned toward Dina. "You can help her find a dress for her reunion."

The rail-thin Goth girl nodded. "High school or college?"

"High school," Dina replied, wondering why that mattered.

Goth Girl gave her a once-over and turned toward a clothing rack against the far wall. As Dina followed her, panic bubbled in her chest. Most of the clothes she saw were in shades of mustard, olive, and rust. When Goth Girl pulled out a cream sheath with subtle ruffles along the hem, Dina's jaw dropped.

"That's perfect," Tracy said, grabbing it from Goth Girl.

She had to admit, it was lovely. But cream? Not exactly slimming. And the back had a huge cutout, which meant she couldn't wear a bra.

"I need a bra, Tracy," she whispered.

"No you don't. Sticky Boobs!"

Goth Girl walked to the accessory area and returned with a package for Dina, who took it as her face went up in flames. They pointed her toward the dressing room and she obeyed without a sound, if only to get out of the awkward situation.

Sticky Boobs.

She stared in dismay at her reflection in the mirror. You'd think these things would be made for large-chested women, as they couldn't afford to go without a bra. Except the models on the boxes were always waifs who looked as if they hadn't even reached puberty yet. And, uh, how sticky was "sticky"? Sticky enough to defy gravity? God, she hoped so.

Once she read the directions and figured out how to apply the sticky boobs, she picked up the dress. The material was soft and slid through her fingers. The ruffles cut against the bias were sophisticated and the plunging back neckline added elegance. But on her? With a shrug, she put on the dress, letting it slide down her body and float into place.

Oy gevalt!

Who the heck was that woman in the mirror?

"Dina? Come on out!"

She blinked, noticing how her reflection hadn't changed. Pushing open the curtain, she exited the dressing room.

Tracy and Goth Girl gasped.

"Oh my God, you look beautiful," Tracy said. "Turn around!"

Dina obeyed, feeling like the ballerina in a music box.

"You have to get this," Tracy said.

Dina bit her lip. "I don't know. I mean, the dress is lovely, but, is it me? I have plenty of 'me' dresses at home that I could wear..."

Tracy marched over and gripped her shoulders. "You are not wearing one of your old dresses to your high school reunion. You're wearing this one."

Goth Girl nodded her agreement. "It's über stunning."

Dina angled herself so she could see her back. "But, it's so..."

"Perfect," said Tracy.

"I don't know."

"Trust me. You want to wow the mean girls from high school and this is the dress to do it. Besides, Adam won't be able to keep his hands off you."

"Kim, can I talk to you a minute?" Adam stood outside in the parking lot Friday evening.

Kim looked around and nodded. "What do you need, Adam?"

He ran a hand through his hair. "Look, I didn't mean to put you in an awkward position the other day, but I'm really confused and was hoping you could help me. Why am I suddenly the bad guy with the paralegals?"

She opened her back door and stuffed her briefcase and purse in the backseat of her minivan. "We're a tightknit group. We're not always treated well by some of the lawyers and we stick together. What you did to Ashley really got to us."

"I swear to you, I didn't blame her without cause. I gave her the motion to be filed. I actually handed it to her before I left and I clearly stated the deadline."

"So you're calling her a liar?"

Adam shrugged. "I wish I wasn't. But I never would have expected her not to own up to her mistake. And certainly not to have all the paralegals rally around her."

"Really? So if a paralegal screws up and forces you all to lose a case, you really think she's going to admit it? We have to have each other's backs."

"Are you saying you'd lie?"

Kim closed her eyes. "No, but I'm saying it's awkward to be working with the boss's son and expect fair treatment, especially individually."

"Wait a minute, hold on. I'll admit I've been careless in the past. I'll even admit to rushing out occasionally. But when I mess up, I admit it. You know that, Kim. I've admitted mistakes to you. And I've never blamed any of you for something I've done. So why are you so willing to believe her over me?"

"Actually, Adam," she said as she got into her car, "I'm trying to stay out of it completely. We do have each other's backs. I've had good experiences working with you and I appreciate all the help you've given me. But in this case, I'm keeping my nose out of everything. If you have an issue with Ashley, or any of the other paralegals, talk to them. Please leave me out of it."

Kim started her car and drove away, leaving Adam alone under the lamplight. Muttering a curse, he climbed into his own car and left. Ten minutes later, he pulled into a bar he and the other lawyers frequented.

"Adam!"

This late on a Friday afternoon, the bar was crowded with happy hour revelers, but despite the noise, Adam could easily hear Ryan, one of the lawyers he worked with. Although going to a bar probably wasn't the wisest choice, Adam wanted to find out from Ryan what he knew of Ashley's work. Maybe if other lawyers were having the same problem, he could use that as proof he was telling the truth. It was weak, but it was the best he could do. Following the voice, and looking out for the raised hand holding a beer, Adam pushed his way through the crowd at the door. He made his way toward the other end of the bar.

"You want the usual?" Ryan asked. Turning to the bartender, he ordered Adam a beer before addressing him again. "Haven't seen you around the office much."

Adam shrugged, took the beer from the bartender, and swallowed deeply. He'd need about twelve of these to release all his tension, but one was a start. "About that. How has Ashley been working out for you?"

Ryan laughed. "What do you mean?

"When you give her deadlines, motions to file, etc. Does she meet them?"

Ryan wrinkled his face. "I think so. I can't remember a time she hasn't. Why?"

"Because I gave her a motion to be filed—handed it to her specifically—and it never made it. She claims I never gave it to her. There was also a problem with a motion I gave her on the Hyde case a month or so ago. Now she's telling the paralegals I'm throwing her under the bus to cover my own mistake."

Ryan took a gulp of his beer. "Sorry, I haven't had any problems with her."

Adam shook his head. Another one who couldn't point to any problems and therefore, couldn't help him.

"I do know she doesn't like working late, but then, none of them do. Wish I could be more help." He eyed him over his beer. "You need to get laid, my friend," Ryan said. "You'll feel a lot better."

Adam shook his head. That was Ryan's answer to everything. In law school, Adam might have agreed with him. Hell, before his father was riding his ass, he'd probably have agreed with him. But now? Now he didn't know what the hell to do.

"Oh, do you see that one over there?" Ryan pointed to a hot blonde in the corner and Adam winced. The blonde didn't appeal to him. He took another swig of beer and shook his head.

"What's wrong with her?"

"Hair's too smooth."

He felt as surprised as Ryan looked. Where the hell had that come from?

"Since when are you so picky?" Ryan asked.

Since my father decided everything I do points to my being a waste of space. "I have no idea."

"Well, if you're not interested, I'm going to check her out." Grabbing his beer, Ryan sauntered over to the blonde.

Adam watched them as Ryan leaned in and said something, the blonde laughed, Ryan held up his hand for the bartender. Adam shook his head. When had he become such a stick in the mud? There was nothing wrong with what Ryan and the blonde were doing. He'd done it countless times.

"How the heck do I get him to pay attention to me?"

A female voice near his ear made Adam jump. He turned toward a brunette with an up do and heavy bangles on her wrists.

"Pardon me?" he asked. What kind of pick-up line was that?

"Ugh, this bartender is impossible to flag down."

Oh. "Here, let me try. What do you want?"

Her lips curved in a smile, but it didn't carry to her eyes. "Martini."

"Shaken or stirred?"

She frowned before giving him a bland smile. Dina would have gotten the reference. He turned to the bartender and raised his voice. "Hey!"

The bartender turned. Adam gave the order. *Not the most elegant way, but effective.*

"You're much better at this than I am." She held out her hand. "Yvonne."

"Adam." She had a firm handshake and well-manicured nails. The bangles on her arm clinked and reminded him of change jingling. The noise could get annoying.

"Are you here with anyone?" She craned her neck to look past him and refocused on his face.

Her voice was raspy. He had an almost irresistible urge to suggest she clear it. "Yeah." He pointed toward Ryan. "You?"

"No, I usually stop by here after work."

So she was a regular.

"So what do you do?"

"I'm a lawyer," he said. "You?"

"I'm a personal trainer. Do you work out?"

God he was tired of mindless conversation. Adam swallowed the last of his beer. Ryan was right, he was picky. Glancing toward Ryan and seeing him still occupied with his blonde, Adam tossed some bills on the counter.

"Well, it was nice to meet you, Yvonne."

"Leaving so soon?"

She placed a hand on his arm. He blinked, trying not to mistake her nails for talons.

"Long week."

As he escaped the confines of the bar, he took a deep breath and tried to force himself to relax. Drinks with Ryan hadn't helped.

Dina's face flitted through his mind and pulled him up short. His hands curled into fists as he pictured her springy hair. His lips curved in a smile as he remembered her obscure trivia and her love of knowledge.

Dina.

He wanted her.

CHAPTER TEN

Dina's phone rang early the next morning, and she cracked an eye open as she looked at the time. Seven-eighteen. Who was calling her this early on a Saturday morning?

"Hey, Dina, it's Adam."

She cleared her throat, hoping she didn't have too much of a morning voice, knowing it was a futile hope, and praying he wouldn't hear it. "Hi, Adam."

"Oh gosh, I woke you! I'm so sorry. I...I wanted to talk to you, and didn't think about the time."

So much for hopes and prayers. "It's okay."

"I'm really sorry. Go back to bed, I'll talk to you later."

"Wait," she screeched before he could hang up on her. "It's fine. I need to get up anyway." That was a lie, but she'd never fall asleep now, so she might as well talk to him. Besides, she'd missed his voice.

"Are you sure?"

"Adam!"

He laughed. "Okay, well, now that you're awake, want to go for an early-morning walk?"

A walk? "A walk? Where?"

"I was thinking on one of the trails. It's cold, but sunny and I thought it might be nice. Although..."

Dina yawned. "Although what?" She heard what she thought was a sigh, and then, nothing. "Adam?"

"Never mind. This sounded like a much better idea last night when I was getting ready for bed."

"It sounds lovely, really. Did you have a particular trail in mind?" She'd never seen this unsure side of Adam before.

"How about the Loantaka Brook Reservation Trail? It's at the end of South Street."

"I know where you're talking about. Should I meet you there?"

"No, I'll pick you up. Can you be ready in an hour?"

Dina looked at the clock again. Seven-thirty. "Sure."

"We'll stop for coffee first."

"Thank goodness!"

He laughed, and the echo of it lingered in her mind long after she'd hung up the phone. Which was ridiculous, because they were nothing more than two people fulfilling a bargain. Thinking of Adam in any other light would just lead to heartache.

By the time she was dressed and ready to go, Dina had just about convinced herself to beg off from the walk. They'd grab coffee together and she'd go back home. There was laundry to do, bathroom cleaning, and grocery shopping.

When he pulled up to her door and flashed his high-wattage smile at her, her pulse thrummed and thoughts of laundry, bathroom cleaning, and grocery shopping dissolved in a poof of cleanser bubbles. He wanted to walk, so she'd walk.

"I missed you," he said, as she climbed into his car. He missed her? Heck, if he wanted her to run, she'd run, without needing anyone to chase her, even.

"It's good to see you too."

They pulled away from the curb into the almost empty Saturday early morning streets, and chatted about their week, Adam paying close attention and asking questions. By the time they'd stopped for coffee and arrived at the trailhead, she was ready to follow him anywhere.

He took her hand as he helped her out of the car and if she hadn't been staring at their hands joined together, she'd swear flames were racing up and down her arm. Meeting Adam's gaze, she saw his eyes darken and a frown line appear between his eyebrows for a brief moment, disappearing before she had a chance to think about why it might be there.

Once she was standing, he dropped her hand and took a step closer to her, until there were mere inches between them. He brushed his hand across her shoulder, lingering for a second or two before moving away.

"Your hair was caught on your jacket collar," he said, a strange huskiness making his voice scrape across the space between them. Stuffing his hands in his pockets, he turned toward the trailhead, and Dina followed.

His stride wasn't overly long, but it was brisk, and she had to race to keep up with him.

"Adam, wait," she said, when he didn't seem to notice.

He turned a sheepish glance toward her and waited for her. "Sorry, I was distracted."

A part of her wanted to ask what distracted him. Another part of her was afraid she knew the answer. So she kept silent and the two of them began walking the paved trail. The air was cold, the sky a clear blue, and the rising sun sparkled in the stream running next to the path.

"Hold on," Dina said, as she pulled her phone out of her pocket. She knelt and took a picture. "It's beautiful out here."

They continued walking, Dina stopping every few minutes as she noticed a pretty leaf or weed or view. Adam waited without a word each time. After photographing a brown leaf floating on the stream, she turned the camera on Adam. He stood staring off into the distance, hands thrust in the pockets of his navy down jacket, a pensive look on his face. Against the stark brown leafless trees, he made a striking shot and she focused the camera, intent on capturing the shot. The click made him turn, and he frowned.

"Did you just take my picture?"

"I did. Do you mind?"

"I wasn't looking at you."

"That's okay," she said. "It was a striking setup. Do you want to see?"

When he nodded, she showed him the photo. His frown deepened. "I wasn't smiling."

"I know, it was candid. You look good."

He raised an eyebrow. "Next time, tell me you want a picture and I'll smile."

She raised her phone. "Okay, smile."

The smile he gave her reminded her of why she called him "Mr. Flashypants." It was broad with white teeth and reminded her of a car salesman. His muscles stretched, but the smile didn't reach his eyes. She took it anyway, since she told him she would, but inside, she preferred the other one. When she showed the smiling one to him, he nodded.

"That's more like me."

She disagreed.

They walked along the stream until the path veered into the woods. Within the shade of the trees, the air felt several degrees cooler and Dina burrowed deeper into her pea coat.

"Cold?" Adam turned and stopped in front of her.

She nodded and he adjusted her scarf, the backs of his fingers caressing her cheeks and jaw. His warm breath tickled her nose and up close, she could see flecks of silver and brown in his eyes. A small scar marked the top of his cheekbone, beneath his eye, and without thinking, she touched it.

He froze, a sharp intake of breath making Dina realize she'd actually made contact. As if the texture of his skin beneath the tip of her finger wasn't enough evidence.

"I'm sorry," she said, drawing her hand away.

"No, that's okay." He took her hand and held it against his cheek. She could see his pupils dilate, feel the rasp of stubble beneath her palm.

"How did you get it?" she asked.

"A fight in the third grade. Tommy D laughed at me for talking to the girl everyone used to make fun of in class. So I decked him. He got me back and we both got detention."

Dina couldn't help smiling. "Aw, you were her knight in shining armor."

He reddened. "You're the only one who thinks that."

"Not true. She probably thinks so as well. Now that I know who my competition is, I'll have to give you my ribbon to carry or something."

At his look of confusion, she continued. "In medieval times, a lady gave her knight a favor, such as a ribbon, and he'd joust for her."

Taking her hand from his cheek, he raised it to his lips and kissed the backs of her fingers. "So you want me to fight for you?"

This was going in a whole direction she didn't want to traverse. So she laughed. "We're too old for fighting. But it's sweet you defended her."

A look crossed Adam's face and she couldn't be sure if it was embarrassment or relief. He squeezed her hand. "Your fingers are icy cold." He rubbed them between his, trying to warm them up, which was weird, since the rest of her was on fire at his proximity. He pulled her back onto the trail and continued their walk. His hand was warm and larger than hers and somehow, it fit.

Their feet crunched on the gravel path. Deeper in the vegetation and hidden among the trees, deer popped up their heads and watched them pass, the younger ones bounding away before they got close.

"Did you get in many fights as a kid?" she asked, as the silence stretched between them.

"That was my only one. My father was so angry, I don't think I was able to sit for a week. How about you?"

"Did I get into any fights?" Dina laughed.

He laughed with her. "What were you like as a kid?"

"You wouldn't have noticed me," she said. "I always had my head in a book. The teacher would have to call my name repeatedly for me to even hear her."

His face took on a dreamy quality, as if he were picturing her lost in her book.

"And now?"

"I still keep my nose in books. The worlds they create are wonderful. I can live anywhere I want, be anyone I want, without consequence."

Adam huffed. "That has a certain appeal." His fingers tightened around her hand, not enough to hurt, but enough to tell her he'd tensed up and she struggled for a way to change the subject. Not knowing what upset him, she didn't want to ruin their walk.

"I bought a dress for the reunion," she said.

"What's it look like?"

She grappled with a way to describe it—fashion wasn't her strong suit. "It's cream, with a ruffle and..." No way was she mentioning the Sticky Boobs.

"And?"

Her face heated as she tried to figure out how to fill in the "and." "Tracy helped me and she says it's perfect, but I'm not sure."

He slanted his gaze toward her and squeezed her hand again. This time, the squeeze wasn't filled with tension. "I can't wait to see it."

His confidence in her appearance should have made her happy. Instead, it only gave her anxiety. She suspected he was used to fashion model-types, not girls with frizzy hair and hips. And even if she passed inspection when he first saw her, once he saw the rest of her classmates, she was sure he'd find her lacking.

Well, she could spend the next few weeks worrying about it, or she could suck it up and accept herself for the way she was.

She just hoped Adam could do the same.

"Adam, your father wants to see you," Diane, his father's secretary, announced as Adam walked into the office Monday morning.

Adam continued walking to his desk, his stomach clenched.

"I think he'd like to see you right away," she said, following Adam.

The woman would have reminded him of a puppy, with the way she followed his father around doing his bidding, if she wasn't so sharp and ferocious. Maybe a rat terrier? With her hair pulled back in a tight bun, small pointy glasses and bright red nail polish, he could see the resemblance. He nodded to her and changed his direction.

Adam knocked on his father's door, not bothering to wait for his father to answer. There had to be some perk to being the boss's son. These days he was hard pressed to come up with any others.

"When are you bringing Dina to the office?" His father spoke without looking up from his desk, his attention still on whatever was on his computer screen.

Two can play this game. Adam sat, crossed his leg over his knee. He waited for his father to look at him.

After a moment, his father met his gaze.

"Why would I bring her here?"

An expression appeared on his father's face that Adam could only describe as patronizing, the kind you give a small child who doesn't understand the simplest of commands. "I thought we went over this, Adam. You need to change your image. Completely. Bringing Dina here, introducing her as your steady girlfriend, would help you do that. It would make you seem more stable and thoughtful."

Bile rose in Adam's throat at his father's blatant use of Dina. And his. Because wasn't that why he was dating her?

"Seems to me that would only prove I slack off, since I wouldn't be working when she was here."

"I don't recall your working on anything so important you couldn't have a small break to show your girlfriend around."

Man, he'd have to look into getting a Kevlar suit made up if his dad was going to continue slinging insults his way, no matter how veiled they might be. He rose from the chair.

"She works so she might not be able to get time off."

"I'm sure she'd love to visit her boyfriend's law office and meet his high-powered coworkers."

Adam returned to his desk, nauseated. His father was manipulating him and using Dina. He was going along with it. Because really, wasn't he going out with her to get his father off his back? A part of his conscience agreed, but there was a small piece that rebelled. Her skin yesterday on the trail, when he'd adjusted her scarf, had been softer than anything he'd touched in a long time. He'd lingered, adjusting the scarf in miniscule movements to try to prolong contact. Had they not been in public and in the cold, he would have removed the scarf, and everything else she was wearing, just to feel if the rest of her was as soft. When she'd touched his scar? Heat had radiated from her fingertip on his cheekbone to the edges of his scalp, down his neck. He'd wanted her to touch more of him.

But those things spoke of physical attraction, which was surprising given how different she looked from those he was normally attracted to. Yet, he'd kissed her in the car on the way back from dinner with his father. If she hadn't stopped him, he'd have gone much further.

But he loved talking with her, hearing how her mind worked, laughing at her obscure trivia. When they weren't together, he missed her. Even if she scared the crap out of him. Because she got him. She knew him better than friends he'd known for years. He liked that. In fact, he was crazy about that.

There was a growing part of him that felt at ease around her. It was comforting to know you didn't have to play a part, even if you couldn't help playing it anyway. Because there had been times when he'd let his inner self shine through—like when they talked about his love of Vikings—and it had been a relief.

So inviting her to his office was going to be difficult. Because he was using her, but he also cared for her. Balancing those two pieces was going to be tricky.

Back at his desk, he picked up the phone and dialed her number.

"Hello?"

Her voice filled him with warmth. He couldn't stop the smile from teasing his lips.

"Hey, Dina. Are you free for lunch?"

"Today? Yeah."

The pleasure in her voice made his request bittersweet. "Good, why don't you come to my office at twelve. We can go to a restaurant in my building."

"I'll see you then."

The busywork he was still handling did little to make the rest of the morning pass, but somehow, the hands of the clock moved along until noon, when his phone rang. Without bothering to answer it, Adam sprinted to the reception desk and stuck his head around the door into the waiting area.

"Hey, Dina, come on in."

He wanted to kiss her hello, run his hands beneath her pea coat, play with her springy hair, but there were people around. Instead, he grimaced. "I'll give you a tour."

His stomach clenched a little as they walked through the office, waving to his friends behind glass walls. He'd do what his father wanted, but fast, and then he'd have the rest of lunch to enjoy spending time with her.

"Have you known him long?" Dina asked, as he pointed out his friend John behind a glass wall.

"Yeah, he's one of my close friends here." Close being relative, of course. He and John hadn't spoken much since Ashley had made her accusations.

"What about him?" she asked, pointing to Paul, another one of his friends who'd also been avoiding him.

"Yeah, we often have lunch together."

He steered her around the paralegal department, rattling off a list of names and keeping them moving until they were near his office.

"Marie, this is my friend, Dina," he said to his secretary.

She waved. "Nice to meet you."

"You too," Dina said.

"And this," he said, opening his door, "is my office."

She took a cursory look around, glanced out his window, and nodded. "Nice."

He shouldn't have been surprised by her reaction. She wasn't the type of woman to be impressed by an actual office, even if it had a window.

She fidgeted. When he opened his mouth to speak, she turned to his bookshelves. Of course. Bending down, she examined the law books on his shelves as if they were the most fascinating things she'd ever seen. He examined the shape of her rear, which he found much more intriguing.

"Are you ready for lunch?"

"Sure," she said.

With his hand on the small of her back, he ushered her out of the office and downstairs to the restaurant off the lobby. She was silent. He didn't know what to make of it. Once they'd been seated and looked at menus, he put his aside.

"So, what did you think of the office?"

"Um, it was very nice." She squirmed.

He frowned. What was going on?

She sighed. "Adam, why did you invite me to your office?"

Well, that was a little trickier. "Because you hadn't seen it. I thought you'd like to."

"The building or the people?"

"What do you mean?"

She blew a strand of hair out of her face. "I mean, did you want me to meet the people you work with or see the place you spend hours of your day?"

He shrugged, confused. "Dina, I don't know what you're talking about."

"Do I embarrass you?"

He stared at her. "Why would you think that?"

"Because every time I'm with you and we meet someone you know, you act like you don't know me. Because rather than introduce me to the people who are your supposed best friends at work, you rushed me by their offices before I had time to even wave."

Oh God. "Dina, you've got it wrong."

"Do I?" She rose and dropped her napkin on the table. "I don't think so. So if you'll excuse me, I'm going to go clear my head. I'll talk to you later."

"Dina, wait!"

He rose to go after her, but was stopped short by a body in his way.

"Hey, Adam, how are you?"

Stephen, a guy in another law firm in the building, came up to him.

"I can't talk now, Stephen, I'm sorry."

"You know, you really need to manage your time better."

Adam stopped short and swore to himself. He couldn't get away from his reputation even if he wanted to. The desire to straighten out Stephen's assumption made him start to turn back, but he shook his head. Now wasn't the time. He needed to find Dina and fix her assumptions first.

But when he looked for her, she was gone.

CHAPTER ELEVEN

The buzzing intercom pulled Dina out of a daydream that evening. The daydream in which she and Adam had a relationship rather than the bargain they'd struck. With a sigh, she rose from the table where her dinner sat untouched and looked at the video screen on her security intercom. Adam's image greeted her and she jerked back.

If I wait, he'll get bored and go away. That would be best for both of them. She needed time to get herself fully on board with what they were to each other—a means to an end. He wasn't interested in her, not beyond body chemistry.

Leaning against the cool steel door, she repeated, "We have an agreement," over and over in her mind.

He buzzed again.

He wasn't getting the hint.

He leaned on the buzzer without stopping.

Oy gevalt. Lovely.

He started making patterns with his buzzing.

He had more of an attention span than she'd given him credit for. Her neighbors, however, had little patience for noise, so unless she wanted them letting him in, she was going to have to answer. Repeating "We have an agreement" to herself one more time, she pressed the button, opened her door and waited for him to climb the stairs.

"You're very persistent," she said, hands clenched together behind her back. His hair was mussed and she wanted to run her fingers through it to smooth it.

"You didn't answer."

She shrugged. Standing this close to him, she could smell his spicy clove aftershave and it was all she could do not to throw herself at him. But they had an agreement, and throwing herself into his arms wasn't part of it.

"Can I come in? We need to talk, and I don't think we should do it in front of your neighbors."

"I don't know. Mrs. MacAvoy loves gossip. It would be a shame to deprive her."

He raised an eyebrow and she held back a smile. What she would give to see that eyebrow raise all the time. She moved deeper into the apartment and let him follow her inside. What would he think of her apartment? It was completely different from his: all colorful fabrics, gravity-defying stacks of books, and mismatched furniture with Judaica scattered around. It probably screamed "single girl" to him, but at least she didn't have a cat. Yet.

She perched on her favorite wingchair, a purple one with daisies she'd bought at a garage sale, and pointed to her gold overstuffed sofa for him to sit on. She'd curl up on it later and inhale his lingering scent, dreaming of what could be. For now, she needed space.

"I'm sorry about what happened at the office, Dina. Truly."

She shook her head. "Don't be. I overstepped."

"No, you didn't, but you did misunderstand."

Their relationship? Of course she did. Was he really going to reiterate their deal? She opened her mouth to stop him, but he held out a hand.

"Let me finish."

She shut her mouth to avoid looking like a fish, or a mouth-breather. Neither was attractive.

He ran a hand through his hair and stared down at his feet for a moment before continuing. "I'm sorry I didn't introduce you to my friends at the office. It wasn't because of you, it was because of me."

Was he really going to use the "it wasn't you, it was me" argument?

"I'm having a problem at the office. I've become sort of a pariah, even with my friends. I was afraid if I brought you into their offices or stopped to talk to them for long, they'd say something about it to you."

"Why are you a pariah and why would I take their side?"

"Everyone else has."

"I'm not everyone else," she said.

It was like she'd stuck a pin in him and let out all the excess air. "You're right. And I'm sorry."

Dina nodded. Why was he a pariah?

He shook his head and mumbled something. She thought she heard the word "father," but she couldn't be sure. "Pardon? Why are you a pariah?"

He fidgeted. "Work politics. But I should have called you my girlfriend when I introduced you to Marie. I don't know why I didn't. Maybe it was just me being careful..."

"No, you were right."

"I was right?"

She swallowed and plunged ahead. "I'm not your girlfriend, not really. We have an arrangement." So getting involved in his work politics was pointless.

"An arrangement?"

"I'm helping you get back in your father's good graces and you're escorting me to my reunion. We might enjoy each other's company, we might have even gone out on a date, but we shouldn't make this into anything more than that."

"Dina—" He looked stricken.

"No, Adam. I'm not your type, and frankly, you're not mine, either." God forgive her for lying. "I overreacted."

"You overreacted?"

She nodded, glad he was finally understanding. "I'm sorry your friends are behaving the way they are. You're probably right, though. Introducing me to them would only have hurt your reputation with them." She didn't need to delve any further into his difficulties at work.

He frowned and looked at his hands.

"I'm glad we got this straightened out," she said, as she rose and led him toward the door. Saying the words, reminding them both of their agreement, was useful. It made things clearer, like drawing a map or an org chart.

He followed her. "Everything will be fine, Adam. I don't usually overreact, and I won't do it again."

He had his "little boy lost" look and it was all she could do not to react to it. She needed him to leave before she wrapped him in her arms. Opening her front door, she waited for him to step back over the threshold. It took him a while, but when he did, she leaned against the doorframe.

"We should grab lunch again sometime," she added.

"Lunch?"

Friends ate lunch together, right? "I promise I won't walk out on you," she said. Smile, she told herself.

"Walk out on me?"

She raised the corners of her mouth, and it lasted while he turned and walked down the hallway, after she closed the door, and until she sat on the sofa he'd recently vacated.

Her stomach fluttered at his scent that remained in the fabric of her sofa and a shiver of desire ran up her spine. Tears coursed down her cheeks.

She'd done it. She'd restored their equilibrium. They were just friends.

Adam climbed into his car and shut the door before opening it and slamming it again, so hard the car shook. He pounded his hands on the steering wheel, the force sending shockwaves up his arms and jarring his teeth. His nostrils flared as he blew air in and out, in an attempt to get his raucous breathing under control.

What the hell just happened?

She wanted to be friends.

The only kind of "friend" he wanted to be with her had "boy" attached to it. No, that wasn't true. He did enjoy her friendship. It added depth to their relationship and prevented it from being a purely physical attraction. Because he loved talking to her, hearing her opinions, sharing himself with her.

But the physical part was also important to him. He was becoming more attracted to her. So far, they'd only kissed, but that one kiss, that unbelievable kiss, haunted him. His lips still burned where they'd touched hers, his insides still turned to jelly when he thought about it. In fact, he'd been hoping there would have been more kissing in her apartment once he'd apologized for his gaffe.

But she'd focused on their arrangement and her overreaction, and here he was pulling away from the curb into rush hour traffic.

She thought he was dating her only to impress his father. If he were one hundred percent honest with himself, he'd acknowledge the partial truth in that statement. But the more time he spent time with her, when he wasn't royally screwing things up with her, the more he wanted to move beyond their arrangement.

His head was another matter. It was still focused on not making a fool of himself, of maintaining the right reputation, of spinning the right message.

But listening to his head was probably what had gotten him into this mess in the first place. As unbelievable as it might sound, it was time to follow his heart.

Dina's phone rang late that night.

"Dina, it's Adam."

She blew her nose, which was stuffy from crying. "Hi."

"Are you okay? You don't sound like yourself."

"It's just allergies." People had winter ones, right? Dust, mold, non-existent cats...

"Are you sure?" His voice was deep with concern.

Dina's eyes watered. "What's up, Adam?"

"Nothing, I just wanted to check in with you. See how you're doing."

He'd seen her that evening. What was left to check in on? "I'm just reading."

"What book?"

She picked up the one closest to her. It was a book she'd read more times than she could count. "*Little House on the Prairie.*"

"Really? I remember my teacher reading that to us in third grade."

"Did you like it?"

"I was more interested in running around the playground than sitting and listening to a story."

Dina smiled.

"Anyway," he continued, "I wanted to thank you for being so forgiving earlier."

"It's okay."

"So, I was looking for a book to read and thought of you, my favorite librarian."

Her insides warmed. "Really?"

"Really. I thought maybe you could recommend something, so..."

They talked for an hour, moving from books to TV to movies. The next night he called just as she was sitting down to eat dinner.

"Hey, how was your day?"

"Sad. There was a homeless woman hanging out in one of the reading rooms. I've seen her before and I leave her alone, other than to smile, because it's a place for her to stay warm and she's harmless, but there was this other woman who objected to her being there so my boss had to make her leave. I felt really bad for her."

"I don't understand how people can ignore someone so obviously suffering," Adam said. "There's an old man near my dad's office and I give him spare change when I see him. I've talked to him a few times. He's a war veteran. He could be anyone. Even you or me."

Dina had swallowed at hearing this unexpected side to Adam. Her chest expanded at his compassion. She'd moved onto the sofa, settling deep into the cushions, as they spent the rest of the evening talking about volunteer opportunities and politics. This evening he'd called to tell her a funny story about a friend of his, but she was getting ready for temple.

"I'm sorry, Adam, but I'm in a rush. Can we talk later?"

Apparently, telling Adam they were just friends made him more inclined to, well, act like a friend and just talk to her. It was nice, but it was also hard. Because the more they spoke, the more attached she was growing—both to him as a person and to him as a man. He was so much deeper than he made himself out to be. This was the Adam she admired.

At least their conversations were over the phone, where all she had to do was ignore her attraction to his husky voice, a voice that reminded her of flannel and leather and the sound an engine makes when it's warmed up. She'd never tell him that—he'd probably object to being compared to flannel, even if it was warm and cozy. As long as it wasn't in person, at least until she could get her mind, her heart and her body on the same page, she'd be fine.

She finished dressing in gray flared suit pants and an orange button-back V-neck sweater. She put on her Jewish star necklace, hoop earrings, and she was set. Shrugging into her black pea coat and swinging her purse over her shoulder, she went to temple, determined to put Adam out of her mind for now.

The chilly wind blew her hair across her face. She entered the foyer of the synagogue with relief. Shivering, she hung her coat in the coat closet and walked into the vestibule outside the sanctuary.

She stopped dead.

Adam.

So much for Shabbat peace. She pasted a smile on her face and walked over to him.

"Shabbat Shalom," she said. "I didn't expect to see you here."

His face lit up in a smile and her heart stuttered in her chest. He leaned over and placed a kiss on her cheek. It shouldn't have affected her—everyone did it—but her knees wobbled.

"I thought it would be a nice place to be tonight."

Her lips trembled and she eyed him askance. "Really?"

He shrugged. "Well, you come every week. There must be something you like about it. I thought I'd try it."

He tried to hide his uncertainty, but she saw it peeking out, like a child sneaking out of bed to spy on the grownups, and her heart melted. "I'm glad you're here. Let's go sit down."

Adam took her elbow as they entered the sanctuary, greeted the ushers, and found a seat halfway down the center aisle. They sat together, Adam's arm across the back of her chair.

"Hi, Dina," Rebecca said. "Can we join you?"

Rebecca, her husband Aaron, and their kids scooted into the row while Dina made introductions. "Adam, this is my friend Rebecca and her family." Adam leaned forward and shook everyone's hand. "Rebecca, this is my friend, Adam."

Dina busied herself in picking up the correct prayer book, but not before she saw Rebecca's appraising glance. The rabbi walked to the *bima* and nodded to the Cantor, who began humming a *niggun*, and Dina was saved from having to say anything further to Rebecca as the wordless melody washed over her.

Throughout the service, Dina kept watch over Adam out of the corner of her eye. He was familiar enough with the prayer book and most of the prayers, and joined in singing many of the songs. His singing voice was beautiful—deep and husky—and made her feel as if he were whispering words of love only to her. He'd moved his arm from the back of her chair, but it now rested next to her. Every fiber of her being told her to move so her arm could touch his, even if it was only through cloth. But they were in temple and they were friends, so she dragged her gaze forward and focused on the service.

When it was over, they joined the entire congregation in the social hall for the *oneg*. Usually, talking to people over refreshments was one of Dina's favorite parts of the service, but this time, Adam was standing too close and she couldn't concentrate.

"Would you like something to drink," he asked, after they'd said the prayers over the wine and the *challah*.

"Water would be great," she said, as much to put some distance between them as to soothe her parched throat. Adam left to find her a drink and Rebecca moved closer.

"So, just 'friends,' huh?" Rebecca asked, her brown eyes almost golden with laughter.

"Yes."

"Are you sure about that? Because he doesn't look at you like a friend, and you don't respond to him like one."

"None of that matters. We can't be anything more."

"So does that mean you're interested in Zach?"

Dina sighed. "I should be. He was great."

"But?"

She shrugged. "But...I don't know."

"I think you do," Rebecca said, as Adam returned with a glass of water.

CHAPTER TWELVE

"Come to dinner with me tonight?" Adam asked Dina, during what she was beginning to think of as her daily phone call.

It being Saturday, he'd called in the morning. Eleven to be precise. After spending time together last night at temple. What was left to talk about? Apparently eating.

"I'm not sure I can."

"Someone else taking you out?"

His tone was light, but she could hear an underlying edge to it, betraying nerves that he covered with a laugh. It could have been interpreted as mean, but she didn't interpret it that way. Adam was many things, including Mr. Flashypants, but "mean" wasn't one of them.

"No. I told Tracy I'd watch the baby for part of the afternoon so she and Joe could get some errands done. I'm not sure how late they'll be." She also wasn't sure she could handle seeing him two days in a row.

"I think you need some adult company."

Adult company sounded slightly obscene when uttered by Adam. "Um, you want to hang out with a baby? Don't you have other things you'd rather do?"

"I'm not doing it for the baby, I'm doing it to see you."

She pressed her hand against her stomach and tried to stop the smile that threatened. Somehow, she didn't think saying no was going to be so easy. And come to think of it, she'd never watched a baby before and she'd been trying to calm her nerves all morning. "Have you spent time with any babies before?"

"I'm a baby expert."

Once again, he was coming to her rescue. "That's great. Because I've never done this before. Why don't you come to Tracy's at two?"

"I'll pick you up instead and we can drive over together."

She gobbled down a tuna and tomato sandwich, and thought and rethought her babysitting outfit—having Adam see her meant her "relax with a baby" outfit needed serious rethinking—several times before Adam buzzed her apartment intercom.

When she climbed into his car, she did a double take. "You do know we're watching a baby, right?"

"I didn't forget," he said, as he pulled away from the curb. "Hello, by the way."

"You obviously weren't paying attention, since you're wearing a white shirt." She pulled her brown turtleneck toward him. "Brown hides stains best. And hi."

He shook his head. "Bleach, my friend. There won't be any problem bleach can't handle." His gaze pierced hers. "You look pretty," he said.

"No I don't. I look like an overgrown chocolate bar."

"There is never anything wrong with chocolate," he said.

She hated when he was right. Dina bit her lip and looked out the window. He apparently was good at laundry. If she were interested in him as a potential boyfriend, that would be a huge plus.

"Dina!" Tracy said as she opened the door, looking like a prisoner about to be sprung from jail. "You brought reinforcements."

Reinforcements? How much trouble could one miniature person be? "I hope you don't mind."

"Not at all," she said, pulling her inside and kissing Adam's cheek. "Thank you both so much for this. Here's where we'll be." She handed Dina a piece of paper with the name and address of three stores and a restaurant. "And here's her schedule."

That list was longer. So long, in fact, Dina's eyes widened as she turned the eight-and-a-half-by-eleven paper over.

"Mackenzie is sleeping, but I'll show you where everything is."

Silently, they got a tour of the apartment and after another ten minutes, Tracy and Joe left. Dina looked at Adam, who smiled.

Flustered, she looked at the list. "It says feed her at one-thirty." She turned and headed toward the baby's room.

"Wait," Adam grabbed her arm. "She's sleeping."

"But the instructions say to feed her now."

"Haven't you ever heard the advice to not wake a sleeping baby?"

"Yes, but I know Tracy. And she wouldn't give us instructions if she didn't want us to follow them."

Adam leaned against the kitchen counter and folded his arms across his chest. "Do you always follow the rules?"

Having shucked his jacket, all that stood between her and his skin—aside from a few feet of air, of course—was a white cotton long-sleeved polo. His stance emphasized his chest and arm muscles, and her throat went dry. She shook her head to clear her mind.

"You don't?" he asked. "Somehow I didn't picture you as a rule breaker."

He was talking to her. "Wait, what?"

"Earth to Dina. I asked if you always follow the rules."

"Oh, um, yeah, usually."

"Then why did you shake your head no?"

Crap. "I don't know."

He took a step toward her, put his arm around her shoulder, and ushered her into the living room. "Okay, it's obvious you're getting a little overwhelmed by the baby. Let's just sit down and wait a little. We can always wake her if we need to, but it's damn hard to *unwake* her."

She let him pull her toward the sofa and she sank into it, running her hand absently over the cloth upholstery. "Maybe I should just call Tracy and ask," Dina said.

"And make her think we have no idea what we're doing?"

Something in his face made her think he might not be joking. "Don't you know what you're doing?"

"Not a clue," he said. "But how hard can this be?"

"Wait a minute," she said, rising and putting her hands on her hips. "I thought you said you were a baby expert!"

"I might have exaggerated a little."

The baby's cries prevented her from responding, which was probably good for Adam.

He'd lied to her.

She rushed into the lavender-painted nursery and reached for Mackenzie, whose face was scrunched up like a withered apple.

"Shh, it's okay," she crooned as she pulled her against her chest.

"What can I do?" Adam asked, standing in the doorway.

He could stop making things up, for one.

She nodded her head toward the supplies. "Can you get out a fresh diaper and wipes?"

Adam rushed to get what she'd asked for and hovered by the table, holding the items in the air like they'd fly away if he let go—or bite him.

"Wait," he said. "Are you sure we should change her? It doesn't say that on the list."

She laughed at the sudden reversal of roles. "Well, I'm pretty sure that if they were able to predict exactly when she'd need a diaper change, she'd be potty trained already, so for this one thing, I'm not so worried about the list."

He looked properly chastised and she changed her mind about his intentions. Maybe he hadn't lied per se. Maybe he'd just exaggerated. A lot. The question was why, which she'd examine after she changed Mackenzie's diaper.

Dina figured out the snaps on the onesie, cleaned her up, and put on a fresh diaper. And still she cried.

"Here, can you hold her? The list said to give her a bottle."

Adam's mouth opened and shut. "How about I make the bottle and you hold her?"

"It's frozen breast milk."

"Come here, Mackenzie. Let Uncle Adam hold you."

With a laugh, Dina went in search of the milk. Three minutes later, she approached the nursery and stopped in the doorway. There was singing and cooing and nose-to-nose touching and all of it was coming from Adam. She double and triple checked, just to make sure there wasn't some TV or radio playing she hadn't noticed before.

There wasn't.

His lips were moving and sound was emerging from them. And while Mackenzie was still fussy, she wasn't screaming her head off.

Adam had calmed her.

Maybe he *was* an expert. Or if not an expert, a natural.

You know what he also was? Bone-meltingly sexy. Whoever said men with babies were sexy knew what they were talking about.

"You going to give me that bottle?" Adam asked in a singsong voice.

She jolted out of her reverie and handed him the bottle, watching as Mackenzie lunged for it and gulped it down. Adam couldn't have looked more pleased if he'd been able to nurse her himself.

When the bottle was empty, Dina reached for her. "Here, I'll burp her."

"No, let me." He tilted the baby onto his shoulder.

"Wait!"

Too late. Mackenzie spit up all over his shirt. Dina tried to hold back a laugh.

"Maybe you should take her after all," he said.

She grabbed the diaper cloth she'd tried to hand Adam before the spit-up incident, flung it over her shoulder and took Mackenzie from him. "Do you want help cleaning up?"

"No, I got it. And hey, at least I'm wearing a white shirt." He winked at her and her stomach fluttered.

Maybe she was hungry.

She patted and rubbed Mackenzie's back until she burped, then looked at the instructions Tracy had left. There was a half hour before she was supposed to check her diaper. Now what?

"Hey, I found this, think she'll use it?" Adam walked in carrying a bouncy thing.

Well, it probably had a name, but Dina had no idea what it was called. There was a seat for the baby and things to play with. And it bounced. Yeah, that would do.

"We can try."

She placed Mackenzie in the seat and Adam spun some of the toys. Mackenzie laughed and bounced as she kicked her legs. Excellent. Problem solved.

They sat on the floor watching her. Adam made funny faces, which also caused Mackenzie to laugh.

"You're quiet," he said to Dina, as he played with Mackenzie's toy.

"Did you know a baby can't taste salt until they're about four months old? It's thought that the delay is related to—"

He grabbed her hand and rubbed his thumb across her palm and she forgot the rest of her sentence.

"What's wrong, Dina?"

She swallowed. "Wrong?"

"You're nervous."

"Why do you say that?"

"Because you're quoting random facts. You only do that when you're nervous."

He was not supposed to know that. "I don't do that when I'm nervous."

Adam arched one eyebrow, making Mackenzie giggle again. "Even she agrees with me."

"No, she's just laughing at your face."

"My…you…!" He tried to frown but couldn't pull it off and Dina laughed. Joking around, she could handle. Seeing Adam with a baby, that was more difficult to deal with.

"Seriously, why are you nervous?" he asked. His green eyes darkened with concern and focused on her, sending midnight-colored lasers direct to her heart, which started thumping.

"I'm not sure what to do with her," she said. Or you.

"She's easy."

Had she imagined a stressor on "she?" "She's a baby who doesn't talk," she said.

"With a mother who provides instructions that rival IKEA's."

True.

He pulled the instruction list toward him while rattling one of the toys on the bouncy thing. It really needed a name.

"We change her diaper in twenty minutes. After that, we have time until she needs to eat again. Want to go for a walk?"

"Does it say we should?"

He smiled. "It doesn't say we shouldn't. And Tracy left us the stroller all set up by the door. In fact, we could probably change her now and leave early."

"No! She said a half hour after eating. We should wait."

"Boy, you really are a rule follower."

"Well, neither of us seems to know anything about babies," said Dina. "We probably shouldn't deviate from the schedule too much."

He squeezed her hand and she tried to join in playing with Mackenzie. When her phone alarm buzzed, she took the baby and went to change her diaper.

"Want help?" Adam asked.

"No, I think I've got this."

She laid her on the changing table. "We can do this, right?" she whispered.

Opening the diaper, she cringed. Mackenzie was filthy and it was everywhere. She thought about calling Adam for reinforcements, but doubted he'd be much help. Screwing up her face, which caused the baby to giggle again, and breathing through her mouth, she cleaned her as best she could before diapering and redressing her.

"Oh, that was nasty," she said, as she returned to Adam. "You should be very glad you didn't do this one."

She handed Mackenzie over to Adam who took her and pointed at Dina's shirt. "Um..."

"What?"

Looking down, she frowned, pulled her shirt to her nose and sniffed. "Oh no!" she said as her face heated.

Adam did a worse job at restraining his laughter than she had done when Mackenzie spit up. "Guess it's a good thing you wore brown."

"I have to go clean this."

Dina ran into the bathroom, thankful there was a door she could shut. It was a good thing she and Adam were only friends, because she'd be mortified if this happened otherwise. And that flush on her cheeks? Must be from the heat. It was going to be scorching hot summer—even if it was only March.

"All fixed?" Adam asked, as she emerged from the bathroom.

Nodding, she focused on Mackenzie, who was seated in the stroller. "Don't you think she needs a jacket?" Her cheeks might still be burning, but she didn't think it was contagious.

Adam dropped his head to his chest. "Oh, yeah."

Together, they unstrapped her, zipped her into her fuchsia jacket, and strapped her back into the stroller.

"Hat?" Adam asked.

"Probably." She looked around and found one on the half wall by the front door. "Okay, I think we're set."

"Yeah, except for *our* jackets."

Right.

As Mackenzie started to fuss, they hurried into their jackets and finally maneuvered the stroller outside, locked the door and began walking down the sidewalk. They settled into a rhythm, the fussing stopped, and Dina breathed a sigh of relief.

"Made it," she said.

"Did you doubt it?"

She glanced at Adam askance. "Honestly? Yes."

"Ye of little faith." He elbowed her gently in the ribs, and she huffed.

Dina pushed the stroller down the sidewalk and Adam rested his hand on the bar next to hers. Their silence was companionable, and for the first time in at least an hour, Dina took in a deep breath.

"Feel better?" he asked.

"I don't know what you're talking about."

He elbowed her again without removing his hand from the stroller. They approached an older woman walking toward them who glanced from the baby to them.

"Your daughter is adorable," the woman said as she approached.

Dina knew she should protest. Adam was just her friend. They weren't even a couple, much less the parents of a baby. She really should say something. But instead, she smiled at the woman and continued walking.

He would have bet money Dina would have corrected the woman. Dina was the one hung up on their just being friends.

Friends.

The more he thought of that word, the more ludicrous it became.

A friend didn't look at a woman with lust in his eyes. A friend didn't ache to touch the other's skin. A friend didn't hunger for the sound of the other's voice.

He had no idea how she felt, because she'd stuck him squarely in the "friend zone," a foreign land with its own language, manners, and rules. He should object to it—he'd heard enough scorn about it from other guys, even if he'd never been relegated there himself. But there was something refreshing about getting to know a woman, really know her, without having to deal with the sexual side of things. Still, he was doing his best to break out of it. Inch by infuriatingly sexy inch. Because the more he got to know her, the more connected he felt to her.

The old woman had drawn attention to their un-friend-like status. He'd expected Dina to draw back in horror before babbling on about some obscure fact about friends, babies or friends with babies.

Instead, she'd smiled.

His heart was still melting.

He wanted to go kiss that old woman, except that probably wouldn't win him any points with Dina. It might draw attention to the idea that they looked like a family, rather than friends. She didn't need any help keeping that in mind. So he forced his feet to continue walking on the cold, hard pavement.

And walked right into a fire hydrant.

"Ow!" He hopped on one foot, gripping his knee with the other, muttering curses under his breath.

"Are you alright?" Dina placed a hand on his arm. Even though he couldn't actually feel her skin through his coat, he imagined he could. He started to speak, cleared his throat, and tried again.

"Yeah, I'm fine." He limped along next to her.

"Maybe we should head back."

"No, let's keep going."

She looked at him like she didn't believe him. "They're probably going to be home soon."

Without waiting for his response, she swung the stroller around and headed in the opposite direction. At home, by the time they'd taken off their coats, un-wrapped Mackenzie from the layers of clothes they'd bundled her in, and stored the stroller, Tracy and Joe walked in.

"Did you guys survive?" Tracy asked, as she un-wound her scarf and put her bags down.

Dina walked toward her, carrying Mackenzie, while Adam limped behind. He watched Tracy's gaze flicker from one to the other. Tracy's mouth twitched. She turned to her husband. As one, they laughed.

"Oh my, you two look like you've been through the ringer."

Adam limped over and put his arm around Dina. She stiffened. He stroked her shoulder with his thumb.

"Nah, we're good. A little spit up, a little poop, a little bruise. No big deal."

She didn't relax into his embrace, as he'd hoped, but she didn't move away either. "He's right. It was fun."

Later, after they'd left, Adam turned to her in the car. "Want to go out tonight?"

She looked down at her shirt. "I'm pretty sure I smell."

Her brown shirt was stained. Her hair was wild. Her lip was caught between her teeth. She'd never looked more beautiful.

He sniffed the air. "I don't smell anything." Then he turned and sniffed his shoulder. "Well, maybe some spit up."

Her smile made her eyes sparkle. Had he never noticed that?

"If you don't mind, I think I'm going to pass tonight. I'm exhausted. Another time?" She grabbed her coat and opened the door as he pulled up in front of her apartment. "But thanks for the offer. And for coming with me today. You were a huge help."

He nodded, wondering what she'd do if he kissed her. Before he could test it out, she climbed out of the car. As he watched her go into her building, he wondered how much longer it would take to persuade her into the idea of a relationship with him.

Because he wasn't sure he could wait.

CHAPTER THIRTEEN

Waiting was hard. Dina picked up her phone and put it down on the table next to her bed three times, before grabbing a book and marching into the living room to read. But her mind wouldn't focus on the words. It was focused on sharp green eyes, tawny hair, and warm skin that smelled like cloves.

She couldn't stop thinking of Adam, which was annoying really, since she shouldn't be thinking of him at all. They were only friends, at her insistence. And even if she did think of him—and friends thought about each other—she most certainly wasn't supposed to think about puddles of goo. Because that's how he made her insides feel, in a delicious, warm, tingly kind of way.

And that couldn't happen.

So she left her phone—her lifeline enabling her to hear his voice once more—where it lay in her bedroom and once again tried to focus on the cozy mystery she was reading. She couldn't remember the plot. She could barely remember the mystery. She did know there was a cat, because the description of it in the book reminded her of Adam's soft cashmere sweater, the one he'd worn the last time they'd eaten together.

Ugh!

It had only been a day since she'd last spoken to him. She'd come to depend on his daily calls. Usually, he called around seven-thirty. Seven forty-five if he was busy. But it was eight-thirty and he hadn't called her yet.

Would he?

Maybe she should call him. Friends did that. She and Tracy were friends and they called each other all the time.

Except Adam was a guy. Would he look at her phone call as an admission of her attraction to him? Because even she was hard put to deny her attraction to him any longer, even if she didn't want to announce it.

They had an arrangement, and acting on her attraction would complicate things and make her seem pathetic.

She flung her book across the room, and then raced to get it. Picking it up off the floor, she brushed it off and examined it to make sure it wasn't damaged. Librarians didn't throw books. It was against their code of conduct. The only thing worse than throwing a book would be to dog-ear the pages. She was pretty sure they'd revoke her masters in library science for that.

Placing the cozy mystery on the end table, she walked back into her bedroom and picked up her phone. This was crazy. She'd call him. She could always plead a wrong number.

She dialed his number and held her breath while she waited for him to pick up.

"Heyyyy, it's Adam! Leave a message!"

Dina exhaled and hung up before the beep sounded, which would have required her to leave a message. Only she didn't have one. Because anything she said would make her sound desperate and clingy.

Later that night, just as she was about to go to sleep, her phone rang.

"Hey, Dinaaaa..."

Adam's voice slurred. He was drunk.

"Adam?"

"I called you before," he said. "No, wait, you called me. Right?"

"Right. But it wasn't important. We can talk to-morrow." Having a conversation with him when he was drunk wasn't fun.

"No, should...should talk now."

There was silence and Dina waited for him to con-tinue. When he didn't, she sighed. "Adam, let's talk to-morrow."

"You have a pretty voice, d'you know that?"

She sighed. "Thank you." Why was he drunk? "Are you having a party?"

"Hah! No, I'm not having a party. A party would be fun. I'm not supposed to have any fun."

This was new. "Why not?"

"Nev...mind."

Dina paused. If you got past the fact he was drunk and you ignored the slurred, sloppy speech, there was something off in his tone of voice. He was trying to be a happy drunk and failing. Why was he calling her when he was drunk? Maybe something was wrong.

"Can I come over?" she asked.

"Why do you wanna come here?"

The Adam she knew wouldn't have asked why. There was definitely something wrong. "I want to see you."

"You want to party? The lib...libar...book lady wants to party?"

She'd laugh if he were sober. "Can I come over now?"

"Shhhurrrre."

Throwing on jeans and a long-sleeved pink T-shirt, she grabbed her keys, black leather purse, and pea coat and ran out the door. The streets of Morristown were quiet at this time of night—it was after eleven—and she made it to the lobby of Adam's high-rise apartment in less than ten minutes. The guy behind the security desk in the marble and mirrored lobby called up to his apartment and nodded to her.

She rode up in the elevator, jiggling her car keys in her hand and tapping her sneaker-clad toe on the gold carpet as the elevator crept up to Adam's floor. She glanced around briefly at the familiar hallway as she got her bearings—black carpet with silver flecks that was plush enough to deaden her footsteps; gray walls with white trim; and geometrically shaped mirrors interspersed along the hallway—as she wondered whether or not this was a good idea.

She knocked on the door and it swung open as if he'd been waiting for her.

"Dinaaaaa!" He reached for her and stumbled and she half hugged, half caught him, pushing him back into his apartment and shutting the door behind her.

He smelled like a distillery and his hair was spiked as if he'd run his hands through it numerous times—the way she'd fantasized doing herself.

"Adam, what's going on?"

"We're having a party!"

She frowned. "No we're not."

"Don't bring it down, Dina. You said you wanted to party." He grabbed her hand and stumble-danced down the hall. He gripped her against him and she could feel his heartbeat against her chest. They banged into the wall and she winced.

"Oh, shit, Dina. Are you okay?" His gaze grew surprisingly clear and his eyes reflected his worry for her for a moment before glazing over again.

"Yeah, I'm okay. Maybe we should sit down, though."

He took her hand and led her into the living room. Once again, the heat from his hand warmed her entire body. She tried not to focus on it.

He sprawled onto a black leather sofa and pulled her down beside him. Now the sides of their bodies were touching, from their shoulders to their hips and thighs. That was even worse.

"Better?" he asked. He hadn't let go of her hand yet and he began playing with it, running his fingers along her palm and wrist, and driving her crazy. Mr. Flashypants was also the King of Distraction.

"Tough day?" she asked.

"Don't wanna talk about it." He frowned, his gaze focused on her hand. "Your skin is so soft."

His body was close enough to her, she could almost hear his heartbeat. Or was that her own pulse racing in her ears? "Thank you."

"Why do you put up with me?"

"What do you mean?"

"I'm just going to chase you away."

"I doubt it. Did you have dinner with friends tonight?" She needed to focus and figure out a way to get to what was bothering him. The direct approach wasn't working.

"Tried to."

"What's that mean?"

"My dad showed up at the restaurant and made a scene." She raised her eyebrows.

He lifted his whiskey glass to his lips, but it was empty, and he started to rise. She pulled at his waistband and he fell back onto the couch. "Oh, is that what you want?" He leaned toward her, his breath a mixture of whiskey and him. She pushed against his chest until he was once again sitting next to her.

"First, tell me why your dad made a scene."

He glared at her, but didn't move.

His eyebrows were caramel-colored, a shade deeper than his hair and she pressed her hands together to keep from running her finger along his brow. "He said I needed to learn my lesson."

"What lesson?"

He lurched off the sofa and over to the sideboard, where he sloshed whiskey into his glass. "Want one?"

She shook her head. Someone had to stay sober.

Apparently, he'd overruled her, because he brought the glass over and handed it to her. "Drink up."

She took a sip and the amber liquid burned her throat. Coughing, she held the glass out to Adam, who banged it on the marble coffee table, relieving her of having to drink any more of it.

"What lesson, Adam?"

He focused his troubled green eyes on her and she wanted to wrap her arms around him, and promise that everything would be alright. He rose, banged his leg on the edge of the table and paced the room. She knew the only way he'd feel better is if he got out whatever was tormenting him. Instead, his jaw was clenched, his body rigid and he wouldn't look at her. Each time their gazes met, his took off in a different direction.

But he continued to return to her and she knew it was only a matter of time before he had no choice but to stop and talk. So she waited.

After a few more circuits around the beige area rug, he sank onto the couch next to her, his forearm covering his eyes.

"What lesson?" she asked again.

"Honoring the family name." His voice was low and a little fuzzy, but understandable.

"Why would he think you weren't?" What kind of father would say that in public?

"Screwed up three cases. No one wants ta work wi me. Giving firm a bad name. Time for me ta get out on my own."

"Did you talk to him? Find out what you can do to fix things?"

"Does'n matter. Can't change his mind."

"You did say you wanted to get a job in Manhattan."

"Ha!" It sounded more like a bark, really, and he jumped up, again. "Like I'll get any sort of accep...acceptable ref'rence now."

"I'm sorry, Adam. What can I do?"

He squinted at her. Looming over her as he was, she felt at a distinct disadvantage, so she rose. Still, she had to tilt her head back to meet his gaze—not that staring at the column of his throat was such a bad thing, especially where it disappeared into the collar of his shirt.

She swallowed. This was ridiculous. She was here, in Adam's apartment, to make him feel better, not to come up with more reasons to fantasize about him. Dina met his gaze.

His eyes had darkened, pupils wide. This close to him she could see the striations of brown and green in his irises, the individual lashes around his eyes and the muscle that jumped around his cheekbone as he clenched and unclenched his jaw. She swallowed again.

"Who are you?" he whispered.

"You know who I am." She wanted to cup his face and stroke his cheek.

As if reading her mind, he lifted his hand, but instead of stroking her cheek, he ran his fingers through her hair, squeezed the curls and released them. His hands weren't gentle, but each tug of her hair sent ripples through her body. He slid his fingers over her scalp and around the back of her neck, and she stifled a moan. Shivers ran down her spine and she inhaled, leaning toward him. Her breasts brushed against his chest. Her head jerked as they tingled on contact.

"Yurre the only one who's ever believed in me, the only one who hasn't left," he whispered. "Why?"

"Because I care," she whispered.

He lowered his head close to her. His lips were so close to hers, their breath mingled and it would take barely any movement at all for them to meet.

He was going to kiss her. Or maybe she was going to kiss him. She couldn't tell at this point. All she knew was it was going to happen. Despite her best efforts to prevent it, despite all her reasons it shouldn't, it was happening.

He was drunk but she didn't care.

When their lips finally met, she melted, like butter left outside on a ninety-five degree day. His mouth was firm and decisive. It brushed hers, back and forth and she opened for him. When she did, he swiped his tongue along her lips and delved deeper into her mouth. She did the same, tasting the whiskey. They explored each other's mouths together, each of them thrusting and receding in equal measure. She remembered learning in biology that the tongue was the only muscle in the human body that worked without the support of the skeleton, but she was loathe to mention that now—if she did, Adam might stop what he was doing and it was too delicious to stop. He brushed his hands up and down her back, and she imagined what it would feel like to have his hands on her bare skin.

She rested her hands on his shoulders, feeling the flex of his sleek muscles beneath her palms, before letting them drift along his neck to cup his jaw, like she'd wanted to before. Her fingers played with his earlobes and threaded through his hair and he groaned against her mouth.

"Dina."

He grabbed her elbows and backed her up against the wall without breaking contact with her mouth, and she was grateful for the support. Her knees felt like a jellyfish and without the wall, and his hands, she would have dissolved onto the floor.

If he never got another lawyer job, he could hire out as a professional kisser. Or maybe not, since he'd have to kiss other women and she wanted him all to herself. She pressed her body against him, her softness melting into his hardness as he grabbed her hips.

She shifted and his breath caught. He pulled away from her mouth and trailed kisses along her jaw and down her neck, sucking her skin, no doubt leaving marks. Letting her head fall back, she gave him access and he continued kissing his way south to her collarbone. She whimpered and ran her hands up and down his ribcage, feeling the play of his muscles beneath his shirt. She hooked her fingers in his belt loops, locking him to her, and rotated her hips against him.

He hissed and pulled the hem of her shirt, loosening it enough to slide his palms beneath it. Finally, he was touching her bare skin, leaving a trail of heat in their wake. She growled and took his lips between her teeth, nipping them and making him chuckle.

"You're as wild as your hair," he said, plunging his tongue once again into her mouth.

Taking a cue from him, she slid her hands beneath his shirt. His skin was warm, and she ran her fingers over the ridges of his abs. When she reached his chest, she played with the hair there, and by the reaction of his tongue, he liked it.

"I want you." His words formed almost silently against her mouth.

Her whole body stilled. He was drunk. Would continuing this take advantage of their friendship?

Adam pulled away from her with great care, one body part at a time, as if he couldn't bear any part of him to be separated from her. Desire and need matched her own.

With a nod, she pulled off her shirt.

He took a step back, swayed and reached for her. His hands landed on her breasts and his thumbs caressed her nipples through her bra. She arched her back as her nipples tightened, and he offered a wolf-like grin.

"You like that."

Overcome by the sensations, she couldn't speak. She nodded and reached for his shirt. Her fingers fumbled with the buttons until he ripped it open, popping the rest of them. Out of the corner of her eye, she saw them bounce on the fluffy carpet, but she couldn't avert her gaze from his muscular chest.

Now she could see what her fingers had touched and she wanted more. Leaning forward, she licked his chest and he gasped.

"Woman, you're killing me." He dropped his head back with a groan and his hands shook on her shoulders.

With a low chuckle, she continued, trailing her tongue and lips across his chest, tasting salt and sweat and man.

Without warning, he pulled away from her, bent down and with one arm around her shoulders and the other beneath her knees, lifted her up as though she weighed nothing.

Dina knew that not to be true.

"What are you doing?" Despite her state of undress, his body warmed her.

"Having my way with you," he said, stalking to the sofa and lowering her onto it. He followed. She leaned against the back of the sofa and he braced his knees on either side of her hips, and stared at her. His gaze took in every inch of her and she realized he had become the hero in her very own romance.

"You're beautiful," he said, and reached out to undo her bra clasp. When her breasts came free he filled his hands with them. If his thumbs had aroused her through her bra before, they almost sent her over the edge now.

She bucked and he tightened his thighs around her, following her body's movements as if he were riding her. Her hands rose restlessly and she reached for him. Shifting beneath him, she felt him harden. Something fluttered low in her stomach.

"I need you now." His voice was hoarse and he leaned away from her, undoing his belt and yanking at his pants.

Oh my God, she was going to see him naked.

Her heart thudded in her chest. She thought about stopping him, but that fluttering inside her increased and all thoughts of stopping or slowing down disappeared. She wanted him, needed him, too. He climbed off her and watched as she wriggled her hips to remove her pants. His nostrils flared at her movements and within moments, they were naked.

Together.

He pulled open a condom packet from the pocket of his jeans and laid her beneath him. She stared up into eyes so green they were almost emerald. Skin against skin, all kinds of tingling sensations pulsed through her, zeroing in low in her belly as he rolled the condom on. He kissed her, open-mouthed and his tongue gave her a preview of what they would do. She rotated her hips and he trailed his hand from her cheek, along her neck, around her breasts down to where her body pulsed. His fingers teased her folds and her breath came in short gasps. He rose and hovered over her, the cool air between them frustrating her. She needed him in her. Now.

As if hearing her silent demand, he lowered himself and entered her, pausing barely a moment for her to adjust before rhythmically moving inside of her. She stretched, trying to accommodate him, wanting to feel the pressure build once again. When he brushed his fingers against her, she gasped.

She ran her hands along his back, reveling in the feel of him as their hips rocked together. His breathing grew heavier and she closed her eyes as her need built. He withdrew partially before plunging inside of her once again, and the pressure that had built within her exploded into shards of light behind her eyelids. His climax followed closely behind hers, his shout echoing off the walls, before he collapsed against her.

Their hearts beat together as slowly their breathing calmed and their sweat cooled. He made lazy circles on her arms as his head rested on her chest. She was blissfully spent and had no desire to move.

If she did, they'd have to talk about what they'd just done and why. They'd have to discuss where to go from here.

CHAPTER FOURTEEN

The first thing he noticed was the pounding in his head. The second thing he noticed was the smell—a mix of alcohol and sex.

Dina.

Images of their time together flooded his brain, but they were fuzzy, more like impressions really. The springiness of her hair, the scent of her skin, some stumbling around.

The utter bliss of making love.

His eyes flew open as he unstuck his cheek from the leather sofa. Sex had never been about love before. But with Dina? It was a possibility. He squinted in the harsh sunlight bathing his living room. He was alone. Forcing down the panic that knowledge always caused him, he sat up, careful not to disturb the rocks in his head. Where was Dina?

"Dina?" There was no answer.

His mind skittered back to yesterday and the debacle with his father. He shut his eyes tightly, as if that would block the memory from returning. He'd much rather think about Dina. But unfortunately, those earlier memories were clear and prolific.

His father, his own father, had fired him.

Even though Ashley had lied.

He shook his head as pain sliced through him once again. He looked for a distraction. Where was Dina?

Looking around his apartment, he didn't find a note or any sign she'd been there. Well, maybe there was. The empty bottles were lined up on the counter—he didn't think he'd had the presence of mind to do that—and his clothes were folded on the recliner.

His clothes.

He looked down. Yup, he was naked. He was definitely hung over if he hadn't noticed he was naked.

Shit. He'd had drunk sex with Dina. The one person he cared about and who cared about him. What had he done? What had he said? Had he told her about being fired? Had he even made sure she was enjoying herself? Come to think of it, how had she gotten here? And now where had she gone?

He started to pat his leg to feel for his phone and would have laughed at the stupidity, but there were too many stupid things in his life that weren't funny. Riffling through his stacked clothes, he felt the hard rectangle of his phone and pulled it out of the pocket. Maybe she'd texted him. He turned it on.

She hadn't.

He'd had drunk sex with her. She deserved more than a text from him. He dialed her number. When her voicemail connected, his stomach dropped.

"Hey, Dina, it's Adam. Give me a call."

He probably should have said more. But what was he supposed to say when he didn't know exactly what he'd said or done. That conversation shouldn't happen on a voicemail, let alone via text.

Sitting in the coffee shop, Dina watched Adam's name appear on her phone screen and let it go to voice mail. This was one awkward phone conversation she was not ready to have. Just as her voice mail dinged, indicating he'd left a message, Tracy walked up to her table cradling her coffee cup like it was a pot of gold.

"Meeting for coffee this morning was a fabulous idea," she said, leaning over and kissing Dina's cheek. "Mackenzie didn't sleep all night and I needed to get away from the house."

"Oh, I'm so sorry," Dina said, stirring her tea. She could only imagine how difficult it had to be being up all night with a baby, and then taking care of the same baby all day. Luckily for Tracy, her husband was a huge help. Someday, Dina hoped to be as lucky. A vision of Adam rising over her flashed in her brain and she shook her head.

"Comes with the territory. Now, tell me what's going on with you. You have a glow."

Dina reared back. "A glow? What kind of glow?"

Tracy leaned forward. "You slept with him, didn't you?"

"Wha...what are you talking about?" Sweat broke out on Dina's upper lip. Could she blame it on the hot tea?

Laughter from her best friend told her the jig was up, and Dina let her head fall into her hands. "I am in so much trouble," she said.

"Why? I'm surprised you waited this long."

"Tracy! We've only known each other a few weeks, and he keeps me at arm's length. Besides which, I don't sleep around."

"I'm hoping there was more than sleeping going on," her friend said with a laugh.

Dina glared at her.

"Was it good?"

Dina shrugged. "Yes and no."

"Details."

Bossy lady. "It was Adam, he doesn't do anything halfway." She smiled. "But he was drunk, so it wasn't as romantic as..."

"You'd fantasized it would be?"

If flames had burst forth from her cheeks, Dina wouldn't have been surprised. In fact, she was surprised the coffee shop's sprinkler system didn't kick on just to be safe. "It doesn't matter anyway, because it shouldn't happen again."

"Why not? And wait a minute, you can't skip over the good stuff. I want details."

"Seriously?"

"Absolutely. I'm an old married lady with a baby. The last time I had sex just for the hell of it, was I don't even know when. I need to live vicariously through my exciting single friends."

"Then you should go make some," Dina said.

Tracy threw her napkin at her. "Don't make me beg."

With a sigh, Dina told Tracy about the phone call, going over to Adam's apartment, trying to get him to talk, and how they ended up having sex.

"And you just left?"

"No, I fell asleep, as did he. Then I woke up. And then I left."

"Why?"

"Because it's going to be so awkward."

"I don't get it," Tracy said. "Lots of people have drunk sex. Why is this such a big deal?"

Dina swirled her tea in her cup. "Because we're supposed to be friends who made an arrangement. I was helping him seem more respectable for his father, and he was accompanying me to the reunion. That's it."

"Okay. And you had sex. Why does that change anything?"

"Because friends don't have sex!"

"Uh, Dina? Yes they do."

"I know, but we weren't supposed to."

"Why not?"

"Because I didn't want to seem pathetic. I really like him, but I'm so not his type and he's not mine. There are still things he's hiding from me, I can tell. And he's only taking me to the reunion because I'm helping him with his dad. Except his dad is mad at him, so it's not really working. Which means he doesn't need me anymore."

"Anyone looking at the two of you knows he's not staying with you because of some arrangement you think you have."

"An arrangement I *know* we have."

Tracy gave her a look and Dina squirmed.

"And leaving without talking to him? You have no idea what he's thinking or feeling. You're never going to get those answers you want if you keep avoiding him. Not to mention," Tracy leaned forward, "you missed out on all the good post-coital talk!"

"He left me a voicemail."

Tracy rolled her eyes. "What did it say?"

"I don't know. I didn't listen to it."

"Give me your phone."

"What? No!"

She held her hand out and Dina gripped her phone in her lap. There was no way she was letting Tracy listen to the voicemail.

"Then listen to it yourself."

Tracy had grown up with three brothers. She was married to a guy who worshipped her. She was a kick-ass mom. Dina had no doubt she'd steal her phone and listen to the voicemail on her own. Flaring her nostrils, Dina pressed play and held the phone to her ear. A moment later, she put the phone in her purse.

"What did he say?"

"Just to call him."

"So do it."

"I will."

"Now. You're not going to feel better, or get the answers you need, if you keep pushing this off. And I think you're reading this all wrong anyway."

"Oh really?" Dina squeezed her hands together. Was Tracy a mind reader now? She did have the cutest baby ever, so perhaps whatever had allowed her to produce that enabled her to read minds too. Pretty nifty trick, even if deep down she didn't believe it.

Picking up the phone, she redialed Adam. If she was lucky, he wouldn't answer.

She wasn't.

"Dina! Where'd you...never mind. Hi."

"Hi."

Tracy mouthed "speaker," but Dina shook her head.

"Where are you right now?"

"With Tracy."

"Can you come over when you're finished?"

"Um, I have errands and..."

"Please? It's Saturday. You can do your errands after. I need to talk to you."

"Can't you just talk to me now?"

"No, this needs to be said face-to-face."

There it was. He was going to tell her he didn't need her anymore. Her stomach dropped. It shouldn't hurt so much, but it did. And he expected her to come over to hear it?

She swallowed the lump in her throat. Tracy squeezed her hand. She'd forgotten Tracy was there. Hanging up the phone, she wiped her eyes. "I don't want to go over. He can't force me, right?"

"Honey, I think you're jumping to conclusions here. How did he sound?"

"Like Adam. Normal."

"Go over and talk to him."

Adam paced his apartment, wiping sweaty palms on his jeans. Something in her voice convinced him that Dina didn't want to come over.

What was it about him that made women leave? His inner voice tried to remind him that he was the one who usually insisted on casual relationships, and that his mom had left because of his dad, not because of him. But there was a part of him that just couldn't believe that inner voice completely.

Why had Dina left? Sex with him hadn't been that bad, had it? He'd never had any complaints before... And even though he didn't remember much, he was pretty sure he hadn't told her he'd been fired. He shook his head. Dina wasn't like the others. First he'd talk to her. Then he'd find out what the problem was. After that, he'd fix it.

The buzzer made him jump. He barked "send her up" into the intercom. Three minutes later, he heard the elevator arrive and he opened his door.

This was it.

His heart sped up as heat rushed through him.

Dina. She had an inner glow that made her cheeks rosy and her intelligent eyes soft. She looked at him like he mattered. She was beautiful, despite the misery giving her eyes a silvery amethyst tint. Her curly hair framed her face, her pale skin was almost translucent, but her shoulders were hunched.

He wanted to take her in his arms and never let her go. He wanted to get on his knees and ask for forgiveness. He wanted to beg her never to leave. He wanted to tell her he might love her.

His body went cold. Love her? He rolled the word in his head and his body temperature returned to normal. The word didn't scare him as much as he expected it to.

But she was looking at him with dread in her eyes, like she was afraid of him.

"Did I hurt you?" His voice sounded like a bullfrog. He cleared it. "Dina?" He motioned her inside.

Confusion crossed her features as she walked in. "Hurt me? When?"

"Last night." His body was frozen in place. If he'd hurt her, he'd never forgive himself.

"No, you didn't."

Gripping the doorjamb to prevent himself from falling to the ground as his knees buckled, he inhaled. Thank God.

She didn't want to be here, with him. She was going to leave him. He'd never get to tell her.

Backing up, he walked into the kitchen. He wanted to lock the front door, but that would be creepy. "Can I get you anything to drink?"

She blinked. "Water would be good."

Someone who wanted water wasn't walking away. Yet. Still, he kept watch on her as he grabbed a glass from the cherry cabinet and the filtered water from the sub-zero refrigerator. Handing it to her, their fingers touched. He felt a charge run up his arm, straight to his heart. He wanted to be the one to get her water, food, whatever she needed, always. He watched her take a sip. He wished he were the glass, because her hands wrapped around it as if she would never let it go. Pointing to the living room, he followed her in. He watched her pause at the sofa before sitting in the recliner.

He swallowed. "About last night..."

"It's fine. I know everything is different now and that's okay."

"Excuse me?"

"Our arrangement. It's irrelevant now."

He must have had way more to drink than he thought.

Running a hand over his hair, he rose and paced the room. "Okay, let's back up. Last night, I was drunk, you came over, we had sex. Does that about cover it?"

She nodded without making eye contact.

"What arrangement are you talking about?"

"The one where I help you with your reputation and you go with me to my reunion."

"Yeah, that's the one I thought you were talking about. Only I have no idea what you're actually saying. Why does one thing have to do with another?"

"Because I'm doing a terrible job improving your reputation and your clodpate of a father isn't changing his mind." She covered her mouth. "Sorry, I shouldn't have said that."

"Do I want to know what a 'clodpate' is?"

Her face heated. "It's an old-fashioned term for idiot. I don't know why it popped out like that."

Adam couldn't help the grin that spread across his face. Leave it to Dina to pick that word. He loved that quirk of hers. Hell, if he was right, he loved everything about her. "That's quite alright. What I don't understand is why you think that has anything to do with our having sex."

"Because you don't need me to help your reputation. So we have no reason to keep seeing each other."

She had the most expressive face he'd ever seen. Every emotion showed in her lovely violet eyes. What shade would they turn if he told her he loved her?

"Why do you think we had sex last night?" he asked.

"Because you were drunk. Which surprised me, because I didn't think alcohol enabled a person to have sex. But you..." She blushed. "You did quite well."

The woman who had "clodpate" on the tip of her tongue said he performed "quite well." He wasn't sure how to take that.

He reached for her hand across the space between the sofa and the recliner. Her skin was soft to the touch. Her fingers were thin and delicate. He held tight to make sure she didn't pull away. "We had sex because I haven't been able to get you out of my mind." *Because I love you.*

Her mouth opened.

"From the moment I met you, I haven't been able to think of another woman. Every time I'm with you, all I want to do is touch you, feel your skin against mine, taste your lips, play with your hair. Yes, I was drunk and that lowered my resolve, but we did not have sex *because* I was drunk."

She remained silent, her eyes wide.

"Why did *you* have sex with *me?*" He swallowed, not sure if he wanted to hear the answer. For some reason, when he was with her, unexpected words tumbled from his mouth. Not vocabulary words like "clodpate," but words from his heart that he kept hidden away from everyone else.

"Because you're irresistible."

Good lord, if he didn't think he'd scare her with the fervor of his desire, he'd leap off the sofa, and take her again right there in the recliner. But the last time they'd had sex was on the sofa, and she was now sitting on the recliner. He needed to make sure she had somewhere to sit in his apartment if he could somehow convince her to stay. Or return.

He wanted their next time to be different than their first—slower, more intentional, sober.

"We're supposed to be just friends." Her voice wavered between accusation and dismay.

"We still are friends, but I've wanted us to be more than friends for a while now."

"What do we do about our arrangement?"

He rose and approached her with caution. Leaning over, he rested each hand on an armrest, effectively boxing her in with his body. He lowered his head until it was a hairsbreadth away from her face. Her lips glistened and a blush rose from her neck across her cheek.

"Screw the arrangement."

CHAPTER FIFTEEN

The last time Adam's face had been this close to hers, they'd been having sex. From the looks of him, most notably his flared nostrils and his dilated pupils, he wanted to have sex again.

She must have smiled, because his lips widened ever so slightly before parting. His eyes hooded, he lowered his head even closer to hers. She could feel her pulse pounding, hear his rapid breathing and a part of her wanted to succumb to desire and let their bodies take over.

But first she needed answers. And this wasn't exactly a position conducive to discussion.

Pressing on his chest, she said, "No."

He reared back and the electric charge in the air fizzled.

"No?"

She shook her head. "You can't kiss me again until you answer my questions."

His shoulders drooped for a moment. But when he met her gaze, she saw relief.

"I thought..." He clenched his jaw. "Well, never mind what I thought. I'll answer your questions. But first I owe you an apology."

She curled up in the chair, now that she had room, and waited for him to sit on the sofa. Instead, he paced.

"Why do you owe me an apology?"

"Because you deserve way better than drunk sex, and while it was amazing, it's not how I had planned our first time to be." He ran his fingers through his hair, making it spiky and sexy.

"You planned our first time?" It wasn't just her.

Adam raised his head. "Planned, imagined, fantasized. And none of those fantasies included my being drunk. I haven't always acted in ways that might convince you, but Dina, you're the one I want to be with, and for more than just sex, although I definitely want that with you as well. I want to go out with you on a real date. I want to go the movies with you and the diner. Hell, I even want to go to the grocery store with you, so we can buy ingredients for a romantic dinner that leads... well." He smiled. "And that didn't happen, especially last night. So I'm sorry."

Her body filled with warmth. She didn't have to relegate him to "friends only." She could be herself. "Well, it's not as if you planned on your father screaming at you in public. He did scream at you, right?"

He gave her a humorless smile. "Yeah. So, what questions did you want me to answer?"

Dina fidgeted. He was willing to answer her questions. It was time to trust him and actually get answers. "So, about your dad..."

All the tension returned to his shoulders. "What else is left to say about him? He's a clodpate, as you so aptly put it, and I'm done."

"Why do I feel like there's something you're not telling me?"

Adam flexed and unflexed his fingers. "Someone lied about whether or not I gave my paralegal something to file. It didn't get filed and I lost the case. The situation took on a life of its own and is hurting the firm's reputation. And it's not the first time a case I've worked on got screwed up. But no matter how much I beg him to believe that I've changed and that it wasn't me who screwed up," Adam swallowed in distaste, "good old 'clodpate' doesn't believe me."

"But he seemed okay at dinner." Not anyone she'd want as a father, but not someone who'd disbelieve his own son.

"He's great at putting on a show."

"Why is he so set on not believing you?"

Adam sighed. "Honestly, I'm cocky, and I probably created part of the problem. I was careless in the past. But I've changed, only he doesn't see it—isn't willing to see it—especially now. Speaking of now, do we have to continue talking about him?"

She wasn't finished. "What are you going to do about your promotion?"

Adam narrowed his gaze. "I'll figure it out. I don't really know. What I do know is I want to kiss you."

He leaned over and pressed his lips against hers, moving his mouth against hers as if he was drawing the kiss out of her in slow, deep pulls. This time she didn't stop him. This time, his mouth didn't taste of whiskey. This time, his lips were gentle. He ran his hands through her hair, massaging the back of her scalp. When she opened her mouth to moan at the delicious chills running through her body, he licked his way into her mouth, exploring her and getting to know her by taste.

It was glorious and she wanted him.

And then he pulled away, panting.

"That was more like it," he whispered, running his thumb along her lower lip.

She wrapped her arms around his neck and reached to kiss him again, but as soon as her lips touched his, he pulled back.

"I can't believe I'm saying this, but no," he said, adding space between them. "We're doing this the right way this time. Nice and slow."

"I can kiss you slowly," she said, shocking herself at her own audacity. She must have shocked Adam too, because he flinched and let out a low laugh.

"Yes, you definitely can." He leaned forward and nipped her upper lip before once again pulling away. "But if we keep kissing, it will lead to more. Right here, right away. I don't want to rush anything. I want to discover everything about you that I missed last night."

Heat pooled low in her belly just listening to him. "So what does that mean?" she asked, her voice trembling with desire. She rose and rested her forehead against his shoulder.

"As crazy as it sounds, it means no more sex until we know each other in other ways. Much. Much. Better."

Adam closed the door of his building behind Dina after promising he'd call her tonight, returned to his apartment and took the first of what he suspected was going to be many long, cold showers. Never before had he denied himself sex as he was doing with Dina. But Dina was special and he wanted to do the right thing with her.

He dialed Jacob's number.

"Hey, want to meet me at the driving range?"

"Sure, when?" Jacob asked.

"One o'clock?"

"See you then."

He pulled into the parking spot, grabbed his golf clubs and walked into the driving range office. Jacob was already there. They walked to their cage, each carrying a bucket of balls. To their right was a teenage girl and her coach; to their left were several boys, each in their own cage. Adam waved at Jacob to go first. His friend adjusted his stance, shifted his hips, and swung his club. The ball soared through the air, coming close to the two hundred yard mark. After ten swings, Jacob stepped aside.

"So, what's going on?" Jacob adjusted his golf glove.

Adam bent to line up the ball on the tee. "My dad fired me." Even uttering the words brought a bitter taste to his mouth. He swung his club, watching the ball skip over the ground and travel nowhere. Just like his career.

"What the hell did the bastard do that for?"

It was satisfying listening to another person speak about his dad that way, even though Dina had a better vocabulary.

"I lost us a case because something that was supposed to get filed, didn't. It's my word against the paralegal's, and well, my word doesn't carry much weight. Unfortunately, having me in the office made others think I was getting special treatment. Especially because all the paralegals think I threw mine under the bus and am relying too much on my name."

He hit another ball. This time it sailed backwards, hitting the roof before rolling back down and landing two feet in front of him.

"Asshole," Jacob said, watching the golf ball.

"Exactly."

He swung his club again. Finally, it sailed straight and true, no more than one hundred yards, but at least it went in the right direction.

"Nice swing."

Adam nodded. He hit another seven balls before switching places with Jacob.

He took a deep breath. "So, I was wondering if you might have any contacts I could speak to," he said, as Jacob pulled out some balls with his club.

"New Jersey or New York?"

The Caribbean. "New York preferably, but I suspect I'm not going to get to be too choosey." He should have known his friend wouldn't make an issue out of helping him.

"Don't panic yet. Your dad's known as a ball-buster," Jacob said. "If you get a job in New York, are you going to commute?"

He shrugged. "I don't know. I've always wanted to live in the city, but lately..."

"What about Dina?"

He was finally in a relationship that might last. Suddenly, the city was less appealing. "We can still see each other if I'm in the city, can't we?"

"So, you're seeing each other now?"

Adam filled him in as Jacob continued his flawless swing. He left out "love." No one would hear that before Dina.

"What's she think about your getting fired?"

"She doesn't know about all of it."

Jacob sliced his ball far to the right. He swung around. "What part doesn't she know about?"

"The being fired part."

"Why not? She knows you well enough not to care."

Adam shrugged.

"Adz, you can't do that to her. You have to tell her."

A jolt of fear ran through him and his mouth dried. He did have to tell her, and based on what she knew already about him and his father, she'd be on his side, not his father's. But what if he couldn't find another job? Whatever respect she had for him would be lost. An unemployed guy wasn't boyfriend material. The thought of her leaving made his palms damp. He had to tell her he loved her first. Then maybe she'd stay. "It's a misunderstanding. I'll straighten it out with her when the time is right. First I need a new job."

"That's a helluva secret to keep from someone you care about."

That was exactly why he couldn't tell her. Not until he told her he loved her, and she loved him back. And even then…"I've got it under control." As long as she didn't press too hard about last night.

They finished each of their buckets. Before they left, Jacob clapped Adam on the shoulder. "I'll email you some contacts, so don't worry about that. But Adam, you need to tell her."

Adam wrapped his hand around Dina's as they walked to the movie theater. It was their first "official" date since his escape from the "friend zone." He was determined to do it right. After showing up with flowers—daisies, which she loved—and complimenting her on her outfit—jeans and a bright pink sweater that made her lips look extra kissable—they'd walked to the movie theater down the street.

He hadn't once let go of her hand, because he hated the thought of being apart from her, even by a few inches. Man, he was a goner.

Inside, he paid for the tickets, awkwardly doing everything with his one free hand, and taking twice as long as if he'd used two.

She looked on and laughed.

Jacob's advice still rang in his ears. So he held on, determined to make himself the best boyfriend she'd known so that even when she eventually learned his secret—and he knew he would have to tell her at some point—she'd stay. And maybe love him as much as he was beginning to love her.

"Would you like popcorn?" he asked after they had their tickets.

"I hate getting kernels in my teeth. But go ahead if you want it."

"Candy? Pretzels? Nachos?"

"I'm good."

"Are you sure?" She was his girlfriend. He needed her to know she could have anything she wanted from him. The voice in his head laughed at him. *Dude, you're toast.*

She turned to him, putting her free hand against his cheek and his heart stuttered in his chest. He turned his face into it, so he could kiss her palm.

"Relax," she said. "I don't eat at movie theaters. It has nothing to do with you. My parents were always obsessive about our eating habits, and it's stuck with me, at least as far as junk food in a movie theater goes."

He kissed her palm again. "You know I think you're perfect, right?"

The blush rising on her cheeks was adorable and he vowed to make sure he caused it to appear more often. She looked away from him. No way. He took her chin in his hand and made her meet his gaze.

"Did your parents give you a hard time about your looks?" His blood boiled at the thought of it.

"I don't think they meant to, but when you're already insecure about your looks, it's difficult to brush off well-meant advice."

He drew her against him and gave her a hug. For as long as she was with him, he'd make sure she knew just how perfect she was. She'd never feel insecure around him again. When it was his turn in the concession line, he ordered himself a bag of popcorn and a soda, and walked with her into the movie theater. The theater had been recently redone, with leather reclining seats, so the experience was more like watching a movie in one's own living room than in a public theater.

As they waited for the movie to start, Adam wished they could share a seat.

She lifted the armrest separating their seats and scooted as close to him as possible. Had she read his mind? With a smile, he put his arm around her and pulled her closer.

"This is better," she said.

He nodded and made small circles on the inside of her wrist with his thumb.

"You're going to distract me from the movie."

He looked at the ads on the screen. "It hasn't started yet."

"Did you know the first movies were under a minute long when they were invented in the 1890s?"

He huffed. "No, I didn't."

The previews started and she faced forward. "This is my favorite part," she whispered.

Lights and colors flashed on the screen, but Adam saw little of it, other than through his peripheral vision. He was too busy watching Dina. Her lips parted as she focused on the screen in front of her. For each preview, he could read her expression as summaries of each movie played—humor, surprise, confusion.

He liked her confusion best. She had this adorable way of wrinkling her nose, making fine lines between her eyebrows and almost challenging him not to touch them. Later, he'd have to figure out a way to make her get those wrinkles back, just so his fingers could be the ones to wipe them away.

When the main feature started—a romantic comedy he'd thought she'd like—she leaned over and whispered in his ear.

"She looks like she could use a plate of pasta more than a boyfriend."

He took a moment to examine the actress. Dina was right. The A-list actress was super skinny and although traditionally attractive, not particularly appealing. He frowned. Before today, he'd always thought she was hot. In fact, a lot of the women he'd dated before Dina resembled that body type. Her neck looked stringy, the veins in her arms ropey. When he held Dina against him, her curves had made him feel she was melting into him, like the two of them were becoming one person, even without sex.

When the actress and actor literally bumped into each other on the street corner, he leaned toward Dina. Her hair tickled his face and he pushed it out of the way, more to give himself an excuse to touch it than because it bothered him.

"He's probably got bruises from her ribs."

Dina buried her head in his shoulder and trembled with laughter. He squeezed her hand, his cheek twitching from trying not to disturb anyone. The smell of coconuts wafted from her hair and he focused on tropical islands, sandy beaches, anything but her silent laughter. Because if he thought about that he'd laugh out loud, and they'd get kicked out of the movie theater. Finally, she took a deep breath and pulled away, and while he was grateful for the absence of her contagious laughter, his body missed her closeness.

They continued to make quiet comments throughout the movie—she pointing out "too stupid to live" moments, he pointing out how the male lead was equally treated as eye candy—until inevitably, the credits rolled and the lights went on.

Somehow, during the length of the movie, their hands had become intertwined and their legs, extended in the red leather recliners, rested against each other. He didn't want to move. Ever.

"That was a pretty ridiculous movie," he said, as they finally rose and filed out of the movie theater.

"Oh, but I loved it," Dina said. "It was so ridiculous that it was entertaining. What I love about movies like that is you know exactly what you're going to get. There are no surprises, because there isn't much depth to the story or the characters, but it's exactly what you need at the time you're watching."

"I'll keep that in mind for next time." He gave her a sideways glance, intrigued by this amazing, intelligent woman who could find meaning and joy in anything she did.

"Good. Although we might need to discuss the genre next time. There are only so many skinny bimbos I can handle at one time."

He took her hand in his. "True. And that's just the guys."

She laughed, and it was the sweetest sound. On their way home, they stopped for frozen yogurt, getting cups to go and eating while walking.

Dina looked over at Adam's cup of yogurt, which was pineapple and coconut. "Um, we may have a problem."

Adam stopped dead. "What's wrong?"

Dina's lips twitched and the pressure in his chest eased. "You don't eat chocolate. That could be a deal breaker."

Adam pulled her toward him and handed her his yogurt.

"My not eating chocolate is a deal breaker?" He drew himself up so he was as large as possible and looked down at her, focusing on her lips. There was a spot of chocolate, and he took his finger, dragging it across her mouth to wipe the chocolate away.

She nodded her head.

With the back of his hand, he caressed her cheek. Her skin was so soft and warmth pooled in his belly. "I would have thought that would be a good thing."

"Wh..." She cleared her throat. "Why?"

He licked his finger, slowly, watching her mouth drop. "Because you don't need to share."

He bent his head toward her and kissed her cold lips that tasted of chocolate. In the background he heard a "plunk," but to investigate would mean pulling away from her and he wouldn't do that. The coconut scent of her hair mixed with the coconut flavor of his yogurt and he couldn't get enough of her. After what could have been hours or seconds, she pushed against his chest and he took a step back, his breath in short gasps.

"I dropped the yogurt."

CHAPTER SIXTEEN

Adam called her every day over the next two weeks. They went out on dates during the week and spent at least one day a weekend together.

And they didn't have sex.

Prior to meeting Adam, Dina would never have characterized herself as sex-starved. She never would have characterized herself as "sex" anything, if she were being completely honest.

She'd had boyfriends—mostly several years older than her, since she used to relate better to older men who appreciated a woman with a brain. She kept a box of condoms under her bed. The box had been opened and several condoms had been used. But sex had never been something she thought about very often.

After meeting Adam?

She thought about sex constantly.

And his desire to take things slow, to woo her, or whatever crackpot idea he had in his head, while lovely, was driving her mad.

That rom-com movie they'd gone to? She'd barely been able to focus. The scent of his aftershave, mingled with the buttery popcorn smell, had almost made her hyperventilate.

The night they'd gone to a karaoke bar? It was a damn good thing the words of the songs had played in front of her, because his arm wrapped around her shoulders had sent tingles running up and down her spine, and if not for the teleprompter, she would have been unable to remember a single word.

She had no recollection of the taste of any of the food they'd eaten, since the only taste she could recall was his mouth and his skin.

And today they were going ice-skating. She'd be lucky if the heat of her desire for him didn't melt the ice beneath her feet and send her plunging into the icy waters below.

At least she'd finally be able to cool off.

Her apartment buzzer sounded, she grabbed her skates and skipped down the stairs to meet Adam. She was going to jump him after skating and convince him they needed to have sex. Today.

Still thinking about all the ways she was going to convince Adam to have sex with her, she didn't see him standing on her front porch until she was on top of him. He grabbed her by the elbows, ostensibly to keep them both from toppling over.

It was the perfect opportunity to press herself against him and kiss his lips.

"Whoa, there," he said against her mouth. "In a hurry?"

To have sex with you. "I didn't want to keep you waiting." *I wonder what sex on the porch would be like?*

He nipped her lower lip and she melted against him, dropping her skates and wrapping her arms around his neck. He groaned, and pulled away.

"Come on, the ice awaits."

Definitely going to melt through it.

With a sigh, she picked up her skates and followed him to the car. "I thought Mennen Arena would be a better option," he said as he pulled out into traffic. "I never fully trust the lake is frozen, no matter how many people are on it."

Well, at least she wouldn't drown when she melted the ice.

Once they parked and paid for ice time, they sat on the bench and laced up their skates. Adam took her hand in his and they both stepped onto the ice. Pushing off with her left foot, she dropped his hand as she adjusted to moving on the ice. Adam was a strong skater, and graceful, too. Dina hadn't skated since she was a teenager and had been invited to some little cousin's birthday party. She'd spent most of the time holding up the younger kids so they wouldn't fall down, and her current skills were rusty. But with Adam's help, after a couple of laps, she had the rhythm and balance down pat.

This time, she seized Adam's hand and squeezed.

Looking down at her, his mouth broadened in a grin. She tripped and he grabbed her waist.

"You okay?"

They were still moving and Adam had her pressed against his side, seeming reluctant to let her go even though she'd regained her balance after a stroke or two.

"I'm fine." This time, she didn't look at his face. It was hard enough to concentrate pressed up against him, feeling his muscles, his warm breath tickling her neck.

His strokes were sure, and he glided with ease. They skated around the rink in silence, until he spun them around. She caught her breath and laughed as the lights in the rink twinkled and his warm body seemed to envelop her. Closing her eyes at the dizzying sensation, she let him spin them across the ice, until finally he stopped in the center.

She opened her eyes to see him looking down at her. "Like that?" he asked.

She nodded and took his hand as he began moving again. "Where'd you learn to skate so well?"

His stride faltered, but he righted himself. Had she not been so close to him, she probably wouldn't have even noticed his misstep. He stared across the rink. "My mother taught me."

"That must have been nice."

He shrugged.

"Did you two skate together often?"

He waited so long to answer, she thought he would remain silent. But he finally answered.

"She took me skating every Saturday. Afterwards, we'd go out for fresh donuts at this local bakery down the street. It's no longer there."

The "neither is she" remained unspoken, but Dina heard it loud and clear. "How old were you when she left?"

He glided with her and from the corner of her eye, she could see him swallow. "Seven."

She squeezed his hand, wanting to say something comforting. But what did you say to someone whose mother had left him?

"For a long time, I blamed myself," he said. "Now I mostly blame my father."

His "mostly" comment told her more than anything else he'd said, because no matter how much blame he'd shifted to his father, Dina would bet a part of him blamed himself. Suddenly, his questions about why Dina stayed with him made sense. Her throat hurt from the urge to cry. Instead, she squeezed his hand again and rested her head on his shoulder for a brief moment before concentrating on remaining upright.

"My dad used to take me to the library every Friday afternoon," she said. "He'd come home early for Shabbat and we'd go borrow enough books to last me through the weekend."

"So that's where you get your love of reading."

She nodded. "To this day, my arms ache from carrying too many books every time I go into the children's section."

"Do your parents still live around here?"

She shook her head. "No, they moved to St. Louis when I was in college. My dad's a professor at a university there."

"And are they as smart as you?"

She glanced sideways at him, but he wasn't making fun of her. "My dad is a physics professor, my mom is a linguist and my two brothers are doctors."

He turned so he was skating backwards, facing her. "Yeah, but are they as smart as you?"

It was the first time someone had heard her family's professions and didn't make some comment about her only being a librarian. It was the first time, for that matter, that a man her own age valued her intelligence. She swallowed. Her heart rate sped up and the tears she'd swallowed before prickled behind her eyelids. She blinked quickly before answering. "We're all pretty smart."

With a nod, he resumed skating next to her. "It's hard living up to family expectations, real or imaginary," he said.

She never thought anyone would understand what it was like to live in the shadow of her brilliant family, but Adam seemed to immediately. A knot somewhere inside, one she'd always felt and had always picked at, loosened. This man, this amazing, complicated man...

"I'm thirsty," Adam said. "Want to stop for a drink?"

It took her a few seconds to process what he said and by the time she did, they were already skating toward the exit. They hobbled over to the refreshment stand, where Adam ordered two hot chocolates and two bottled waters. Finding an empty table in the back, they sat and people-watched.

Or rather, Adam people-watched.

Dina Adam-watched.

His innate understanding of her, and his demonstration of vulnerability, made him even more attractive to her. He tipped his head back and gulped most of the water in the water bottle. His Adam's apple bobbed and the light shone on his skin. His hand wrapped around the bottle, the same hand that cupped her jaw when he kissed her, or her neck when he drew her close. His lips pursed around the mouth of the bottle, water moistening them, and she licked her own lips with desire. He returned the bottle to the table and the clap of the bottle against the Formica made her jump.

She drank her own water, slaking her physical thirst, but leaving her sexual desire unfulfilled. Her hot chocolate was steaming and she played with the cup. She didn't need anything to make her hotter.

"Not a fan?" Adam asked. He nodded toward her cup.

"Oh, it's hot, I'm letting it cool a little." *And me.*

"What do you think their story is?" he asked, indicating a couple two tables over. They were both on their phones, looking to everyone else as if they weren't paying any attention to each other.

"Brother and sister," Dina said.

Adam stared at them a moment longer. "Nope. I think they're sending each other dirty texts."

Dina choked on the hot chocolate she'd just sipped and her eyes watered. Adam leaned over to help her and she waved him away. Her throat stung from the heat of the liquid, but she got herself under control and wiped her mouth with a napkin before speaking.

"That was unfair."

"Why?" he asked.

"Because you can't tell a person something like that while they're drinking."

"Should I have texted it instead?" he asked with a wink.

She rolled her eyes. "You're impossible." But her neck heated at the thought of the content of those texts and she tried to distract herself. "Do you have any?"

"Dirty texts?" He pulled out his phone and Dina squeaked.

"No!" People around them turned their head and she ducked, hearing Adam chuckle softly. "Siblings. Brothers or sisters."

His relaxed exterior changed once again, tightening and growing wary. His jaw vibrated, as if he were clenching and unclenching his teeth. "No, just me."

"I'll bet that has its advantages."

He shrugged, staring into his hot chocolate. "I never thought about it really. What's it like having siblings?"

"Complicated. It's like being in an unending competition, where the stakes are constantly raised."

"At least they provide a distraction."

She waited for him to explain further, but he remained silent and she could almost see him raising his walls. Only this time, they weren't quite as high. She'd knocked a few down and she was determined to tackle the rest. If he'd let her.

Adam forcibly relaxed each part of his body—his neck, his shoulders and his hands—and tried to clear his head. He'd given away more about himself than he'd intended, but he'd learned more than he'd expected about her as well.

"Let's get out of here," he said.

"Why? Don't you want to skate some more?"

"Not unless you do."

He led her out to the car. He went to turn it on, but she stopped him with her hand on his upper arm. "Why don't you like to talk about your family?"

His hand gripped the key and he forced himself, once again, to loosen his grip. His chest tightened and his gaze travelled from the key to her hand, up her arm to her violet eyes, unblinking and kind. Crap.

"There's nothing to say."

"You don't act like a man with nothing to say."

The air in the car grew heavy and he needed space to breathe, but short of opening the car door, there was nowhere to go. He pulled at the chest strap of the seatbelt, until he felt more pressure on his other hand. Now it was between both of hers and she was stroking it, like one would a frightened puppy.

He had nothing against puppies, unless he was being compared to one.

Swallowing, he tried to grin at her, but it came out as more of a grimace. "You've met my father."

"And I'm still here."

Good point.

"It's not your fault your mom left."

He rubbed his other hand, the one Dina wasn't holding, across the top of his head. He needed a haircut. "You can't possibly know that."

"It's never the kid's fault. Have you talked to your dad about it?"

He choked on a bitter laugh he tried to swallow. "He likes the conversation even less than I do."

"That must have been hard for you to deal with."

He didn't know how to answer that, or even if it required an answer. So he focused on her hands wrapped around his. They were cool, but soothing. They didn't add to the heaviness around him. In fact, they centered him. "It's done."

She stared at him a moment longer and he wondered what she saw. But she gave nothing away and finally, she let him have his hand back. He wasn't sure if he was disappointed or relieved.

Without a word, he started the car.

"Come back to my place," she said. Her voice was low, but it wasn't a question. If it had been anyone but Dina, he would have said it was a command.

Not in the mood for an argument, and really, what was there to argue about, he drove to her apartment and parked in front. She climbed out of the car and waited on the sidewalk until he joined her. Then, taking his hand once again, she led him into her apartment.

Once inside, his mouth went dry and for the first time, he didn't know what to do. He wasn't a moron when it came to women. He could read the signs, and Dina's clearly pointed to sex. From the way she'd touched him frequently, to the way her tongue had just slid across her lips, and the way she gave him so little personal space as she stood next to him.

She held her hand out for his coat and when he gave it to her, she held his hand just a moment longer than necessary.

They'd had sex once and it had been great. But he was trying to change, to show her and himself that he was different. He wouldn't have sex with her again until they'd spent time getting to know each other better.

Returning to his side, she placed a hand on his arm. His muscle twitched and her fingers tightened. Her gaze was focused on his arm, and his was focused on her. She pulled away and left the room.

He couldn't afford to get attached and have her leave him. It's why he never went for serious relationships with women. Casual flings? Sure. Him leaving first? Definitely. But Dina? Did she deserve someone like him? Probably not.

"You're thinking too hard," Dina said, returning with a bottle of wine and two glasses. She gave him the bottle to open and when their fingers touched, he felt a jolt of electricity arc between them. Standing this close to her, he could see her individual eyelashes framing pupils that were wide with desire.

She wanted him. He wanted her. What was the problem?

"I seem to think a lot around you," he said, pouring the wine and clinking his glass against hers.

Was she always this blatantly sexual? Another reason why they needed to get to know each other better. She kept her gaze trained on him, took a sip, swallowed, and then ran her tongue once again across her lips. His groin tightened. Before he could force his brain to figure things out, she stepped toward him and took the glass out of his hand.

Oh God. She pressed her body against him and rose on tiptoe to kiss him, creating a torturous friction between them. His hands, which had been suspended in some kind of midair limbo, dropped to her hips.

Meanwhile, her hands brushed against his backside and squeezed.

He groaned, and when he opened his mouth she slipped her tongue inside. She tasted of chardonnay, she smelled of coconut and he was done for. So much for waiting. Lifting her up, he carried her across the room, heading toward her bedroom. She wrapped her legs around his waist.

Adam leaned against the wall and all of a sudden, her hands were everywhere—his hair, his neck, his back, his chest. She nibbled his ear and trailed kisses along his jaw. Blood rushed to his groin and he felt lightheaded, a buzzing sound in his ears so loud he couldn't think. He just knew he had to have her right here, right now.

And she seemed to agree. She fumbled with the buttons on his shirt, pushing the fabric back and off his shoulders, rubbing her fingers across his chest and driving him mad. He lowered her to the floor and pulled at her jeans, and she pulled at his at the same time. A moment later, both pairs were down. He ran his fingers beneath the waistband of her panties, dipping down further and feeling how wet she was for him already. He hardened painfully, his cock jumping against her as if of its own volition. She quivered against him and angled her hips toward him.

"Are you sure?" he ground out.

"Yes."

That one word was all it took. He grabbed a condom from his wallet, hands shaking as he unwrapped it and slid it on. Using the wall for support, he slid into her, trying to go slowly, but with her gripping him and rocking against him, it was almost impossible. She was so tight and her muscles clenched around him. His panting mingled with hers and sweat dripped down his back. God she felt good. His legs shook and he braced himself as he plunged inside her, deeper still. His focus narrowed until all he could feel was her, all he could smell was her. She screamed her release and everything around him went dark until suddenly he was over the edge. Red and yellow lights flashed like a hundred fireworks lighting up the night sky and he roared.

When their breathing eased and his heart rate slowed, he lowered himself, with her still in his arms, to sit the floor and pulled her into his lap. She smelled of sex, coconuts and her, and he inhaled deeply, leaning into her neck.

"Why didn't we do this sooner," he asked.

She punched his arm. "Really?"

Smiling against her skin, he let her hair cover his face. God he loved her curls.

Her fingers drew small circles on his back and a deep sense of peace settled over him.

"This is good, right?" he asked.

"This is very good."

"I wish I had better news for you," Jacob said.

Adam's every muscle tensed.

"I extended some feelers. People are hiring." He trailed off and tapped his pencil on his desk.

Adam frowned. It wasn't like his friend to be this uncomfortable. "That's good. I can take it from here if you just give me the contact info."

Jacob shook his head, leaned forward and stared at him. "I can't. Because as soon as they heard I was checking things out for you, they suddenly lost interest. I even tried not mentioning you, but they're all talking about how your firm is bungling big-name cases. I'm sorry, Adam. You need to give it some time to let things settle."

Adam thrust himself out of his chair and stalked around the office, rubbing his hand over the top of his head. He wanted to shout. No, he wanted to kill his father.

"What the hell did he do to me?"

"I don't think it was your dad, Adz."

"Who else could it have been?"

Jacob spun around in his chair. "What about the paralegal? Could she have told someone?"

Adam turned toward the window and looked out, images of his father, the paralegal, and his former office shuttling through his brain. "I don't know why she would. I mean, I know the paralegals in our office talk, but between different law firms? I can't imagine that happening."

"Your dad's an ass. Sorry."

Letting out a laugh that was far from amused, Adam turned back to Jacob. "I need a new career plan."

"Well, if you can figure out who's spreading the news, maybe you can do something from that angle."

"The horse not only left the barn, but it left the state. It doesn't matter if I can find out who's after me. The news is out there. Shit, I am not letting them end my career!"

"I don't think you should ignore who might be trying to hurt your career. I think it's worth looking into."

"Oh, I'll definitely be looking into it, don't worry about that."

Jacob flipped a pencil through his fingers. "How are things with Dina?"

For the first time, Adam smiled. "Good." *Great.*

"Have you talked to her?"

He could play dumb and pretend he didn't know what Jacob was talking about, but he didn't think he could pull that off. "Not yet."

Jacob shook his head. "How serious are you two?"

Adam pulled at his collar.

"That serious? Have you had sex yet?"

"Twice."

Jacob let out a breath, fluttering papers on his desk. "Oh boy. I hope you know what you're doing."

"If I tell her, she'll leave."

"If you don't, she might anyway."

"I can manage it."

Jacob walked with him to the door. "Go through your dad's employees and see who jumps out. And tell Dina."

CHAPTER SEVENTEEN

Dina walked through the door separating the conference room of the county library from the public portion of the building and stopped so quickly the person behind her rammed into her back.

"Sorry, Jack," she said to her colleague, moving out of his way and over to where Tracy was pouring herself a cup of coffee. They were both attending an all-county librarians' meeting and had gotten an early start this morning. Now, they were in the middle of a fifteen-minute break.

"I swear I thought I just saw Adam heading into the reference room." She shook her head. *She must be imagining things.*

"That's weird. Are you going to go look for him?"

"Maybe during the next break." She stretched her back. These meetings were always long, but informative. *That would be a really funny coincidence.*

"Uh oh, trouble in paradise?"

Dina laughed. "Of course not. We don't track each other's every move." She grabbed her cup and a small plate of fruit and returned to the conference table. Her pulse increased. What was he doing at this library?

You'll never know unless you ask. At the next break, she headed to the reference room. Sure enough, Adam sat in front of a computer, a stack of papers next to him.

Smiling wide, she walked over to him. "Hey, I didn't know you were planning to come here today."

Flipping the papers over, he jumped and turned toward her.

Her curiosity increased.

Banking surprise, he smiled back, but his neck was red.

"I didn't expect you to be here, either. I'm doing some research." He clenched his hand on top of the papers.

His law office didn't have a research department? "Tracey and I are here for a meeting. What are you researching? Anything I can help with?"

He spread his hand out. "No, I'll be done in a little bit. Want to do something when I'm finished?"

She admired his hands, even as she wondered what he was doing. "I can't. I have a hair appointment for the reunion."

"Don't do anything to your hair." Adam's voice rose and those around them glared. He lowered his voice, but his tone was no less commanding. "It's perfect just as it is."

"Really? I was thinking of getting it straightened. The curls are all over the place."

"Those curls are you. Don't change them." He looked almost fierce as he stared at her, his fingers flexing and straightening as if he were running them through her strands.

Dina fingered her frizz, not understanding why springy hair was his thing, but feeling warmth in her belly that he cared. "I still have to get it trimmed though."

"Not much."

"Seriously, you're crazy."

His green eyes glowed as if he looked deep into her soul. "Don't let the mean girls change who you are."

His understanding pulled her up short, before a tingling followed the trail of warmth. No matter what happened at the reunion, he'd have her back. If they promised to be silent, would the other people mind if she and Adam had sex right here? With a sigh, she pulled away. "I'll let you get back to your research, whatever it is. Call me tonight?"

"Only if you text me a picture of your hair after your appointment."

"Only if you tell me what you're researching."

He shifted in his chair. "Law stuff. How's your meeting?"

Why was he suddenly so eager to change the subject? "It's fine. What kind of law stuff? Must be pretty outside the box if you have to do it at the county library rather than your office."

He swallowed, shifting his gaze around the room. "It's just...it's nothing. Don't worry about it. Want to come over tomorrow and watch a movie?"

"You're changing the subject, Adam. What's going on?"

He sighed. "Can we talk about this later?"

She nodded. "Come over tomorrow and we'll watch a movie at my place. I've got the perfect one."

The next evening when Adam entered her apartment, she held up a DVD. "I just came across this again and it's amazing."

"*Mr. Smith Goes to Washington*?" Adam frowned as he read the back cover.

"Have you seen it?"

He shook his head.

"It's about a naïve politician battling corruption. It's great."

A strange look crossed his face. "Sure, if this is what you want to watch."

She ran her hand up and down his arm. Beneath the cotton shirt, tension hardened his muscles. "I thought you'd enjoy this, but if not..."

"No, it's fine. Sit with me."

She put the movie in and sat next to Adam. He put his arm around her shoulders and drew her close to him, so she was leaning against his chest. His fingers played in her hair.

"I like what you did with this," he said.

She'd had about two inches chopped off, and the rest of it shaped. She smiled and turned her face into his hand, kissing his palm. "I'm glad." Against her back, she could feel him exhale, as if he'd been holding his breath. Something was bothering him, but she had no idea what. His list of secrets was getting longer and she wasn't sure how much longer she could wait. Maybe if she could relax him with the movie, they could talk.

It didn't work.

Dina wasn't sure if it was the specific movie, although his attention and focus indicated he liked it. Maybe it was the time of day, although a Saturday night didn't usually bother him. Perhaps it was her, yet he hadn't once moved or suggested she sit further way. Whatever the reason, he remained as tense as when he arrived.

Watching the movie hadn't achieved her goal.

She wished she knew some obscure fact about keeping secrets from your girlfriend. Maybe that would help break the ice. Because he'd walled himself off from her and it was starting to make her nervous.

"Good movie," he said, stretching.

"I love Jimmy Stewart. My grandmother used to watch his movies all the time and I remember sitting with her on Saturday afternoons. Did you know that the word 'Philadelphia' was misspelled on his Oscar?"

Adam laughed. "I'll bet you were adorable as a child."

She shook her head. "No, I had these huge glasses, I asked tons of questions and drove everyone crazy. Except her. She would answer anything I asked."

"Is she still alive?"

Dina shook her head. "No, she died a few years ago. What about your grandparents?"

"They died before I was born, although I was named after my mother's father."

"Did your mother ever talk to you about him?"

He leaned back and took her hand. "Not that I can remember. There wasn't a lot of conversation in my house."

That explained a lot. Maybe he just didn't know how to open up.

"That's a shame. Talking keeps the bad things from festering and creating more stress."

"I seriously doubt that." He'd pulled away from her and there was a wariness about his face.

She wanted to draw him close and reassure him that whatever was bothering him would be easier shared, but she didn't want to spook him.

"It's true," she said. "Kind of like the anticipation of something is worse than the actual event. Bringing it out in the open makes the burden lighter."

"Or it convinces you of the merits of what you worried about in the first place."

Somehow, she didn't think he was talking about the grandfather he'd never met. "But isn't it better to just get it over with?"

His mouth whitened around the edge of his lips and he stiffened. "No." He rose and stalked toward the DVR, kneeling before it. He tried to look busy, but Dina could read him. He was fiddling.

"What's the worst that can happen?" she asked.

He kept his back to her, his muscles straining against his shirt.

At any other time, Dina's throat would have gone dry at the sight. However, knowing he was, in effect, straining against her attempts to know him better, made his muscles decidedly less attractive.

Adam rose and turned toward her, but kept his gaze focused somewhere behind her and to her left. He opened and closed his mouth several times before clenching his fist and focusing on her. He thrust his hand through his hair. "I know what you're trying to do. I know I need to talk to you, and I will, but I need time. Please, I need you to trust me. Can you do that?"

Her stomach twisted and she swallowed. He hadn't done anything to abuse her trust, but how much time did he expect her to give? And what was so important that he needed time to prepare? With a nod, she gave in. For now.

CHAPTER EIGHTEEN

Adam called her on Monday, acting as if nothing had happened. Acting, actually, like his Mr. Flashypants self. It was like he'd erected a wall around himself and behind that wall, nothing had happened. He kept his conversations light and avoided the painful topic.

Dina spent the week stuck in a fog. Her reunion was next weekend, and Adam was supposed to go with her, but if he thought she was going to bring it up, he had no idea who she was.

Dina didn't know what to do.

"Did you tell him how mad you are at him?" Tracy asked on Wednesday. They were taking a lunch break at a sandwich shop down the street from the library.

"No, because every time I figure out what I want to say, he changes the subject or teases me and makes me laugh, or has to run."

"That's ridiculous, Deen. He should know how you feel."

"Yeah, but I also have a pretty good idea how I made him feel."

"So what, you're his girlfriend. If he won't be honest with you now, there's no future for you."

Dina stirred her soda with the straw. "I know you're right, but there's a part of me that doesn't want to mess with this. For the first time, I'm dating someone who likes me. Me. What if I screw it up?"

Tracy reached across the table and covered Dina's hand with her own. "If he's truly worth it, he'll understand."

"Okay, after the reunion. Despite what I said in the beginning, I'm really looking forward to having him go with me, and I don't want things to be tense there. It's already going to be nerve-wracking."

Adam shut off his computer and rubbed his face. He had a list of New York City law firms that looked promising. He'd done a search of Ashley's name in relation to the firms and couldn't find any connections. If he couldn't use Jacob's connections, that didn't mean he couldn't find a job. The tricky part was going to be the references, but maybe with some bargaining, his dad would consent to giving him a good one, if only to get his son off his back.

His son. The words were bitter on his tongue. What kind of a man treated his son this way? Adam thought he'd given up caring long ago, but his father's actions created a dull ache in his breastbone, and he couldn't get rid of it no matter how hard he tried.

Screw it. Lots of people didn't get along with their family and they survived. He would too. He had a plan—submit résumés, take Dina to the reunion, get a job offer, tell her he loved her and come clean to her about being fired. In that order. Because he'd look a lot less pitiful if he had a great job to prove his worth to her. She'd see him as a man who'd overcome adversity, not someone who'd been beaten down by it.

He'd convinced her to go out with him through sheer force of will. Once his future was set, he'd convince her she loved him the same way. And her reunion would be the place to show her how indispensable he was. He just had to hold everything together for a few more days.

Dina's nerves were crackling by the day of the reunion. Not only was she stressed about Adam and his secrets, but on top of that, the thought of willingly putting herself in the same room as her high school classmates had been looking less and less appealing as the reunion approached. And now it was here. She was too nauseated to eat a real breakfast, but her stomach needed something in it to prevent the flip-flops it was doing. Settling for dry toast and tea, she curled up on her window seat and looked outside.

This early on a spring morning, the only people out were the joggers and the dog walkers. Her toe tapping jostled her tea and she squeezed her eyes shut. Exercise was just what she needed to work through her anxiety.

After changing into leggings and a long-sleeved Smashing Pumpkins T-shirt, she plugged her ear buds into her phone, laced her bright orange running shoes, and left her apartment. Was she really ready to face the girls she'd gone to high school with? Rather than heading toward the main street, she headed deeper into the residential part of town, admiring the converted Victorian mansions and taking in the newly sprouting elm trees that lined the sidewalks. Shouldn't she be over her dislike of them by now? A few had leaves just starting to emerge and the light bright green added hints of color to an otherwise grey morning. She nodded at passing joggers and smiled at passing dogs, and their owners, and by the time she returned to her apartment, she had calmed down some.

After showering, she puttered around her apartment. Feeling a bit like a squirrel who hops from tree to tree and acorn to acorn, she tried to focus on her cleaning, but kept being pulled away and distracted by as little as a background humming noise from the air conditioner or a passing conversation in the hallway. Deciding she needed something to take her mind off things, she called Tracy and asked her to come over, making tea in the meantime.

"What's wrong?" her friend asked when she arrived, baby in tow.

"This is stupid. I shouldn't bother going tonight." She twirled her hair around her finger, smiling at Mackenzie.

"Wow, this is really bad." Tracy handed her a cup of tea.

"Why am I even bothering to go?" The heat from the mug warmed her hands and she wrapped them around it, inhaling the chamomile-scented steam.

"To your reunion? Three reasons: Hot dress, hot guy and payback."

Dina choked on her tea. "Seriously? I'm afraid no one will remember me or care whether or not I'm there, and it's probably a sign of some mental illness that I'm still even thinking about my high school horrors, and you say 'payback'?"

Handing her a napkin, Tracy perched on Dina's sofa. "Deep breath. Look, the ten-year reunion is all about payback. It's everyone's chance to prove themselves outside of the cloistered high school world they grew up in. You're going to walk in looking sexy and fabulous in your dress, with a gorgeous man on your arm, and everyone is going to come up to you."

"No one is going to come near me because they're not going to remember me and I'm going to look stupid in front of Adam."

"No, they're all going to come up to you, especially because they don't remember you, in order to figure out who you are and how you got so lucky. Trust me," Tracy said. "And besides, Adam likes you—I've seen how he looks at you. He won't care if the two of you are the only people in the room. In fact," she said, rising and heading toward the door, "I think he'd probably prefer you two being completely alone so he can undress you."

CHAPTER NINETEEN

Adam's mouth dropped when Dina opened the door. At least, he was pretty sure the goddess in white was Dina. She had the same violet eyes that intrigued him, but this time they were accentuated by subtle green shimmery eye shadow. She had the same curves that made him want to bury himself inside her, but this time they were emphasized by white fabric that somehow managed to hug her curves and flow at the same time. His gaze jumped to her head. Her hair. Her crazy, curly, outrageous hair was perfect. She'd pinned back her curls, but allowed enough of them to escape that they framed her face and once again, made him want to grab them. Instead, he clenched his fist at his side. He'd dated enough beautiful women in his lifetime to know better than to touch their hair when they'd obviously spent time getting ready for an evening out.

But Dina? Dina was stunning.

She was also blushing, and he realized with a start he'd been standing on her doorstep without uttering a word for far too long.

"Hi," he said. Brilliant.

"Hi."

So maybe she was as affected as he was. But by him? She was the last person to fall for any of his supposed charms, which was one of the things he treasured about her.

"You look...beautiful."

She dipped her head. "Thank you."

He held his hand out for her and when she placed her hand in his, the world shifted, like a house settling into a storm, and peace encompassed him. "Come on, we're going to have fun."

She raised an eyebrow at him and they walked to his car in silence. Once inside, he pulled onto the street and began following his GPS.

"Did you know Princeton was founded before the American Revolution?" she said. "The Lenni Lenape Indians—"

"Dina?"

She stopped, lips parted, and turned toward him.

"Relax," he said, reaching across the console and taking her cold hand in his. "It's going to be fun. I promise."

Out of the corner of his eye, he watched her chest rise and fall, like she was taking her last breath of fresh air.

As he stopped at a traffic light, he turned to look at her. "We are going to have a great time. And you are going to be the star."

Her body relaxed, even as her expression told him she thought he was crazy. "We'll see."

For the rest of the ride, she blurted out ridiculous facts about clothing—the Greeks and Romans thought trousers were worn by barbarians, traffic lights—the first one was installed in 1914, and hair gel—the first type was Brylcreem, invented by the British in 1929. No matter how many times Adam tried to change the subject or engage her in what he considered "normal conversation," she always retreated to obscure facts. So he let her ramble and admired the sound of her voice.

An hour later, when they pulled up to the hotel in Princeton, Dina remained seated in his car after he'd turned off the engine. She stared out the window at the façade of the building. Or maybe she was watching the people enter. Could be she was plotting the perfect angle to make her escape. He couldn't tell because her body had stilled, and her breathing had softened.

And she was silent.

"Dina?"

She didn't answer. He craned his neck to look at her—at her eyes, glassy and focused inward; at her hands, clasped tight in her lap; at her mouth, compressed into a firm line.

"Dina."

Like someone awakening, she opened her hands, released her lips and turned to him. "Are you ready to go?" she asked.

"It's going to be fine."

She gave him a bright smile, one that didn't reach her eyes. It reminded him of the smiles he often gave. "We should go inside now."

He reached for her hand. It was icy cold and he rubbed it between his. She stared down at their entwined limbs like they were aliens. And although he honed in on the softness of her skin, the delicacy of her bones, he suspected right at this very moment, she thought nothing of their touch. With a sigh, he pulled away and opened the door.

Inside the hotel, they retrieved nametags from the registration table in the black and tan lobby. Manned by three women, none of them showed recognition when Dina picked up her tag, nor did they interrupt their conversation with the guests who stood behind him waiting for their turn. But that wasn't too unusual. Not everyone remembered their entire class, even if they were on the reunion committee.

Following the sound of music playing, they entered a ballroom decorated with enormous crystal chandeliers. Gold tablecloths covered round tables with centerpieces of green balloons. A Welcome Class of 2007 banner, also in green and gold, hung over the DJ station on the far end of the room. In the center was a dance floor, where couples mingled and danced. To the left was a mirrored wall, lending enormity to the room. Wait staff zigzagged through the crowd, offering hot hors d'oeuvres. A banquet table on the right was filled with cold appetizers, and a crowd surged by the bar.

"Would you like a drink?" Adam asked.

When she nodded, he cupped her elbow and led her toward the crowd. He watched her scan nametags, with only a discreet frown indicating her reaction to anyone. But still she remained silent.

"Pick a person," he said, as he handed her a gin and tonic with lime.

"What do you mean?"

"Pick someone for us to go up and talk to."

"I don't want to do that."

"Okay, then I will." He started to walk toward a cluster of people and she grabbed his arm. Only the fact that he'd anticipated her reaction, and kept his drink in his other hand, prevented him from sloshing his beer everywhere.

"Wait! Please don't," she said.

He turned to her and stepped close enough to see worry etched in her violet eyes. "Come on. The first time is the hardest. After that, it gets easier."

"But no one is going to have any idea who I am."

"So what? We'll introduce ourselves, talk about our jobs, say how nice it was to see them and move on. It's easy."

"It's embarrassing."

"Okay, then, let's play a game. Pick someone."

When she looked at him askance, he held his hand out to the room. "Come on, pick someone."

With a quick scan, she pointed to a couple nearby.

"Do you know them?" he asked.

"I can't see their nametags, but I don't think so."

"Perfect. What do you think they're doing now? I mean career wise."

She studied the red-haired woman and the brown-haired man. They were well-dressed, if not ordinary, with him in a suit and her in a black sheath dress. They each held a soda in their hands and she was scanning the crowd.

"Doctor and lawyer?"

He shook his head. "Accountant and teacher. Now we find out who's right." Before she could protest, he pulled her by the hand toward them.

"Adam Mandel. This is Dina Jacobs. Nice to see you here."

"Cory and Steve Tindal," Steve said. "Did you attend school here?"

"I didn't, but Dina did."

Steve undressed her with his eyes, while Cory pasted a blank look on her face. Adam wanted to punch them both.

Dina squeezed his hand. "So, what are you doing now?"

"Well, I graduated from Penn State and I'm a lawyer," Cory said. "You?"

"Harvard undergrad and University of Illinois with a Masters in Library Science."

Adam's chest swelled with pride as she readily admitted her intelligence. From the looks on Cory's and Steve's faces, they were impressed. He felt Dina soften next to him.

"That must be why I don't remember you," Cory said. "You must have been in all the honors and AP classes."

As they moved on from the couple, Adam snagged two eggrolls from a passing waiter.

"That wasn't actually too bad," Dina said before biting into the crispy hors d'oeuvre. "Especially since I was right."

"I'll get it right eventually," he said. "Who should we target next?"

They met a second couple and a foursome before Dina stopped in her tracks. "Uh, let's go over there," she said, pointing away from the people they were heading toward.

"What's wrong with that group?"

"I think I recognize them."

"And that's a bad thing?"

"I'm not sure."

"They just saw you, so we're about to find out." He put his arm around her shoulders and faced the woman walking toward them. If Barbie was a living person, she would be it. Blond hair teased and sprayed to within an inch of its life, big boobs, tiny waist, endless legs. But for once, he wasn't attracted to her. At all.

"Oh my gosh, I love your dress," Barbie said with a squeal. "Where did you get it?"

Dina gave her the name of the store and Barbie scrunched up her nose. "I've never heard of it." She leaned toward Dina's nametag and he'd swear she mouthed the words as she read them.

"Dyna Jacobs? I'm not sure..."

"It's Dina with a long E. We were in a marketing class together sophomore year."

He felt the tension enter her shoulders and he massaged them.

"Oh, Dina! Meg, Stacie, come here! It's Dina Jacobs."

Her voice could grate cheese and even Adam winced as she yelled. All around them, heads turned and Meg and Stacie minced over.

"Dina? I don't remember any Dina," Meg said, her brassy red hair-from-a-bottle overflowing her shoulders and emphasizing the swell of her breasts in a low-cut black tube of a dress.

"Yes you do, girls," Barbie said. "She was in marketing with us."

"I was drunk in marketing," Stacie said. Adam tried not to stare at the rolls of fat squeezed into a red dress at least three sizes too small. When she rubbed up against him, he stepped to the side, pushing Dina, who stumbled.

"Sorry," he muttered.

"I'd remember you, though," Stacie said, eyeing him and down. "Want to get me a drink?"

He stepped back at her blatant flirting. Dina was right here. "Love to, but Dina and I have something to do first. Nice meeting you all."

With a firm grip on her upper arm, he half dragged, have pushed Dina across the room. They stopped at the banquet table, where Adam grabbed a cocktail napkin and wiped his brow.

"Wow."

Dina shook her head. "I told you."

"Please tell me your entire school wasn't like that."

"My entire school wasn't like that."

"I'm serious."

"I am too. There was a group of them—those three were part of it—who drank and partied and were in the service of Venus with anything that breathed..."

His lips twitched.

"What?"

His nostrils flared.

"Adam, what?"

His eyes watered.

"Are you okay?"

He burst out laughing. Through streaming eyes, he watched concern, confusion and annoyance flash across her features. By the time he'd controlled his laughter, she stood in front of him, arms crossed beneath her breasts, toe tapping. She reminded him of the stereotypical "sexy librarian" and he sobered.

"What was so funny?"

"The service of Venus?"

"Yes. It's an old term to describe you-know-what, and we're in public, so it's not like I'm going to say it out loud."

She was right. They were in public. Out of the corner of his eye, he could see people moving toward them, stopping some distance away. But he didn't care. For once in his entire adult life, he didn't care what others thought. For the first time since his mother left, he wanted to commit himself to a woman he cared about, to let her into all parts of his life. He reached for her and his fingers brushed the undersides of her breasts as he grasped her forearms. His breath quickened and he drew her forward. When their toes touched, he looked at her and wondered how he could ever have thought someone like Barbie or any of those other blatantly sexual, vocabulary-challenged women could ever be appealing. Everything he wanted in a woman was right in front of him. Class, humor, beauty and brains. She made him feel good about himself. She made him less afraid. She gave him hope. It was time to tell her.

"I love you." Saying the words didn't scare him anymore. They filled him with peace. "I love you, Dina."

She had to have misheard him. There were people gathering around them, their voices mingling with the sounds of the music, making it hard to hear. "What?"

"I love you."

She hadn't misheard him.

"Did you know that when two lovers stare into each other's eyes, their heart rates synchronize?"

Adam's body vibrated against hers as he laughed silently. "Relax, sweetheart, I love you."

He had to be crazy, because who declared their love for someone at a high school reunion? She watched surreptitious pointing from Stacie and some of her friends. Had they heard what he said? Did they think he was crazy? Except...he didn't look crazy. He looked like Adam.

At the same time, he didn't. He looked sure and settled and solid. Not like Mr. Flashypants. More like Mr. Dependable.

That must be what all the other people were noticing. Her heart raced in her chest and she swallowed. Her mouth was dry and her arms, where he held on, were warm and cold.

"You do? Why?"

He laughed at her again, but only for a short time. More like a moment, really.

"Most women wouldn't ask that question the first time their boyfriend declared his love for her."

"Most boyfriends don't declare their love at a reunion." *Surrounded by women so much more beautiful than I am.* She took a quick glance around, surprised by the number of women staring at her. Was it so hard for them to believe a guy like him could like—or love—a woman like her?

He let go of her arm and caressed her jaw with his finger, making her forget about everyone else, before tipping her face to meet his gaze. "Most boyfriends are not in love with a woman who calls sex 'the service of Venus'."

She melted a little. "You keep saying that word."

"I've said a lot of words. Can you be more specific?"

"The 'love' one."

"Is there a problem with it? Is there some archaic vocabulary you'd prefer me to use instead?"

"No, I just don't understand why."

He hugged her to him and she inhaled his clove scent. The music, flashing lights, laughter, conversations and pointing melted into the background.

"That is a longer conversation for a different time," he said. "But know this. I do love you, and I don't say that often."

Her heart fluttered in her chest. He loved her. She loved him too. Should she tell him now? Would he think she was just saying it because he said it to her? It was too important for it to be handled trivially.

He leaned down and brushed his lips against hers, stopping all thought of conversation. In fact, all thoughts flew from her head as he deepened the kiss, sending trails of heat down to her belly and making her breasts tingle where they pressed against him. Before she could do more than kiss him back, he pulled away, his eyes dark, his nostrils flared.

"That's another thing we'll continue at another time," he said.

Taking her hand in his, he turned toward the buffet table and grabbed two plates.

She blinked, trying to focus on something other than his lips. Or his butt, which faced her as he spooned a variety of foods and sauces onto her plate. Sauce. Most of the food had sauce and she was wearing white. Lovely. With a sigh, she took the plate and held it gingerly, scanning the room for an empty table.

"Let's sit there," she said, pointing to a table next to the dance floor. He joined her and they ate with fingers entwined, as if he were loathe to let her go. She didn't taste the food, had no idea what she was eating, but focused on Adam and how to tell him she loved him.

Just when she'd decided to come out with it, two more couples joined their table. She sighed, not in the mood to be friendly to people who had no recollection of her. But these four people stared at her and at Adam, their gazes tracking the two of them like spectators at a tennis match. Did she have something on her face? Was seeing two people in love that strange?

Adam squeezed her hand and leaned forward. "Hi, I'm Adam Mandel and this is my girlfriend, Dina Jacobs. Great reunion, isn't it?"

The women shrugged and the guys raised their glasses to their mouths and looked at each other before answering.

"I guess it depends on what you're looking to get out of it," the large guy with a square head said.

The skinny guy put his arm around his date and Dina frowned.

"So, did you all graduate from here?" Adam asked. Another reason she loved him—he was trying so hard for her.

The women ignored him and turned to Dina. "We both did," the date of the blockhead answered. "I'm Cheryl and this is Ann. We're friends with Stacie. You were in marketing with us, right?"

Dina nodded, realizing Cheryl had spoken more to her with that sentence than she ever had in four years of high school. It was weird. It was even weirder that she wasn't looking at Adam, the person who had asked the question in the first place.

"What are you doing now?" Dina asked. If Cheryl was being friendly, she might as well respond. Next to her, Adam put his arm around her shoulders and Ann stiffened.

"I'm an office assistant at an investment firm," Cheryl said. "You?"

"I'm a librarian."

Cheryl nodded. "You always were really smart." There was no scorn on her face. Instead, Dina detected admiration. She looked at Ann, who looked…sympathetic?

"And you?" she asked Ann. "What are you doing?"

"I'm a teacher, can you believe it?"

Dina smiled. "We all change."

In fact, Dina was having a hard time detecting the vapid, nasty girls in these two women and her judgment softened. Because she'd changed, too.

The music changed to a slow song and Adam leaned toward her. "Want to dance?"

Yes. She rose and the other women leaned down to their dates. She assumed they were going to join them on the dance floor, but instead, Cheryl and Ann called her name.

"Dina, we're going to the ladies' room. Want to join us?"

There was an intensity in their expression that Dina didn't understand. She turned to Adam, who shrugged. "Go ahead."

"But I'd rather dance with you."

He touched her cheek. "We can dance to the next song. It's good for you to socialize." He sat back down and took a drink, and Dina nodded and followed the women to the ladies' room, if only for curiosity's sake.

The door had barely swung shut when they pulled her into the room and off to the side.

"The guy you're with," Cheryl said. "How long have you two been dating?"

Dina pulled back. In the mirror, her shock at the question reflected back at her, but it wasn't nearly as strong as her feelings. This woman barely knew her. How could she ask her such a question?

"About six weeks or so." She turned to go, but a manicured hand on her arm stopped her.

"Does he work at some law firm named Mandel and something?"

This time it was Ann who spoke. Neither one of them had given two thoughts for her in high school. Why the heck was she bothering now?

"I don't think it's any of your business."

Women were opening the stalls and staring at them as they approached the sink and Dina's face heated. Cheryl and Ann drew her over to the side.

"Listen," Cheryl said. "I know you don't know us. But we should probably warn you about Adam. You're reaching his expiration date."

"What are you talking about? How do you know him?"

"He works at the same firm as Ashley Peters," Ann said. " She was part of our group in high school."

"So what?"

"According to her, he goes through women like water," Cheryl said.

"How do you know that?"

"Because we're still friends."

"Okay, so what?" Dina asked. The whir of the air dryer was beginning to give her a headache. Or maybe it was the mixture of perfume, hairspray and scented lotion. She rubbed her temples, wishing she could rub the women away instead. She had a man to tell she loved him.

"He's never dated anyone longer than six weeks."

The shriek filled his eardrums, causing the DJ to stop the music mid-spin. Conversations halted mid-word and as one, people's heads turned toward the person guilty of releasing the glass-shattering racket.

"It's you!"

Adam watched the crowd part and a model-thin woman in a slinky black dress and sky-high heels stalked toward him. His stomach dropped.

"What are you doing here? Don't you torment me enough at work?" she asked, stopping close enough to him he could see her tremble. Her skin was pale, her ruby lips outlined in a thin white line of anger, and her brown eyes crackled in fury. And that anger was directed at him.

Adam's foot hit the floor and he gripped his drink so hard he was certain the glass would shatter. Forcing himself to act calm, he placed his glass down and wiped his lips with a napkin before folding it and sticking it in his breast pocket.

"Ashley," he said. "What are you doing here?"

"I belong here," she snapped, getting up close in his face. "The question is, why are you here?"

"I'm here with my date." The last thing he wanted to do was embarrass Dina. For once in his life, his main concern was someone else. He held his hands up and she glared at him, before looking around at the gathered crowd.

"Pfft. I bet you tried to impress her with your position at your daddy's law firm. Maybe I should tell her about the real you. About how your father—"

He reached for her arm. "Ash—"

"Don't touch me!" Her drink sloshed over the side of the glass and splattered on the floor.

A buzz started in the crowd, or was it in his head? He blinked. A sea of faces stared at him, while two guys walked over and flanked Ashley. A third approached him.

"Listen, buddy, you need to leave her alone," guy number three said. He had the beer belly of a former frat boy/football player and a buzz cut, with a thick neck and beady eyes. He'd lost his suit jacket—or maybe he'd never had one to begin with—but his tie was worth less than Adam's silk socks.

"I'm not doing anything to her," he said. "Never have."

"Never does anything *for* me, either. He leaves work to go party, giving me all his busywork and then blames me when he forgets to do something," she said.

The crowd should have gotten bored by now, returned to their food, drink and dancing. But it looked like he was the latest entertainment of the evening. Where the hell was Dina?

Shit. Dina. He needed her in order to leave, but he didn't want her anywhere near this. She'd never understand and she'd be mortified. He was supposed to have helped her deal with tonight and instead, he was causing a scene. Beads of sweat popped on his brow and he reached for the napkin he'd slipped into his breast pocket.

The crowd parted again and two women approached, their arms around Dina. As they got closer, he recognized Cheryl and Ann, the two women who'd asked her to join them in the bathroom in the first place. It was a woman thing he'd never understand, but at the time, he'd been glad they'd included her. But now, Dina looked green. Was she sick or had the two women said something to bother her? He pushed away from Ashley and rushed over to Dina.

"You okay?" he asked, his hand cupping her cheek.

"Stay away from her," Cheryl said. "You're just making things worse."

Ashley joined them, as well as the various men associated with them. With Dina surrounded by so many people, it was hard to figure out what was going on. All he knew was that she was upset and he wanted to back up time by about fifteen minutes. He didn't want her knowing about Ashley.

Unless she already did.

He didn't want to think about that, but once the idea entered his brain, it took up residence. He didn't want Ashley anywhere near Dina, but the four women looked as if they were best friends. He didn't want to face Dina if she knew about Ashley's accusations, but she was staring at him.

If only he could read her expression. Or her mind. That would be helpful. But he couldn't. And unfortunately, everyone around them had gone silent, so whatever he said to Dina would be heard by the crowd. And more importantly, they would hear Dina's reply.

"Dina, would you like to go?" His voice sounded raspy to his ears, as if he'd dragged it over an artificial turf. All he wanted was to get the two of them out of here, or at least away from these people.

She shook her head no and his world stopped. He reached back for the bar he'd been leaning against, forgetting momentarily that he'd stepped forward when the guys had come up to him. He stumbled, and righted himself. She didn't want to go with him. She was choosing them over him. Like his mother. Roaring sounded in his ears and his breath came in gasps. He tossed a quick look over his shoulder, trying to find a clear path to the door, but people had surrounded them and there was no way out.

Cool pressure on his hand startled him and he looked down.

Dina.

"I don't want to leave. I want to dance with you."

CHAPTER TWENTY

The DJ started the music as soon as she walked out onto the dance floor with Adam. "I Gotta Feeling" drowned out the voices, but it couldn't eliminate the images flashing through her mind—Cheryl's and Ann's concern, Ashley's anger, Adam's desolation.

It was his desolation, the hollow look in his eyes that replayed more often than the other images. And made her push down her own fears and ask him to dance, rather than find out what the heck everyone was talking about.

Possibly because they were the only people on the dance floor, the DJ switched to a slow song. Now they had a reason to look as if they were holding each other up. She'd never felt Adam so stiff, not even when they were at dinner with his father. It was like dancing with a stone statue. His hands were on her waist and although it wasn't painful, he gripped her like he thought she would run away. She wouldn't. Against his chest, she could feel his heart pounding. And looking up at his face, his blank expression was set. She ran her fingers along his nape, trying to ease some of the tension. When he glanced down at her, she spoke.

"Relax. We're dancing. Don't let them get to you."

"Dina, I—"

"It's okay. I don't know what happened back there, but they ruined my entire high school experience. I'm not letting them ruin tonight."

He pulled her close—or maybe his body just relaxed enough to make her feel like he did—and rested his cheek against her hair. His breath puffed against her neck, sending shivers down her spine. She felt him bob against her as he swallowed—once, twice, three times—and she focused on keeping them moving to the music and running her fingers through his soft hair.

As she looked around the room, other couples joined them on the dance floor, the lure of the music too much to resist. Yet they kept a safe distance away from them, as if afraid of catching something.

The DJ changed the song to "Hips Don't Lie," and although everyone around them picked up the speed, Adam found a slow tempo hidden in the song and kept them dancing to it. All around them, bodies undulated to Shakira's song, yet she and Adam swayed to their private version of the music.

But when the song ended, Adam took a deep breath—she felt it against her body—and pulled her off the dance floor. They grabbed their things from the table and headed toward the exit. Once again, her tormentors/rescuers/troublemakers confronted them.

"Dina, are you sure you want to leave with him?" Ann asked. Why was this woman, who hadn't spared two thoughts for her in high school, looking out for her now?

"I'm fine, Ann."

"That's what I thought," Ashley said, her expression sharp, lips pulled back in a sneer.

Adam ignored them, walking toward the exit with single-minded purpose, and Dina increased her pace to keep up. At the door, she turned to take a last glimpse of the banquet room. The decorations were festive, but the people inside were no more known to her now than they were when she was a student ten years ago.

She'd come, she'd seen and now she was leaving.

Adam handed her his keys when they reached the parking lot. "I think I had more to drink than I should have."

She frowned as she removed her heels. He hadn't appeared drunk, but maybe he drank more than she thought while she was stuck in the restroom with the harpies. Why else would he let her drive his car? Taking a quick glance at his form in the passenger seat—eyes closed, head back, legs stretched out, she focused on the workings of the car and the road as she navigated them home.

The ride was silent. She wanted to discuss what happened back there, but if Adam needed to sleep off the alcohol, there was no point in trying to have a reasonable discussion. Her questions, which increased in number with every mile marker they passed, would have to wait.

He opened his eyes when she pulled up to her apartment and he climbed out of the car.

She reached for him, but he took a step back.

"Why don't you come inside so we can talk?" she said.

He shook his head. "No, I need to get home."

"I thought you had too much to drink."

He stuffed his hands in his pockets. "I'm fine now, just tired. It's not far to my place from here. Don't worry."

She gave him his keys and he took them, stepping forward to kiss her forehead. "We'll talk later," he said.

"Soon."

But he pulled away without acknowledging what she'd said. And the concerns she'd batted away at the reunion came roaring back.

Adam paced the confines of his apartment. The space, which had once seemed so large, now restricted him, making him claustrophobic. Floor-to-ceiling windows, white walls, clean lines of expensive leather and marble furniture the saleswoman had picked were all supposed to convey light, air and minimalism. Yet with one evening at a reunion, one scene at the table, one conversation among many, it all evaporated. And now he couldn't breathe.

Dina was going to leave him. And if he were half the man he thought he was, he'd show her the way out.

He shivered and jacked up the heat on the thermostat. But regardless of the temperature in his apartment, he couldn't shake off the cold seeping into his bones.

Ashley had gotten to her first. Well, maybe not Ashley, but her minions, which was worse. Even if he were innocent, as he maintained, the accusation was enough to damn him. And the fact that he was known for obsessing over his reputation was another strike against him. Add in his father's disbelief, and he was toast.

His reputation was in tatters. Why would anyone, much less Dina, want to be with him? She was going to leave him, just like his mother had. His stomach tightened and bile rose in his throat. He'd vowed never to be in the position of letting someone leave him again. And here he was, back in the same damn situation. At least this time he knew the reason.

But even if he wasn't to blame for losing that particular case, everyone knew his own father had fired him. They had even bled into Dina's life—what were the odds she'd gone to high school with his adversary? The silence in his apartment was deafening. Even his neighbors were silent.

He pulled up short. What were the odds?

He shook his head. If it were anyone else, he'd think they were setting it up. But this was Dina. She was wicked smart, passionate, funny. She was not manipulative. And she would never have been able to pull this off. He'd seen her face, heard her voice—she'd been as surprised as he was. She'd been an unwitting pawn in all of this, not the chess master.

However, it gave him the perfect out, enabling him to leave so he didn't have to watch her leave him. Because no matter what the truth was, no one would stay with him after this. And if he played his cards right, he could ensure that he would be the one to do the leaving.

Dina frowned at her phone. She'd texted Adam twice—once in the morning and once this afternoon, and he hadn't responded to either text. After last night, she was concerned about him. Maybe he was sleeping it off? But it was four o'clock. Even a drunk would be up by now.

And Adam hadn't seemed drunk.

When it rang, she tossed it up in the air, before answering it. "H...Hello?"

"Dina, it's me. What's wrong?"

Tracy's voice usually made her happy, and she tried to swallow her disappointment when it wasn't whom she was hoping to talk to.

"Sorry, Trace, I was waiting for a phone call."

"So was I. You didn't call to let me know how the reunion was."

Dina gripped the phone. "I'm sorry. It was...eventful." She scrunched into the couch, drew a green afghan her mom had knit over her knees and told Tracy about last night. "I'm not sure what surprised me more—the way the popular girls acted like we'd been best friends for years, or the way Adam just shut down. He didn't even give me a chance to defend him. Adam is many things, Tracy, believe me, I know. But he's never indicated he wasn't interested in pursuing a relationship with me. He's never suggested he'd up and leave if we got serious. That's not his style. But he won't let me talk to him or ask him what's going on."

"Wow. My tenth wasn't nearly so eventful, unless you count the drunken posturing going on by the homecoming king and queen. As for Adam, are you sure he's as into you as you think?"

Blood rushed to her head at Tracy's lack of loyalty. "Absolutely, Tracy. He's big on image, but behind that, he's caring and loyal and decent. There's no way he'd go to all the trouble of taking me to my reunion just to break up with me!"

"Hey, easy. I'm sorry. I didn't mean to upset you. I just don't like seeing you hurt."

Dina took a deep breath. "Okay, sorry, didn't mean to jump on you. Yes, I'm positive. No matter what image he projects to others, he's serious about me. And I'd feel it or sense that vibe, even if I didn't see it directly."

"You're right. He doesn't give off that vibe at all. It's some coincidence though that you went to high school with his paralegal."

"I know. It really is a small world. Now if only he'd call me so we could talk this through. I have no idea what's going through his head."

"Din, don't wait around. If he's not answering you, call him."

She glanced at the clock. "You're right. I will as soon as I get off the phone with you."

When Dina dialed Adam, she expected her call to go to voicemail, but he picked up after three rings.

"Dinaaaa!"

Oh brother. Her hands trembled as she held the phone to her ear. "Adam. Are you okay?"

"Suuuuure."

She cringed at the way he was speaking. "You don't sound it." His voice was off. And he was giving her the attitude she hated.

"Like you'd expect anything else?"

Her skin tingled and her stomach felt heavy. "Adam, what are you talking about?"

"Come on, Dina, you're too smart to act this stupid."

Her throat tightened and the room tilted. Reaching for something to grab onto, her hand found the arm of the sofa and she sank into it. "You're not making any sense. Do you want me to come over?"

"No, I don't want you to come over."

Although they hadn't been on the phone long, it was as if time dragged, with each question and response elongating and distorting. She swallowed and gripped the phone tighter.

"Then why are you calling me?"

Adam's humorless laugh echoed in her ear. "You're the one that's been texting me all day."

So he'd gotten her texts and ignored them. "Because I wanted to talk to you about last night."

"I have no need to talk to you about last night, or anything else for that matter."

Sweat dotted her forehead. "Adam, I really don't understand what's going on."

"Oh, for once the idiot gets to play the smart guy and enlighten the genius!"

His words stung. "You're not an idiot, Adam."

"I must be, if I fell for your trick."

Her mind raced as she tried to figure out what he was talking about. "What trick?"

"You set me up."

"What?"

"Last night. You had me thinking this whole time you were dreading your reunion, that you'd never fit in with any of your classmates, when this whole time you were in league with Ashley."

"What? No! That's not true!"

"Come on, Dina. You went to school with her. You think it's just a coincidence? How stupid do you think I am?"

Her mouth dropped and her heart raced. "Adam, I swear. Everything I told you was true. Those girls never knew me in high school. I didn't even know Ashley worked with you."

His voice lost all the "drunk Adam" tone and hardened. "Forget it, Dina. Don't pretend anymore that you don't know my father fired me. You even pretended to try to help me improve my reputation, when all along you knew, and you helped Ashley make it public. Well, congratulation. We're done."

Tears welled and overflowed down her cheeks as she dropped the phone and sank to the ground.

His own father fired him and he thought it was her fault.

CHAPTER TWENTY-ONE

For the third time after hanging up with Dina that afternoon, Adam vomited. He'd convinced Dina it was her fault. He'd broken up with the one girl he loved. And he was a bastard. Because none of it was true.

But at least he'd been the one to leave first.

His stomach gurgled and flopped and once again, he hunched over the toilet. The cold porcelain did little to ease his torment. This was worse than being drunk. At least he knew he'd feel better once the alcohol was purged from his system. But this? There was no way to purge his vile behavior from his system.

When his phone buzzed, he groped blindly for it, skittering his fingers across the tiled floor until they bumped against the vibrating phone.

"Hello," he rasped.

"Adam, it's Jacob. You sound awful."

Wiping his mouth, he sat back against the wall. "Yeah, I feel like crap."

"Sorry. I was going to see if you wanted to meet in the city for some pool. Aviva's out with her mom tonight, but doesn't sound like you'll make it."

Adam roused himself and ran his hand over his face. "Yeah, I don't think that's a good idea. Next time."

A weight sat on his shoulders as he put down his phone. He wasn't sick. There was no physical reason why he couldn't spend the evening with Jacob. In fact, it would probably be good to keep his mind off of things. Except Jacob would ask what was going on and he'd have to explain why he broke up with Dina.

He didn't have a good public reason, because Jacob would see through the argument he used—that Dina had set him up. And then he'd have to tell Jacob the real reason—he was afraid Dina would leave him if she knew the truth, so he made sure to leave first. Knowing Jacob, and his sense of right and wrong, he'd back Dina, which meant he'd lose a girlfriend and a best friend. He couldn't handle that. So he'd have to keep his distance from Jacob until some time passed and he got a new girlfriend.

That thought almost made him start heaving again, but he forced his stomach to calm. Keeping up appearances and never letting anyone leave before he did was getting old.

"Oh, sweetheart!" Tracy pulled Dina close, squishing the baby between them until she started to whimper. Caressing the child's face, Dina pulled back, wiped her eyes and sat at Tracy's kitchen table.

The same one she'd sat at with Adam when they'd babysat. She blinked, trying as much to banish the image as the tears.

"What are you going to do?" Tracy asked.

Dina glared at her friend and gripped the edge of the table. "Not a freaking thing. I'm done. He hasn't explained anything to me and he thinks I set him up. I wouldn't know how to fix things even if I wanted to."

"You don't want to?"

"The guy who supposedly cares about me thinks the worst of me as soon as something goes wrong. Why would I want to be with someone who can't give me the benefit of the doubt?" She fiddled with the baby's rattle and squeezed her chubby fingers.

"No, you're right. Only...maybe there's some reason he jumped to that conclusion. Maybe there's something you're missing."

"Trace, he never even told me his father fired him. I don't want to spend any more time on this. I just want to forget he ever existed."

Of course, that was going to be as possible as switching night with day. Everything reminded her of Adam.

Tracy pushed a cup of tea toward her and she held the hot mug between her hands, trying to warm them up. She'd been freezing for two days now, ever since Adam had broken up with her. Nothing helped.

"I can't believe he said those things to you," Tracy said.

"Me neither. I should have stuck with my gut instinct with him. I knew he was a phony. I called him Mr. Flashypants," she said with a sob. Clearing her voice, she continued. "He never was my type."

But as she left Tracy's house and returned to her own apartment, her inner voice whispered to her.

Yes, he was.

A week later, Adam adjusted his tie, combed his hair and shot his cuffs. Stepping out of the restroom in the black and grey marble lobby of the third largest law firm in Manhattan, he strode to the elevator and punched the button for the fifth floor. When the doors opened, he stepped into a rose and gold carpeted reception area and approached the desk. An older woman with perfectly coiffed white hair looked at him over reading glasses perched on an aquiline nose.

"May I help you?"

"I'm Adam Mandel. I have an interview with Matthew Stevens."

"I'll page him."

She pointed to the buff leather sofa, but Adam paced instead. This was his third interview this week. He should be thrilled the headhunter had found law firms looking to hire, but after the previous two interviews, he wasn't holding out much hope.

The door opened.

"Adam? I'm Matthew. Come on in."

Adam followed the older gentleman down a labyrinth of hallways until he reached the corner office. Unlike his father's, which was dark and stately, this one was airy with floor-to-ceiling windows and filled with clean lines from a glass table that served as a desk, sleek modern furniture and geometric rugs. He sat in the black leather mid-century modern chair Matthew pointed to and rested his right ankle on his left knee. The pseudo-relaxed pose was supposed to hide his anxiety.

"So, Adam, I took a look at your résumé and you're in a good position to be looking for a new job. But I have to say, I'm a little concerned about something."

Adam's stomach knotted. He had his answers prepared, but he'd hoped to get further into the interview process before using them. "What are you concerned about?"

"The reason you're leaving your father's firm. Thomas, your headhunter, has given me great candidates consistently, which is why I called you in for an interview, but I've heard the whispers about you riding on your family's reputation and missing deadlines, resulting in your losing cases. I'm not sure I can afford to hire someone like that."

Adam moved so both feet were on the floor, leaned forward in his chair and met Matthew's gaze square on. "I didn't do it." He held up his hands. "Rather, the very first time, months ago, I botched something I was working on. It was my fault. I was careless. But the other two? I swear that I gave everything to my paralegal to file. I have no idea how the filing didn't happen. I know she says I never gave anything to her, and maybe I'd be inclined to believe her once, but twice? I've learned my lesson and in the future, I'll either file the motions myself or wait around for proof things were actually filed, even if it means staying in the office all night. I know you have no reason to believe me, but I'm telling you the truth."

"Then why did you father fire you?"

The million-dollar question. "I can't say for sure. I know that he has to look out for his firm's reputation and he can't afford to lose clients." He shrugged. "When your name is on the door, the only way to convince a client a mistake won't happen twice is to fire the lawyer who supposedly screwed up, even if that lawyer is innocent." Or your own son.

"You didn't ask him?"

Adam ran a hand over the top of his head. "My father and I try to keep our relationship in the office separate from that of a father and son. He had to do what he thought was best for the firm in general."

Matthew sat back and twirled a pencil between his fingers. "But if things happened as you say they did, why would this go where it did?"

"Because the paralegals were starting to rebel. They were talking publicly that they were being thrown under the bus. The firm can't function without them, and if they left, it would be hard to hire others."

"And did you? Throw her under the bus?"

"No. I never even talked about it publicly. If I were going to do that, I would have."

"Okay. Look, you know that legally I can't refuse to hire you based on your reputation. So let's look at your experience."

They spoke for the next thirty minutes about cases he'd tried, goals he had and what the firm was looking for. When Matthew rose to shake his hand, Adam got to his feet.

"Thank you for taking a chance and interviewing me," Adam said. "I know it would have been easier to simply pass on the whole thing."

"You seem like a good guy who made some errors in judgment. Let me get back to you in a few days."

Adam left the interview in a better mood. Out of all three interviews, this one seemed the most likely to give him a shot. As he walked to Penn Station to catch the train, he thought once again about Dina. He'd been able to talk about what happened to his potential employer. Why couldn't he talk to her about it?

Because he still was afraid she'd leave. That she'd believe the worst about him. If people who knew him

well could doubt him, Dina would too. And if not immediately, eventually. Especially if he couldn't get a
job.

Of course, he'd left that part out of the interview.
And maybe, if he was lucky and got this job, he could
go crawling back to Dina and beg her forgiveness.

CHAPTER TWENTY-TWO

For the fourteenth consecutive day since she and Adam had broken up, Dina took a walk through Morristown. Unable to stay still for long, lunch breaks were the worst. She'd spend the entire hour staring at the door of the library, expecting Adam to walk in and beg her forgiveness. So she walked, trying to focus on anything—items in store windows, how cold it was when the wind blew, pity for the homeless woman sitting in the green—anything other than Adam.

But today, she couldn't stop her mind from picturing a reunion. She'd be coming out of a store and bump into someone. That someone would be Adam and he'd grovel until she forgave him. Not that she would, but it was nice to imagine. A passing car honked and she jumped, startled out of her reverie. Her stomach dropped—she'd walked up to Adam's office. Or rather, his former office. Spinning around to head the other way, she banged into someone.

"Watch where you're going," a deep voice said.

When she looked up at his face, she blanched. It wasn't Adam. But it was worse. She'd bumped into his dad.

"S...sorry." The smell of his cologne transported her back to dinner at his house, when Adam had been solicitous of her even as he was being humiliated by his dad. Her throat tightened.

He stepped back and frowned. "You're Dina, right? My son's girlfriend."

Oh God, he remembered her. "Sorry for bumping into you."

"That's alright. How are you?"

She nodded, hoping he'd take the action for an answer. "How are you?"

"Very well. I'm on my way back from a client meeting. How's Adam? I haven't spoken to him in a while."

She swallowed, ignoring for the moment the sad fact father and son didn't speak. She wasn't sure she could have this conversation, not without dissolving into a puddle on the sidewalk.

"We're not together anymore."

He ushered her into the lobby of the building and the warm air slammed into her, making her gasp.

"Oh, that's too bad. You were a great influence on him."

She bit her lip. "I have to get back to work."

"You're too good for him," he said. "I knew it from the moment I saw you. I hoped it would work out, that he could change, but I had my doubts."

The conversation would have been awkward if she had still been dating Adam—what kind of father spoke ill of his son to the girlfriend—but now that they were broken up, it was even worse. The physical resemblance she'd noted vaguely at dinner was highlighted now in the harsh winter sunlight. The space their bodies took up was similar and their tone of voice, while not exact, was close enough to make her ache. All she wanted to do was forget Adam, and his father was making her want to defend him.

Her blood pressure rose and her head began to pound. Adam did not deserve defending. Not after the way he'd treated her. How dare his father make her feel this way?

"Adam is a grown man. He's capable of whatever he wants on his own. He doesn't now, nor has he ever, needed me."

With that, she turned and walked back into the cold, but not before seeing a glimmer of admiration in his father's eyes.

Damn them both.

Adam sifted through his email and shook his head. Still no word from any of the seven firms he'd interviewed with. The knot in his stomach tightened. No callbacks, no questions, nothing. He supposed it was better than a rejection, but there was little solace in that thought, since he still didn't have a paycheck coming in and he was loathe to ask his father for a loan. Just the thought of approaching the man made his shoulders ache from tension.

However, if he didn't get a job soon, he might have to. Bile rose in his throat and he swallowed the bitter taste.

Switching gears, he looked on his computer at his bills coming due. He had enough saved in the bank for this month and possibly next, but sweat gathered on his upper lip as he looked at his list of expenses: rent on his "luxury" apartment, his BMW lease and law school loan. Those were the biggies. But then there were his everyday expenses: food, phone, cable and clothes. And others he couldn't think of right now. His friends expected him to socialize a certain amount, and while he'd cut back after his breakup with Dina, they wouldn't let him continue to live the life a hermit for long. Although he didn't need expensive work clothes right now, he still had a look to maintain, especially during interviews. And a guy had to eat. He might be jumping the gun a little, but he was starting to get nervous.

Should he look for a different job to tide him over? It would keep him from having to ask his father for money, but what would he do? Bartend? He'd seen help-wanted signs at plenty of the bars he frequented. The places did great and were always packed, which meant good tips and plenty of work. But it was one thing to be a patron. It was something completely different to work there and let his friends and acquaintances see him. What would they think of him? Temp work? He wasn't qualified for much, and what if he was placed in the office of a former client? God, the embarrassment would be awful.

No, he'd have to wait it out a little longer. If he didn't get a job offer in two more weeks, he'd evaluate his other options. In the meantime, he'd wait.

His ringing phone pulled him out of his worries about the future, until he saw his caller ID. His father. Crap. He was tempted to let it go to voicemail, but the slight, but improbable, chance that he was calling to offer him his old job back made him answer the phone.

"Adam, we need to meet."

Should have let it go to voice mail. "About what?"

"Things I'd rather not discuss on the phone."

Great. A crick formed in his neck. "I'm busy, Dad. I'll give you a call when my calendar clears up."

"No, we'll set something up now. Your calendar can't be that full, you're not working for me and I haven't heard of anyone else hiring you yet."

Score one for good ole dad. "Okay, when?"

"Sunday, eleven o'clock. The house. And don't bring any of your women."

Adam hung up the phone and banged his head against the wall. Just when he thought things couldn't get any worse.

Dina burrowed under the quilt as she sat on the hearth in front of the lit fireplace, hands wrapped around her steaming teacup, and still she couldn't warm up.

"Deen, come back over here," Tracy said, juggling the baby on the sofa. "You're going to catch on fire."

She shook her head and stared into the flames. The yellow edges reminded her of Adam's hair, and tears leaked from her eyes. Dammit, she should be done crying over that jerk.

"Why did Adam's dad upset you so much?" Tracy asked.

Dina had dragged herself back to work after her lunch break and hidden herself in one of the storage rooms for most of the rest of the day. When Tracy had found her, she'd pulled her up and brought her to her house. Joe had taken one look at Dina, grabbed his jacket and left the house, with just a quick kiss for Tracy. Dina didn't want to talk about it, had given Tracy only the barest of details, but she was her best friend and deserved to have her questions answered. With a sigh, she turned toward Tracy.

"Because he made me feel sorry for Adam and I don't want to feel sorry for him. I want to hate him, and I do...mostly."

"I still can't believe he thinks you set him up."

"I know. He was the one who forced me to take him to the stupid reunion. Why would I have resisted so hard if I wanted to set him up?"

"You know," Tracy said, "for a lawyer, he's not being logical."

Dina shrugged and brought the tea to her lips. The liquid burned her throat, but she didn't care.

"And for a guy, he's being a dick."

She sputtered and choked on the tea that was already half-swallowed. Her eyes watered further and Tracy rushed forward to pat her back.

"I'm sorry, I didn't mean to make you choke."

Dina rested her head on Tracy's shoulder and stroked the baby. "That's actually the best thing anyone has said to me since he broke up with me." She played with the baby's feet in their footy pajamas. "I'm angry, I'm hurt, and I want to be allowed to feel those things. But running into his father made me feel bad for him, and why the hell does he get my sympathy? I'm the one who was wronged. I shouldn't care at all what his father thinks of him."

"Would be nice if we could just turn a switch in our brains," Tracy said. "But you're a good person, so of course you care. Plus, you love him."

She swung around to face Tracy. "What? I don't love him." She had thought she did. She'd been trying to figure out the right time to tell him. And then he'd accused her of trapping him and those feelings had died. It proved she hadn't really loved him, didn't it?

Tracy tilted her head and gave her a look like she didn't believe her.

"I don't. I might have thought I did, or could, but if those feelings can disappear when he makes an accusation at me, how true could they really have been?"

"Or, it's because you really do love him that you feel sorry for him. I don't think you'd feel so emotional over a guy you didn't love."

Dina turned back to the fire. It wasn't fair. She'd finally fallen in love—head-over-heels, every cliché ever written about, in love—and it was with Adam. Golden-haired, way above her everything, Adam. And what was more amazing? He loved her back. In fact, since she hadn't had a chance to tell him her feelings, he loved her "first." She should have been giddy. She should have swooned. She should have at least gotten to hug herself. Instead, she'd missed out on everything because of Ashley.

And this was what Tracy chose to focus on?

"You're not making me feel better. So I loved him. Big deal. I didn't even get a chance to tell him or to spend time thinking about how he loved me. It's moot at this point, because he hates me. I'm angry, and he and I are finished."

Tracy put the baby down in her playpen and gave Dina a hug. "I'm so sorry, sweetie. Whatever you're feeling for him is justified. And you're right, he's the one who's in the wrong here, not you. Also, he has no idea what he's missing. His dad is an even bigger ass than he is, so don't let his behavior make you question yours."

Dina's phone rang and Tracy reached for it. "Want to answer it?"

She shook her head no. There was no one, other than Tracy, whom she wanted to talk to.

"I think we need a girls night out," Tracy said.

Dina shook her head. "No, I don't want to go anywhere right now."

"I know that, and I can't with Peanut, here, anyway. But Saturday night you and I are going out. There's a film festival at the university. We'll go and forget all about Adam and his dad."

"Okay." Dina gave Tracy a hug and kissed the baby. Her smell carried her back to the day she and Adam had babysat and she blinked. She was not going to cry. Not again. She would think of something else—anything else—and somehow get over Mr. Flashypants.

Except as she made her way home, something Tracy had said earlier stuck with her. "For a lawyer, he wasn't being logical." She replayed the sentence in her mind, as she got ready for bed. Once under the covers, staring out the window into the darkness, she tried to figure it out. He wasn't being logical, like his profession required him to be. Therefore, his reaction was more personal. She bolted upright. From a personal perspective, Adam was always concerned about his reputation and afraid of what others would think of him.

He'd accused her of setting him up, which aside from being wrong wasn't logical. And he'd know that. So what was he afraid of her finding out?

CHAPTER TWENTY-THREE

By the next morning, Dina still hadn't figured out what Adam was afraid of, but she'd received two more phone calls from the unknown number that had called her while she was with Tracy. Whoever it was hadn't left a message, which meant it was a telemarketer. A very annoying one.

When the phone rang a third time, Dina grabbed it and barked, "What?" as she walked from her parking spot toward the library.

"Dina? Oh I'm so glad I caught you," the female voice on the other end said.

"Who is this?"

"It's Cheryl McAdams. From high school. We were at the reunion together."

"How did you get my number?"

"I asked the reunion chair. Listen, I really need to talk to you and Adam."

Fat chance. "I'm sorry, I'm on my way into work."

"Are you free tonight? We could meet for dinner."

"I really don't think..."

"Please, it's super important. It's about Ashley."

No way. "I have no desire to waste anymore time on her, Cheryl. Please stop calling me."

"Even if she lied?"

Dina caught her breath so hard she choked. Tears flooded her eyes and her nose ran and she dropped her phone into her bag as she rummaged for a tissue. Ashley lied?

Wiping her eyes and nose one last time, she put the phone back to her ear. "What are you talking about?"

"Oh good, you're still there. I heard this horrendous noise and I called and called your name and you didn't answer and—"

"Cheryl!"

"What?"

"Ashley lied? How do you know?"

"Oh, right. Sorry. Yes, but this is too important to discuss over the phone. Please meet me for dinner tonight."

Dina's glance shifted from the library door to her car and back again. If she had to meet Cheryl in person, she wanted to do so now, so she didn't have to spend the entire day wondering about their conversation. Because even if she and Adam were no longer together, her curiosity was too strong for her not to pursue this.

"Okay."

They fine-tuned the details and Dina went into work, confident she'd get nothing done today. She was right. In spades. By lunchtime, she'd filed three books in the wrong place, had looked up the wrong information for her research project and had repacked the books she was supposed to unpack.

Brian, her boss, came up to her as she was searching for her lunch in her bag. "Dina, everything okay today?"

"I'm sorry, Brian. I'm distracted today. I'll get a grip, I promise."

"Everyone has an off day once in a while, but you've been off now more than usual. I'm concerned about you."

She ran a hand through her hair and it caught in her frizz. Wincing, she untangled her fingers and massaged her scalp. "I know. I'm sorry."

As he walked away, she shook her head. She had to find a way to get over Adam. Maybe her conversation tonight with Cheryl would help. She paused, her sandwich halfway to her mouth. Cheryl had invited her and Adam to dinner. Should she call him and ask him if he wanted to go?

No, she'd sound desperate.

But it was about Ashley, who had ruined his life.

Except she didn't know specifically what, other than she lied, which, if she were honest with herself, didn't mean much. She could have lied about anything.

It was probably better to wait until after she met with Cheryl and listened to what she had to say before deciding whether or not to tell Adam. For all she knew, it might not be important, and it was silly to involve him for nothing.

That evening, after an even less productive afternoon than morning, Dina walked into the sushi restaurant where she was meeting Cheryl. It was a favorite of hers, and when Cheryl had expressed a willingness to come to Morristown, Dina had given her the name and location of the restaurant. She was about to give her name to the hostess when movement caught the corner of her eye. Cheryl sat in a corner booth and was waving her arms, trying to flag her down. Gritting her teeth, Dina thanked the hostess and walked over.

Cheryl gave her two air kisses before sitting back down and pointing to the empty seat across from her. Stashing her purse next to her, Dina sat and took the menu from the waitress who appeared at the table, even though she already knew what she was going to order. It gave her hands something to do, if nothing else.

"Oh, you really do look like a librarian," Cheryl said. "It's adorable."

Not quite sure what to make of that statement, Dina nodded. "Did you know Casanova was a librarian?"

"Uh...wasn't he some sort of lover?"

"He was also a scam artist, alchemist, spy and church cleric."

Cheryl looked at her askance and Dina could feel a flush creep up from her chest to her face. Why was she trying to have a conversation with this woman? She had no desire to be friends with her—they were completely different types of people. If she were smart, she'd keep her mouth shut—except to eat—and let Cheryl say her piece so she could leave and be done with this ridiculous dinner.

"I guess being a librarian gives you access to all kinds of information," Cheryl said after a few moments had passed with agonizing slowness.

"Pretty much everything is good here," Dina said. "My favorites are the dragon roll and the spider roll."

"I don't really like eel—too rubbery. Oh, they have California rolls! My favorite!"

And now she knew exactly what kind of sushi "lover" Cheryl was. As soon as they'd ordered, Dina sat back and waited for Cheryl to tell her why they were here. She tried not to fidget, but she couldn't stop her foot from swinging like a clock pendulum on steroids. When the toe of her shoe made contact with something solid, she hoped, for a nanosecond, it was the table leg.

"Ouch!"

Oops. "I'm sorry," she said. "I guess I'm anxious to find out what you wanted to tell me."

Cheryl grimaced as she rubbed her leg through her black wool trousers. "That's okay. Yeah. So, you know how Ashley accused Adam Mandel of not actually giving her the forms she needed?"

"You mean the motion."

Cheryl waved her hands. "Yeah, whatever, the motion."

"Yes."

"Well, she made it up. All of it."

"Why?" Dina leaned forward. "Why would she do that?"

"Apparently, Adam is competing with someone else at the firm for junior partner. The guy—I don't know his name—is nervous because Adam's dad is the head of the firm. And Ashley has a thing for him. So she decided to help the guy by messing up Adam's cases. I guess this isn't the first one she didn't file on time. She mentioned doing it a couple months ago and then again this time."

"Oh my god, I can't believe she'd play with someone's reputation and career like that! You know he got fired, right? From his *Dad's* firm!"

"She's a witch and she cares only about herself and her own interests. Well, and the other guy, although knowing her, it probably won't last."

Dina sat back as the waiter delivered their sushi, but she couldn't bring herself to eat. Her stomach roiled at the destruction Ashley had caused.

She squinted at Cheryl. "Why are you telling me this?" Her heartbeat increased as she waited for her answer.

Cheryl's expression hardened and Dina caught a glimpse of the mean girl she remembered from high school. "She tried to steal my boyfriend."

"But I thought she was into the other guy at the firm?"

Cheryl shrugged. "With Ashley, there's always someone."

If this was the big league, Dina wanted no part of it. She wanted to stay in her own world, where people acted like adults, where girlfriends trusted their boyfriends and vice versa, where communication and not deception solved problems. But she couldn't say that to Cheryl.

Dina picked at her food as Cheryl went into all the evil ways Ashley had tried to steal Cheryl's boyfriend. Dina nodded and made sympathetic noises, but wasn't required to do more, which was good since Cheryl left her little time to speak. Finally, when she took a break to breathe and pop the last piece of the California roll in her mouth, Dina turned the subject back toward Ashley's accusation.

"But why are you telling me this? Why not go to the law firm or even Adam?"

"He's your boyfriend. You should be the one who gets to do it."

Cheryl was being her version of nice to her? Dina wasn't sure if she should be thankful or wary.

"But they're never going to believe me. It's hearsay."

Cheryl grabbed her phone and tapped the screen a few times. "Give me your number again."

"Why?" She bit her lip. She didn't mean to sound as if she didn't want to give it out...well, she didn't want to give it to Cheryl, but she should have hidden her feelings better. Except, Cheryl didn't seem to care.

"Because I'm going to send you a screenshot of a text Ashley sent me."

Dina gave her the number and a moment later, her phone binged. When she opened the text, she gasped.

> Don't forget, ladies, lying and manipulation are the norm in the law profession—I should know!

There was more, but red spots appeared in Dina's vision and prevented her from reading any further. Her anger at Ashley's careless disregard for the truth and for Adam threatened to overwhelm her.

"Hey, relax," Cheryl said, reaching for her hand. "We'll pay her back, don't worry."

Cheryl spent the rest of dinner discussing all the ways she'd paid back different people who had wronged her—her mother for being uninvolved in her life and whom she now refused to visit; her ex-boyfriend who'd cheated on her and whose current girlfriend she mailed old photos to; her old boss, for whom she'd moved around all kinds of files when he'd let her go; and of course, Ashley.

By the time Dina left, she was in desperate need of a shower. She didn't want to be as spiteful as Cheryl and she had no desire to continue any kind of a relationship with her. But if she passed along this information, she'd probably have to see Cheryl again to obtain proof or something. And would she seem like she couldn't let Adam go by bringing this information to his attention? Would she be showing him how much his accusations hurt her and would that be the assumed motivation?

Whatever Dina had expected her rabbi's office to look like, it wasn't this. Pale grey walls with bright white trim, a large window with multi-colored beads instead of curtains, and a glass topped chrome table instead of a desk. White bookshelves covered two of the four walls and were filled with Judaica books, modern textbooks and a variety of other books Dina was itching to explore. Interspersed with the books were modern art paintings and black and white photographs of Israel. The one free wall featured colorful Jewish prints and her rabbinical ordination certificates. The overall effect was one of friendliness and approachability, which shouldn't have surprised her at all. Because the rabbi was friendly and approachable, which was why Dina had requested a meeting with her.

Only now, with the prospect of having to discuss the situation, Dina was having second thoughts. She sat on one of the two raspberry colored leather chairs and clasped her hands together to keep them from trembling.

"It's so nice to see you, Dina," Rabbi Ackerman said, leaning forward and smiling at her. "And I wanted to thank you for the book recommendation you gave me Friday night. I ordered it on Sunday and started reading it yesterday. It's excellent!"

Dina's face warmed and her hands stilled. "I'm glad you're enjoying it. You know, if anyone ever wants to start a book club at the temple, I'd be happy to help."

"That would be wonderful. But I don't think that's the reason you wanted to talk to me today."

Dina gripped her knees before forcing herself to relax. "No, it's not. I have a dilemma I was hoping you might be able to help me with." She outlined what happened with Adam, being careful not to name names, and finished with her conversation with Cheryl.

"My problem is I don't know what to do with the information."

"Why not?" the rabbi asked.

"Because Adam and I aren't together anymore and honestly, after the way he treated me, I don't want anything to do with him."

"I can understand that, Dina. But you know information that will help clear his name."

"He's not under arrest and believe me, these women are so gossipy, that information will get back to him anyway."

"Then why are you here?"

Dina shrugged. "I guess I feel guilty doing nothing. I don't want to be spiteful, but I don't want to come across as this desperate girl trying to get back together with him."

"Do you really think he'd take it that way?"

"I don't know. Women throw themselves at him all the time."

"Did you?"

Dina's mouth dropped. "No. If anything, I tried to avoid him."

"And yet he still went out with you."

Her eyes filled with tears and she blinked them away. "It doesn't matter now."

The rabbi nodded sympathetically. "Look, I suspect you have plenty of girlfriends who can give you relationship advice. How about I give you advice from a Jewish perspective. I am a rabbi, after all." She winked at Dina.

For the first time since she walked into the rabbi's office, Dina relaxed.

"In Deuteronomy, it tells us 'Righteousness, righteousness you shall pursue.' Because the word 'righteousness' is repeated, some say that we may not use unjust methods in pursuit of a just cause. Kind of like the end doesn't justify the means."

"So leaving it to others to allow word to filter back to Adam would be wrong?" Dina asked.

Instead of answering, the rabbi continued. "There's another story, in Leviticus, where Moses chastises Aaron for not following his instructions. Aaron suggests that perhaps Moses didn't quite understand what God told him, and Moses agreed that Aaron could be right. When we study this text, Moses admitting he might be wrong is huge, because if he's misinterpreted God's words here, where else might he have done so? By admitting he's not perfect, he's giving the Hebrews an opportunity to go against him. But Moses realizes that his duty is to tell the truth."

"So I have to tell him."

"I think you do. And I think you knew that deep down."

Dina sighed. "I did. I just kept hoping there was a way around it."

Sitting back in her chair, the rabbi thought a moment. "Well, there is one thing. His father is the one who fired him, right?"

Dina nodded.

"So could you bring the information to his father? Of course, you'd have to be sure his father would tell him; otherwise you'd have to tell Adam anyway and then you'd be exposing a fault in his father to his son, which isn't very righteous."

"His father is many things, but even I can't imagine he wouldn't tell his son the truth."

As Dina left the rabbi's office, she thought about their conversation. Adam's father wasn't the nicest man, but he wouldn't want his company to suffer. He'd want to expose the truth so his reputation would be pristine. All she'd have to do is meet with him, expose

Ashley's lies, and frame it so it was a matter of honor to tell Adam. They'd both win. Adam's father would know the truth, as would Adam, and she wouldn't have to see him.

It was perfect.

CHAPTER TWENTY-FOUR

Dina paused in front of Adam's father's house. Her "perfect" plan might not be so perfect after all. She'd called his father at work and asked to meet with him, telling him she had news to share that was too important to discuss over the phone. Instead of picking a time during the week as she'd expected, he'd invited her over to his house today, Sunday, at eleven o'clock. Reluctant to go to his home, she'd tried to offer alternatives, but he'd been adamant. So here she was. At least she was guaranteed not to run into Adam.

The house intimidated her. The man intimidated her. This lifestyle intimidated her. Every fiber of her being wanted to turn around and leave, forget about what she knew and go back to her cozy apartment to curl up with a book.

But she was righteous and had a duty to tell the truth.

Dammit.

Finding her backbone, she pushed the door chime and listened to it echo throughout the house. Mere moments later, the marble door opened and the same formal woman stood in the doorway. There was no smile of recognition, no welcoming gesture. *I guess hired help is paid to be neutral.*

"Hi, I'm Dina. I'm here to see Mr. Mandel."

"Come in." She stepped back and motioned for Dina to follow her. This time, she wasn't led into the living room. She was shown to a room off of the foyer. Decorated in shades of blue and cream, with white orchids on the table and a small Queen Anne sofa, it had a more feminine touch. Dina sat on the sofa and gazed at the Monets on the wall as some of her nerves dissipated.

"This was my wife's favorite room," Mr. Mandel said.

Dina startled at his silent appearance and rose to greet him. "I can see why," she said, holding out her hand to shake his. "It's lovely."

"My son never sets foot in here."

She did not want to talk about Adam anymore than she had to. "I'm sure it's a reminder she left. Thank you for seeing me today."

He sat in a blue and cream striped wingback chair, across from her and the woman who'd answered the door brought in a tea service. When Dina nodded to the silent question, she poured tea and handed Dina the sugar, before arranging a cup for Mr. Mandel.

When she'd left, Adam's father leaned forward. "You said you had news for me?"

The bone china teacup rattled as she placed it on the saucer and she wished there had been alcohol added to it to steady her nerves.

"I have proof Ashley lied about everything."

"Ashley…?"

"The woman accusing Adam of never giving her the motions she was supposed to file." Did he really not remember who she was?

"You know her?"

"I went to high school with her, although I never knew her, other than by reputation."

"What's your proof? Because I was never able to find out any information. The paralegals in my office presented a united front and defended her."

She told him about the reunion and about Cheryl and Stacie and Ashley and all the rest of the "mean girls." She recounted her dinner with Cheryl and finally, she handed him her phone.

"The screenshots are of texts Ashley sent her group of friends. Ashley is currently trying to steal Cheryl's boyfriend and this is Cheryl's way of getting payback."

"And these girls are your friends?" His disdain showed on his face and even though it was undeserved, Dina winced.

"No, they never were. I didn't have friends in high school. I was too smart to fit in. They used me back then to try to pass their classes and they're using me now to get revenge."

"Then why are you helping them?"

She met his gaze and refused to cower. "Because in this instance, the truth is more important than anything else. I'm not a part of them, I never was. And I'm not participating in their payback. I'm simply passing along information that you need to hear."

"What about what I need to hear?"

The voice made her drop her teacup, which shattered in the saucer and spilled tea on the table before dripping onto the Aubusson rug. Mr. Mandel yelled for the maid, but Dina froze, staring at Adam.

He never visited his dad. That was the only benefit she'd seen to meeting at his house. He wasn't supposed to be here. Her body temperature plummeted before ratcheting up and making her sweat. She opened her mouth, remained silent, and closed it again.

The woman entered with a rag and cleaned up the mess. Adam remained in the doorway, leaning against the jamb, feet and arms crossed. Only the tic of his jaw told Dina he wasn't as relaxed as he pretended to be.

When all traces of the spilled tea were gone, Mr. Mandel settled back in his chair and focused his gaze on Dina, seeming to ignore Adam. If only it were that easy for her.

"Why?" Mr. Mandel asked.

Dina frowned, trying to keep her focus on him. "Why, what?"

"Why are you giving me this information?"

"Because it's the truth. Adam didn't shirk his duties or lie. It wasn't his fault on either of the accounts. She made it up. And with the proof, you can get him his job back."

"What's in it for you?"

The question came from Adam and she had to control her breathing before she answered. "Nothing."

Mr. Mandel was staring at her like she was a brand new species of insect. She refused to squirm.

"Thank you for bringing this to me," Mr. Mandel said. "Can I get a copy of these texts?"

"You can have them. I don't ever want to see them again." She sent him the screenshots and when he confirmed receipt, she deleted them from her phone. "If you'll excuse me, I have to go. Thank you for the tea and I'm sorry about the mess."

As she passed through the doorway, Adam grabbed her arm, but she yanked it away.

"Don't touch me."

"Dina."

Hearing her name on his lips was like a knife through her chest. Without waiting for him to say anything else, she rushed out the door and drove away.

"What the hell did you do?" Adam shouted to his father as he watched Dina leave him—again. Dammit. He'd set this whole thing up so he'd been the one to leave. And now his father had interfered. The familiar hollow feeling filled his chest and bands of pressure squeezed, making him picture an empty bag with a tie around it, slowly squeezing all the air out of it.

"What did *I* do?" his father asked. "There you go again, blaming all your problems on everyone but yourself. Why don't you ask yourself that question?"

His father strode out of his mother's parlor, into his office and grabbed a bottle of scotch off the sideboard. Adam hated this room almost as much as his mother's parlor, except he'd enter this one. He followed his father and watched him pour a fingerful into a Glencairn tumbler and toss it back. He could almost feel the burn in his own throat, but he shook his head. He wasn't drinking. Not until he got answers from his father.

"What was Dina doing here?"

"I believe you overheard at least part of what she said. She told me she had something to tell me."

"And you just happened to invite her over right before the time you'd told me to arrive?"

"Two birds, one stone."

"What the hell is that supposed to mean?" Adam paced the room, too agitated to sit still.

"It means you need to fix things with Dina and she was going to be here."

"I need to...who the hell gives you the right to butt into my business?"

His father loomed over his desk, fists planted on either side of the leather blotter, a frown twisting his face. "I am your father and you are royally screwing up your life. It's high time you settled down and made something out of yourself."

"I was *making something* of myself just fine until you fired me on a whim."

For the first time since Adam had arrived at the house, a look of discomfort passed across his father's face. He'd learned from years of experience, the best way to best his father was indirectly.

"The accusations were hurting the firm."

"The accusations were false, as Dina just proved." He glowered at his father and watched his face suffuse with color.

"I had no way of knowing that."

"Yet somehow, Dina was able to find out?" Adam staggered back. Were his accusations true? Had she really been working with Ashley? "How could she have known, Dad? Unless she was working with Ashley all along." The last sentence came out in a hoarse whisper and he sank into the chair across from his father's desk.

"If you believe that, you're dumber than I ever thought you were," his father said.

Adam remained silent.

"You're kidding me." His father rose from behind his desk, came around and leaned against it, mere inches away from him. "Adam, think about it. Can you really picture her and Ashley working together? This is Dina we're talking about. The girl who spouts obscure facts Ashley wouldn't recognize in an encyclopedia and covers more skin than Ashley ever has in her life. Come on!"

"They went to high school together. Ashley used Dina to get good grades. Who knows what else they've done?" But even Adam recognized the absurdity of his statement. He dropped his head to his chest. "Okay, scratch that. Dina's not that type of woman."

"Damn right. And you owe her an apology for thinking that way."

He was right. "What about what you owe me?"

"I owe you one as well. I'm sorry. I couldn't face the idea of the firm suffering and I let it blind me to how I was hurting you."

His father had never shown this side of himself and Adam rose, sticking his hands in his pocket and shrugging off the unexpected emotion. "It's fine. I'm used to it."

"Adz."

Adam stiffened at the unused childhood nickname. He hadn't heard it since before his mother left.

"Don't let my mistakes ruin your life, son."

"It's a little late for that, when your own father fires you."

His father's gaze bore into him. "I'll take care of reinstating you and making things right at the office. But I'm not talking about your job."

"What gives you the right to think you have a say in anything else?"

A brief flicker in his father's eyes was the only indication he'd scored a hit. "She did come to me with the information."

And that was the million-dollar question. Why hadn't Dina come to him?

"Don't push Dina away, Adam. Not for me, but for you. She's the best thing that ever happened to you. Find a way to make it work."

He couldn't listen to his father anymore. There were too many things zooming around in his head—Ashley and her accusation, Dina, how the hell Dina knew the truth, why she'd gone to his father instead of him, his mother, his father calling him 'Adz.' He needed to get out of this house, where memories threatened to overwhelm him.

Striding out of his father's office, he raced to the front door, but his father stopped him in front of his mother's parlor.

"I miss her too, you know."

The raw emotion in his father's voice struck him like a physical blow. Daring a glance at him, he looked in awe at his father's moist eyes. He couldn't handle his father or the implications of his statement. He had to escape. Throwing the front door open, he ran to his car, gunned the engine and sped down the driveway. The thrum of the engine echoed the racing of his pulse. He hugged the curves in the road, watching trees pass in a blur, knowing he was going too fast but not caring.

When he reached the straightaway, he slowed, taking deep breaths as if to calm his car as well as his heart.

He had to talk to Dina.

Dina lay curled in a ball on her bed, the shades drawn. She'd spent an hour talking to Tracy, or rather, sobbing to Tracy. Her throat was parched, her eyes were gritty and her limbs felt heavy. She had the "Adam Flu." And she was pissed.

He was an ass. There was no reason for her to feel this bad after clearing his name with his father. The truth was supposed to set her free, or some crap like that. It was supposed to make her feel better.

It didn't.

Maybe if Adam hadn't shown up. But he did and the sight of him shredded her heart.

Her intercom buzzed and she roused herself enough to stumble out to the kitchen. Tracy was a sweetheart to come over.

"Hello?" Her voice was hoarse.

"Dina, let me in."

The masculine voice was not Tracy. For a millisecond, she tried to convince herself it was Tracy's husband, but she knew better.

"Go away, Adam."

"Dina, I want to talk to you."

She leaned against the wall. "I don't want to talk to you. Go away, Adam."

"Please."

"No."

She returned to her bedroom and burrowed under the covers as she listened to the intercom continue to buzz. There was nothing to talk about.

After five minutes of near continuous buzzing—she could almost picture him leaning against the button like some crazy combination of debonair movie star and petulant toddler—the noise ceased. Dina raised her head. The silence was disturbing and a relief at the same time. Exhaling, she made herself more comfortable among the light blue and yellow throw pillows and soft white comforter.

And then the knocking started.

"Oh no," she said. "Oh no, no, no, no, no!"

She threw back the covers and stormed to her front door. Through the peephole, she saw Adam. Which of her neighbors was she going to have to kill?

"Go away, Adam!"

"Dina, I need to talk to you. Please let me in."

"No."

The knocking turned to pounding, and as she leaned against the door, the wood vibrated against her back.

"Dina, come on."

"Adam, if you don't stop, I'm calling the police."

Her phone buzzed in her pocket and a text from Tracy appeared.

> are you okay

> adam is here. he wants me to let him in

The knocking ceased and Dina waited, sure it would resume. But after a few minutes, she heard his footsteps recede. Her phone buzzed again.

> I told him to stop

> so did I. how'd you do it?

> I have my ways. do you want me to come over?

> no, I'm okay now

> call me if you need anything

Now that he was gone and her anger had subsided, Dina started to shake. She was tired, hungry, sad and a host of other emotions she couldn't name. She paced the confines of her small apartment, overcome with a desire to leave, which warred with her fear of running into Adam. He'd come to her apartment and managed to get inside. Tracy had somehow convinced him to leave, but what if he were outside waiting for her?

She raced to the window and peeked outside. Neither he nor his car was in view, and she backed away. She had no idea how Tracy had convinced him to leave, but he was gone, and it was time to go back to her own life.

And somehow finding a way to get over Adam.

CHAPTER TWENTY-FIVE

Getting over Adam was going to be a lot harder than Dina expected. The following morning, Dina woke up to four text messages from him.

Dina, it's Adam. can we talk?

please, I really need to talk to you

I know you're angry and I'd like to make it right

Dina, I'm sorry

She turned off her phone and got ready for work.

Tracy took her out to lunch and while they waited in line at the bagel store for their sandwiches, Dina turned her phone back on. Another three messages from him, which she deleted without reading.

"Do you want me to tell him to stop texting you?" Tracy asked.

"I'm just going to ignore them. He'll get tired and stop eventually."

"And you're sure you don't want to hear what he has to say?"

She leveled a glare at Tracy. "Do you have any reason why I should?"

"Nope, just checking."

"Then no. And I still need you to tell me how you got him to leave my apartment."

"I just told him that if he wanted his reputation fixed, getting a complaint filed with the cops wasn't the way to do it."

Dina stared at Tracy for a few seconds. She suspected there was more to it than that, but she didn't have the energy to push. And this was Adam. He was always concerned about his reputation. Besides, she was tired of focusing all her attention on him. She wanted a distraction.

"I want to go to the movies," she said after placing her order. "Want to go with me?"

"Sure, what are we seeing? And when? Because I need to make sure Joe is around for the baby."

"Something funny. I need to be entertained."

"Okay," Tracy said. "I'll have tuna on a blueberry bagel," she said to the guy behind the counter. "Look at what's playing and let me know."

"I can't believe you ordered that," Dina said. "Blueberry with tuna?"

"Don't knock it til you try it. It's really good."

Dina shuddered. "No thanks, I'll leave it to you. And I'll pick a movie tonight and let you know."

As they sat down to eat, Dina's phone buzzed again, and she shut it off.

"You're sure?" Tracy said, eyeing the phone.

"He'll get bored. It'll pass."

"Okay. In the meantime, I should probably plan on only using your home phone to reach you, huh?"

Dina laughed. "For the time being."

The next morning, a pot of basil, tied with a yellow ribbon, arrived for Dina at the library. She frowned as she pulled the card from the envelope.

"If it be a sin to covet honor, I am the most offending soul."—Adam

"Mmm, that smells so good," Tracy said as she walked by. "Where'd you get it?"

"Adam."

"He sent you basil?" She started to laugh. "So he went from stalking your apartment, to texting non-stop, to sending you an herb?"

Dina started to giggle. "It's so strange."

"There has to be a reason. Let me think about this one."

"Trace, there's a card, too."

Tracy's mouth dropped when she read the card. "Did you know he was this odd when you were dating him?"

Dina blinked. "No."

"Don't cry, sweetie. Let's enjoy the game." Tracy picked up the pot and brought it to her desk.

Without the overpowering scent of basil, Dina was able to breathe again and after a few attempts, she focused her thoughts on organizing the children's programs for May. Just when her stomach started to rumble, Tracy returned with the pot.

"I figured it out. He's actually pretty clever, you know."

"Do I want to know?"

Tracy put her hand on her shoulder. "It's up to you."

Dina sighed. "Fine, tell me. Why is he sending me herbs?"

"Not 'herbs,' a specific herb. Flowers and herbs and trees all have specific meanings. Basil means 'good wishes.' Colors do too, and yellow is for apologies. The Shakespeare quote is also an apology."

"Yeah, I got that part."

"He put a lot of effort into this one."

"Still doesn't change my mind." Dina rubbed the yellow ribbon between her fingers.

"I never said it should. Do you want this or do you want me to keep it?"

"You keep it." Memory of all the gold flowers he'd sent her for her reunion flashed through her mind and she shivered. It had been thoughtful, but over the top. And thinking of them made her remember the disaster of the reunion.

"Want to grab lunch?" Tracy asked.

"No thanks, I brought my own today. Besides, I haven't been focusing on work very well and I need to get stuff done. These piles aren't going away nearly as fast as I'd like."

"Okay, see you later."

When she finally left work and returned home, there was another plant outside her apartment door. This time it was a bouquet of carnations. Pink ones, tied with a blue bow. She picked them up and dialed Tracy as she unlocked her door.

"He did it again," she said without even saying hello.

"What did he do?"

"Left me a bouquet of flowers outside my door."

"Really? What kind? Color? Tell me!"

"You don't need to sound so excited about it."

"I'm sorry, Din. I'm putting aside my feelings about him and separating them from my fascination with this game he's playing."

"That's just it, it's all a game to him."

"So have fun with it."

Dina sighed as she unwrapped the bouquet, filled a vase and put the flowers in the water. "They're pink carnations tied with a blue bow."

"Is there a card?"

"Oh, I forgot to look. Hold on." She sifted through the wrapping until the hard edges of a card dug into the pads of her fingers. "Yeah, found it."

She pulled it out of the envelope. "This one says, 'A fool thinks himself to be wise, but a wise man knows himself to be a fool.'"

"Oh, *As You Like It*!" Tracy said. "I love that play! Okay, I'll research the flowers and get back to you. Unless you want to..."

"Nope, all yours."

"Okay, gotta run, baby's crying. I'll call you later."

Maybe it was the basil, but she had a sudden desire for Italian, so she made herself pasta with a red sauce for dinner, along with a salad. She was just finishing up when Tracy called her back.

"Carnations mean 'alas for my poor heart'—kinda dramatic, don't you think? Pink means love, obviously and blue is the color of trust and peace."

"Ha! And I don't mean that in a funny way. He wants me to believe he loves me and that I should trust him? He's insane."

"But creative, Dina. You have to give him that."

"Somehow I think you're silently rooting for him."

"No, but I'm making notes for Joe. He could learn a thing or two from Adam."

"Careful what you wish for, Tracy."

"I know. And I'm looking forward to tomorrow."

"Oh my god, you think this is going to continue?"

"Of course I do!"

"How long?"

"Depends on how long it takes for you to talk to him."

"Oh brother."

Tracy was correct. For the rest of the week, twice a day, Adam sent Dina bouquets. On Tuesday, he sent her chamomile with "No legacy is so rich as honesty" and white clover with "The course of true love never did run smooth." Tracy researched the meanings—chamomile for 'patience' and white clover for 'think of me'—while Dina researched how to make chamomile into tea.

On Wednesday, she received daffodils with a pink bow and "I hold the world but as the world, Gratiano; A stage where every man must play a part, and mine is a sad one." That night, there was a delivery of daisies in pink tissue paper and "Love all, trust a few, do wrong to no one."

Thursday brought ferns and forget-me-nots—obviously he was going through the alphabet, she thought to herself. The cards were getting more dramatic, too. "Love to faults is always blind, always is to joy inclined." She was tempted to send him a text with the rest of the quote: "Lawless, winged, and unconfined, and breaks all chains from every mind" but she didn't want to encourage him. She almost choked when she read the second card, "No legacy is so rich as honesty."

By Friday, when he'd sent her holly for hope and white jasmine for sweet love, she'd had enough. Especially when she read the cards, " Now, God be praised, that to believing souls gives light in darkness, comfort in despair" and "O God, O God, how weary, stale, flat, and unprofitable seem to me all the uses of this world!" Creativity was one thing, but she was starting to think he was mocking her.

Later that night, she was sure of it.

"Jake, it's not working." Adam paced his apartment and ran his hand over the crown of his head. When Dina had refused to answer his calls or his texts, he'd called Jacob in desperation and told him everything. His advice had been to woo her. So he'd spent the past week wooing her and still she hadn't called.

"What have you tried?"

Adam filled him in.

"You need to apologize to her, Adam."

"I would if she'd talk to me."

"Then you need to force the issue. Unfortunately, you've given her the message you don't trust her. That's hard to overcome. You've shown her you want her back, but you need to show her why."

Adam swallowed. "She knows I want her back. What more do I need to do?"

"You need to open yourself to her." Silence stretched across the line. "She's not your mom, Adam."

His breath hitched and his stomach dropped to his knees. "I know that."

"Do you? Because it sounds like you pushed her away before she could leave you. And you haven't done anything to convince her that was a mistake."

"I sent her flowers. And herbs. With meanings."

"Which she probably understood because she's brilliant. So you've appealed to her mind. But you need to appeal to her heart, Adam."

"Her heart? I don't even know how she feels about me." He'd told her he loved her, but she'd never responded.

"Then ask her."

"And what if I don't like the answer?"

"At least you'll know. Knowledge is much better than fear, Adam. Trust me. And her."

Adam hung up the phone and continued to pace. He didn't know if he could do that. Trust her? He'd trusted his mother and she'd left him. Jacob might say Dina wasn't like his mother, but how could he be sure? He passed his bookshelf, where a photo sat of his mother, holding his four-year-old self on her lap. They both smiled for the camera. He picked it up and examined it. The gold frame had intricate designs on it and the swirls somehow reminded him of Dina's apartment, which was weird, because nothing about the apartment was similar to his mother's decorating style.

She had loved perfectly matched antiques, orderliness and calm. Dina's apartment was boho chic, with mismatched everything that somehow coordinated and conveyed warmth.

His mother's smile didn't reach her eyes. When Dina smiled, you knew she was happy. Her nose crinkled, her frizzy hair vibrated and her eyes shone. Her entire body softened.

Had he ever made his mother happy? He assumed so. She hadn't been a bad mother. She just turned into an absentee one. But he remembered them playing on the swings, making bubble people during his bath time, snuggling together when she read him a story. He also remembered trying to impress her so she'd stay longer—she was always having to go somewhere or do something and he would beg for one more story, show her one more amazing rock he'd found or ask for one more hug. But she'd always left soon after.

With Dina, he never had that underlying fear. When he was with her, she showed how much she liked being with him. He never worried about having to impress her or begging her to stay. He never wondered if she'd let him see her again.

Dina and his mother were completely different people. And it was time he gave her what she deserved. His trust.

CHAPTER TWENTY-SIX

That night, after watering the white jasmine, she'd rushed to get dressed and raced to temple. Walking in five minutes late, she tried to slide into her seat unobtrusively while the rabbi was reading one of the opening prayers. A movement to her left caused her to look up just as Adam slid into the seat next to her. Her mouth dropped.

"What are you doing here?" she hissed.

He leaned forward, pulled out the prayer book and opened it to the correct page. Handing it to her, he reached for another book for himself before answering her.

"Attending services."

"I don't want to talk to you."

He looked over at her and held her gaze for a moment. "Then don't. It's rude to talk through services anyway."

God, he was infuriating. She'd move, but that would call attention to her and to him, and she'd already walked in five minutes late.

For the rest of the service, Dina couldn't focus on anything but Adam—his proximity to her, his smell, his deep voice slightly off-key. When they *davened* in prayer and bowed before the ark, she noticed the tips of his shoes, highly polished, like him. When they stood, his shoulder brushed against hers, as if he knew how hard it was for her to be away from him.

When the service finally ended, he turned to her. "Shabbat Shalom, Dina."

It was the traditional thing to say to each other on Shabbat. It would be rude not to respond.

"Shabbat Shalom, Adam."

He turned and walked out of the sanctuary and into the social hall for the oneg. She followed him, despite her desire to make a run for it. Unfortunately, Rebecca and her family weren't here tonight and the rabbi had seen her, so if she left, it would be obvious. She sighed and took her cup of wine to say the prayers. When they finished, Adam took her empty cup and threw it away for her, even though she hadn't asked him to. After the prayer over the challah, the rabbi walked over to her.

"Hello, Dina."

"Shabbat Shalom, rabbi."

Adam leaned forward. "Shabbat Shalom, rabbi. I'm Adam."

The rabbi looked between the two of them. "Nice to meet you, Adam. I think I've seen you here before with Dina?"

Dina's cheeks heated.

"Yes. She's angry at me right now, and we're not together, but I'm hoping to change that."

Dina couldn't prevent her jaw from dropping.

The rabbi's eyes twinkled with amusement. "I like your honesty," she said, with a wink at Dina. "But perhaps you should be talking to her instead of me."

"I intend to," he said, pinning Dina with a look that promised he'd get his way. "But in the meantime, I'm waiting."

"Going to be waiting a long time," Dina muttered under her breath.

The rabbi chuckled. "Well, as it says in *Pirkei Avot*, 'Do not be contemptuous of any person, and don't remove yourself from anything, for every person has his moment and everything has its place.' Good luck, Dina."

The rabbi walked away, leaving Dina and Adam alone.

"I don't appreciate your speaking about me to my rabbi," she said to Adam, looking straight ahead and counting the stripes in the wallpaper on the far wall. Anything to avoid his gaze.

"You used to not like when I kept our relationship quiet," he said. She could feel the air around her constrict as he took a step closer to her, an almost physical charge zinging between his chest and her arm.

"I am not getting back together with you," she said, opening and closing her hands at her sides as she wished for something to do with them, other than strangling him. There were too many witnesses.

"I just want to talk to you."

"You already are. And I'm not interested in having a conversation with someone who doesn't trust me."

"Then I'll wait," he said and took a step back. A coolness wrapped around her like a shawl, and for a brief moment she wanted to pull him closer to her. But that would be ridiculous. Because she was still angry at him.

A man Dina recognized as someone from Brotherhood approached.

"Hi, I'm Dave," he said to Adam and held out his hand as he nodded to Dina. "Welcome to Temple Tikvah. Are you interested in Brotherhood events? We have a breakfast coming up in a week."

Adam shook Dave's hand. "Oh yeah? That sounds great. I'd love information about it. I'm Adam Mandel, by the way, a friend of Dina's."

"Nice to meet you. Dina, the breakfast is actually open to everyone, if you'd like to join us."

She plastered a smile on her face. "Thanks, I'll think about it."

As Dave walked away, she stalked to the door. This was ridiculous. She couldn't take any more of it.

Adam rushed to keep up with her, his long legs making it easy.

"Leave me alone, Adam. You've had your fun."

He jumped forward until he could block her way. She thought about skirting around him, but he folded his arms and looked at her like he'd like nothing better than to pick her up and dangle her in the air if she tried to get away.

"I'm not having fun, Dina. I'm trying to apologize. But you won't let me."

"No you're not. You're trying to make an impression—with me and those ridiculous flowers, with my rabbi and with everyone at my temple. But what you don't get is I'm not interested. I'm done. So you need to stop and leave me alone."

She removed her heels and ran out of the synagogue, leaving Adam in the shadows.

On Monday, Adam passed the library on his way to his father's office. He shook his head as he remembered Friday night in the synagogue. For a man who'd refused to allow a woman to ever walk out on him again, he sure was failing when it came to Dina. Because she'd walked out on him twice so far.

Each time she left, the invisible bands around his chest tightened. And this latest time had left him with the knowledge that not only wasn't there anything he could do about it, most likely, he was going to have to suffer through it several more times, because as he'd said to her rabbi, he was hoping she'd come back to him and he was going to be patient. And you didn't lie to a rabbi.

He parked his car in the parking garage, in the spaces designated for visitors to his father's firm and swallowed the bile the rose in his throat. His father's secretary had called him to this command performance, in a suit, no less. He pulled on his blue silk tie before readjusting it in the rearview mirror, left his car and took the elevator up to the firm's floor. There was no need to give his name to the receptionist, but he did anyway. There was nothing stopping him from walking in like he belonged—except he didn't. So he waited for direction and tried to keep his toe from tapping or his fingers from fiddling with his tie.

A moment later, his father's secretary opened the door. "Come on in, Adam. Your father is in the conference room."

Adam followed her down the warren of hallways to the glassed-in conference room. At the head of the teak table was his father. Seated around the table were the senior partners and standing behind them were the partners and junior partners. Adam swallowed as his throat went dry. When she opened the door, there was no other recourse than to enter. James was there as well.

Great, I've been invited to watch James as he's given the junior partner position. Thanks, Dad.

He leaned against the wall, hoping not to be noticed.

His father rose and the room grew silent.

"About a month ago, a former paralegal claimed—for the second time—that my son had not given her a motion to file. Two different cases, two different outcomes, neither of them good. Despite my son's protests otherwise, she swore he'd never given her the material. She also said he was throwing her under the bus. As a result, the entire paralegal department banded together in her defense. She had a plausible story, he had a problematic reputation and while there was no way to verify her claim, there was no way to refute it, either. And so I, as the head of this firm, fired my son. I put the well-being of this firm above my love for my son," he paused and cleared his throat before continuing, "something for which I will be forever ashamed."

Adam's pulse pounded in his ears. It was the only sound, as the rest of the room was silent.

Noah looked down, before raising his head and meeting the gaze of everyone in the room. When he reached Adam, he paused, nodded and continued.

"It took another woman, my son's ex-girlfriend, to make me see the error of my ways. In the process, she provided proof—proof I should have been able to find—that Adam is completely innocent. His accuser made up the story in order to try to get another man in this firm the promotion, and hopefully, to get him interested in her."

Adam staggered and reached behind him to hold onto the wall. His father had just admitted a mistake to everyone in this room.

"Prior to the accusations, both Adam and James were being considered for junior partner. The accusation, and his subsequent dismissal, removed my son from consideration. The accuser's retaliation included poisoning other firms against my son, making it impossible for him to find another job."

Everyone turned to look at each other, and Adam saw the shock on their faces. A few, who noticed him, looked sympathetic. Some, like Paul and John, who had avoided him, looked embarrassed.

"As of today, we are suing Ashley Peters for slander. We are taking out a full-page ad in all the major law publications refuting the charges, standing behind Adam and restoring his reputation. I will be asking Adam for a list of all the firms he's submitted résumés to and will personally call their managing partners to explain the situation. Then Adam will have a choice. He can return to work here as a junior partner—James, you will keep your new title as well, however you will be on probation because of your ties to Ashley—or he can work for any other firm he chooses. The choice will be his. But should he choose to rejoin us, he will be welcomed by all with open arms."

One by one, everyone in the room began to clap, until the sound of hands together was deafening. Those who were seated, rose. Those who knew Adam was in the room turned toward him and eventually, everyone was clapping at him. He bowed his head until the room silenced. Then, he walked to his father.

"You and I have had our differences over the years," he said, " and I suspect we will continue to have them. But it takes an honorable man to publicly admit when he's wrong. I appreciate what you've said, and I'd be happy to accept the position of junior partner here. However, as much as I owe my father respect for what he has said today, I would not be here if it weren't for Dina Jacobs. She believed in me from the very beginning, even when our relationship was new and she could have easily walked away and assumed the worst. But she didn't. And after we broke up, which was completely my fault, she had a choice. She could have kept her knowledge to herself, written me off and forgotten all about me. But instead, she went to my father. Now, as I'm sure all of you have figured out, my father isn't the easiest man to confront."

A smattering of laughter met Adam's remark and he smiled.

"But she didn't let him intimidate her. She went to him and told him of his error, and she did it in a way that made him listen to her and even believe her. I'm sure most of you will believe me when I say that's not an easy thing to do. But she did it."

He looked at his father and for the first time saw admiration—for him.

"My father's biggest regret might be not believing in me, but mine is not believing in Dina. You all gave me a standing ovation welcoming me back. My wish for my time here is not only do I continue to remain worthy of your welcome, but I continue to learn from you all—to believe in people and to give them second chances. Thank you."

En mass, people crowded around him, shaking his hand and congratulating him. Everyone said he had guts to make that speech. Most said they'd always believed in him, even though he knew they lied. A few apologized and those were the people he valued in the office. But the one person he wished more than anything could have heard him wasn't here.

And she was the only one who mattered.

Dina sat in the waiting room of her doctor's office, passing the time on her phone while waiting for her physical. She scrolled through social media, updated Goodreads and moved on to Instagram. With the waiting room packed, the doctor was already behind, and Dina moved on to Reddit.

And stopped.

One of the highlighted videos caught her eye. It was Adam, speaking to a crowd. She stared at it. His father was next to him. The video had been liked several hundred times.

She should ignore it. Who cared what it was about?

She did.

She pressed play, lowered the volume and held her phone to her ear.

Tears streamed down her face.

This man who was so concerned about his image was confessing to everyone he worked with what a horrible person he'd been to her. She wasn't there, he wasn't doing it for effect. He was simply owning up to his mistake publicly.

And there was nothing simple about it.

She replayed it two more times, trying to find something to dislike about it. But there was nothing. Of all his gestures—the texts, the phone calls and the ridiculous number of flowers and herbs—this was the one that got her.

And she could no longer ignore him.

CHAPTER TWENTY-SEVEN

Adam sank onto the sofa after work and turned on the baseball game. Outside, noise from the street below was muted, but he could hear the low bass of passing cars and the higher tones of the commuter train as it slowed on its way from Manhattan. It was the train line he would have taken if he were working for a big Manhattan firm, but he wasn't. He was working for his father again, and this time, he was happy about it.

Opening a diet soda with a pop and a fizz, he gulped the carbonated liquid and leaned his head back on the leather cushion. He'd put in a twelve-hour day at the office, working through lunch and not leaving before seven. After the warm welcome he'd received the other day in the conference room, his friends at work had accepted him once again. In fact, everyone had, even the paralegals. Sure, there were still some people who kept their distance, including James, but they were in the minority now. And professionally, he was satisfied.

As the game went to commercial, an ad for a Manhattan law firm appeared, and he thought about where he might have ended up if things had been different. And for once, he didn't have some deep desire to be in the city. Now, looking at the commercial, the law firm seemed cold and impersonal, whereas it used to seem to be the embodiment of his professional dreams. But that all changed once his father backed him up.

Had he really been so desperate for his father's approval? He shook his head. They still had a lot to work out, but knowing his father supported him meant a lot. Now if only he could fix the hole in his heart.

He looked to the side. If he had his way, that part of the couch would not be empty. Dina would be sitting there. Of course, if she were, they probably wouldn't be watching baseball...or maybe they would? She'd never been selfish enough to prevent him from doing what he liked, and she'd always tried to join in. He remembered the books she'd given him on superheroes and how he'd initially reacted to them. He'd been so consumed with what others thought, he hadn't recognized the gesture for what it was—someone who was thinking only of others.

God, he missed her. He'd spent weeks trying to get her back, to show her he was sorry, to demonstrate how much he cared. And she'd refused all of his overtures. His hands chilled and sweat beaded his brow.

How was he going to get her back? If he thought he'd been afraid of her leaving him, it was nothing to knowing she wasn't coming back.

His efforts hadn't been good enough. He'd lost her.

He took deep breaths, trying to control his heartbeat. He would be okay.

The knock at the door startled him and he splashed soda out of the can as he rose. He took a peek through the peephole, blinked and looked again.

He opened the door.

"Dina." There were so many things he wanted to say, but the sight of her, here, on his doorstep, left him speechless. Her beautiful frizzy hair was pulled back into a low ponytail. A pink scarf gave her cheeks a rosy glow. And the scent of coconuts filled the air, making him want to fold her into his arms and inhale her.

"Adam. I hope you don't mind my just showing up—"

"Not at all. I'm glad you're here." Her expression was wary. He'd never seen that expression in them when she looked at him and his chest ached. After everything he'd done to show her how much she meant to him, she still had doubts? If only she'd been in his father's office to hear his speech.

He stepped out of the doorway and motioned her inside. She followed, not touching him and leaving a margin of space around her, like a personal "Do Not Touch" zone. The Dina he remembered had never done that before.

Leading her into the living room, he pointed to the couch he'd vacated, imagining his wish of her sitting next to him coming true. But she sat across the coffee table from him, as if she needed the physical barrier between them. Bands of pressure tightened around his chest.

"Sit down," he said. "Would you like something to drink? Eat?"

She shook her head no, making her curls bounce, making Adam's fingers itch to touch them. He sat on his couch on top of his hands and stared at her, drinking her in. There were so many things he wanted to say to her, and he didn't know what to say first. It was as if all the words he wanted to say rushed from his brain toward his mouth at once, couldn't all fit, and sat behind his lips, trying to jam forward and getting stuck.

"I heard what you said," she said, gripping her fingers until her knuckles turned white.

What he'd said? When? Where? He wracked his brain trying to figure out what she meant. Oh, his phone calls.

"You mean the messages I left on your voice mail."

She bit her lip. "No. I deleted those."

The bands around his chest grew tighter. He cleared his throat. "Oh. The texts?"

She shook her head. "No, I still have those, but I meant the video."

Oh God, there's a video? Images of Kardashian sex tapes filtered through his mind. What the hell had he done? "What video?"

She pulled out her phone, tapped on the screen and held it out to him. His breath expelled in a whoosh of relief, before he inhaled sharply, making himself choke. Dina half rose as if to help him, but he waved her away, rubbed his streaming eyes and sat back on the couch. "Where did this come from?"

She shrugged. "I found it on Reddit."

Only now did her earlier words sink in. *I heard what you said.* Never mind where the video had come from, she'd watched it.

In his head, he knew that admitting he'd been wrong was the right thing to do. It was honorable and honest and some might even say, brave. And although he'd chosen to do it in a roomful of people he worked with, it had been easier than one would think because Dina wasn't there. He'd only had to say his side of the story. She hadn't been there to respond or reject him.

But she was here now. He should be thrilled because he'd been trying to talk to her for weeks without success. Her showing up at his apartment was unexpected, but meant she wanted to talk to him too. His heart pounded and his throat went dry. He reached for his soda and took a long swallow. God, what he'd give for a beer right now. But he'd been overdoing it lately and the last thing he wanted was to blow this time with Dina. So he focused on her and tried to calm the bouncing ball of fear in his chest.

"That was quite an apology you gave," she said.

"I meant every word, and more."

"Why did you tell them? They don't know me."

He leaned forward, resting his elbows on his knees. "My dad made this big speech about me. About how I was innocent. And about how you were the one to prove it to him. He was honest, and I felt I needed to be too. Including about how badly I'd treated you and how sorry I was. Because I wanted a fresh start. And I couldn't have one unless I told them everything."

She rose and he opened his mouth to stop her from leaving. But she was only pacing and he kept his gaze trained on her, ready to jump up and block the door if she left, or better yet, fall to his knees and beg her to stay.

"I don't understand what happened the night of my reunion. One moment, those women were telling me ridiculous lies, the next moment you shut down and then you accused me of being in collusion with them."

Collusion. God, he loved her. Even if she didn't love him back. "Those 'ridiculous' things were accurate." At her look of surprise, he held up his hand. "No, I didn't lie about giving her the material to file. I didn't throw her under the bus. But the women were right about the personal stuff. Before you, I never committed to anyone. "

"I know."

Now it was his turn to look shocked.

She laughed. "Come on, Adam, your personality, at first glance, screams player. I'm sure you've done plenty of things with plenty of women before me. I don't care about any of it, as long as it happened *before* me."

He swallowed, afraid if he spoke, he'd pop whatever bubble there was supporting this fantasy and fall splat back into reality.

"What I do care about is everything else," she said.

He ran a hand over his head. How could he possibly explain this to her? He'd show all his insecurities at once. Taking a deep breath, he took the plunge. "We were dancing and I told you I loved you and you didn't reply." A squeak made him look up and he held up a hand. "No, don't. It's fine. You didn't have to say it then, or at all for that matter. I didn't tell you because I wanted you to say anything. I told you because it's what was in my heart and I wanted you to know. But then the accusations started and I saw you with them and I didn't know what they'd told you. And knowing my reputation, I was afraid you'd believe them."

"I never knew her, never liked any of her friends, and no reunion is going to change that. I'd never believe them over you. They mean nothing to me."

"I know that now, but I panicked."

"Why?"

"Because I was afraid you'd leave me. I was so twisted up inside over my dad firing me, I let it bleed into my relationship with you. I'm so sorry."

"You should have had faith in me. And if you had doubts, you should have told me."

He nodded. "I know. I knew you weren't really with them. I accused you of being on their side because that way I could leave you first."

"Why?"

He nodded. "You're the first person I've ever fallen in love with. I mean, really fallen in love with. Dina, I love everything about you—your hair, your smile, the way you don't take me too seriously, your vocabulary and the crazy facts you know. All of it. And it terrified me. Because I was afraid when you knew the whole story about Ashley, you'd leave. It was okay you didn't tell me you loved me—I had time to change that—but if you'd walked out on me, it would be the second person I'd loved who'd done that and I couldn't have lived with it. So I left first."

"You didn't think I'd believe you if you told me the truth?"

"My father didn't."

"Your father is an ass."

Adam laughed. "I used to think so too. Now I'm not so sure."

"And I'm not your mother."

Adam froze. "What?"

Dina moved onto the couch next to him, exactly where he'd wanted her to sit when she'd first walked in. Only now he wished she were anywhere else. His heart pounded in his chest and the bands of pressure squeezed so hard, spots flickered in front of his eyes. He didn't want to talk about his mother.

His hand grew cool and he looked down to see Dina's hand covering it, her thumb stroking across his knuckles.

"I'm not your mother. And her leaving had nothing to do with you."

"You don't know that."

"No, I don't. Only your father does, and he could probably give you the answers you're looking for. But I do know that children are never the cause of their parents' problems. Whatever her reasons for leaving, it was not a lack of love for you."

Adam gripped Dina's hand. "I have this irrational fear that if I let go, you'll disappear, like when Darth Vader killed Obi Wan." *Oh God, tell me I didn't just say that.* What was it about her that made all his defenses shut down? She'd think he was a coward, a geek coward, which might be even worse. He let his head fall forward, not wanting to see the laughter in her gaze, laughter that would be directed at him.

"Hey," she said, her voice low and thoughtful.

When he raised his head, her mouth was serious, her gaze somber. She cupped his cheek with her free hand. Her skin was soft, smooth and cool, providing another touch point he didn't want to lose, and he covered it with his other hand. "You can hold on for as long as you'd like. I'm not going anywhere, even when you let go. And I'm not going to turn into any Force ghost."

The bands of pressure in his chest loosened and calm settled over him for the first time in as long as he could remember. He let go of the hand on his cheek and pulled her close, inhaling the coconut scent of her hair as he tried to keep his breathing steady.

"I love you," she whispered against his ear.

He pulled away. "You don't have to say it. I don't deserve it."

She stroked the side of his face. "I've wanted to say it for weeks, but I was scared. And then when you said it to me at the reunion, I didn't just want to prattle it back to you like some talking parrot. My feelings mean too much for me to do that."

"Why?" When she frowned, he hurried to continue. "No, not why do your feelings mean something. Why would you possibly love me after the way I treated you?"

"Because I can see through you. I see who you are inside." She touched his chest and he wished for her skin to touch his. "I don't care about the rest of this—your money, your looks, your job, although I'm glad you have one because it makes you happy and everyone needs to make a living. But that's not why I love you. I'd love you if you were a janitor on a bicycle."

The image made Adam laugh and he hugged her to him, kissing the part in her hair. After a moment, he grew serious again. "But after the way I've treated you?"

She pulled away and he tamped down the automatic fissure of fear. She was still here. She said she wouldn't leave. He had to believe her.

"I hate the way you treated me. You forgot who I am and what about me makes you love me, and while you're very good at apologizing, that can't happen again. I can't be with someone who doesn't trust me, and I won't be with someone who thinks so little of me they'll drop me anytime something gets hard."

"How do I fix this? Because you mean more to me than anyone and I don't ever want to let you go."

Dina bit her lip and Adam wanted to draw her into his arms and hold her close. But he'd learned he had to give her freedom, trust her to come back to him, even on the little things, like pulling away from him to think. So he sat and he waited.

"You showed me you're sorry and what I mean to you by your calls and your texts and the flowers and herbs that all had meanings behind them."

"I'm glad you understood it."

She smiled. "Tracy helped at first. Then I caught on. It was impressive. A little over-the-top, but impressive."

He nodded.

"And you showed me you're not embarrassed by me with your speech to your co-workers."

"I never expected it to go online," he said.

"You've given me more than enough reasons to forgive you, and I do. I think I need us to take things slow, to talk and to see how things go from here."

He nodded and they sat in silence for several minutes. Their only contact was the touch of their hands. Adam concentrated on the way her skin felt against his. Although her hands were perpetually cold, her touch sent a path of warmth up his arm, straight to his heart. The apartment was silent, except for the sounds of their breathing and the hum of the refrigerator in the background, and he had the urge to mingle more than the sound of their breath.

"Would kissing you be moving too fast?" he asked, glancing sideways at her.

Her hair swung as she shook her head, and it was all the encouragement he needed. Wrapping his arm around her shoulder, he threaded his fingers through her hair as he drew her head toward him. Their lips touched, their breath mingled and at last, he was where he belonged.

When they finally pulled apart, she stared at him. "You know," she whispered, "I might be willing to compromise on the speed."

He bent his forehead until it touched hers. "Whatever you want, for as long as you want, I will be yours and you can be mine."

And it was enough.

The End

Acknowledgements

I can't believe I actually have to say this, but this book was written by me, not some AI bot or whatever. A reader's time is too precious to waste.

.

About Jennifer Wilck

Jennifer Wilck is an award-winning contemporary romance author for readers who are passionate about love, laughter, and happily ever after. Known for writing both Jewish and non-Jewish romances, her books feature damaged heroes, sassy and independent heroines, witty banter and hot chemistry. Jennifer's ability to transport the reader into the scene, create characters the reader will fall in love with, and evoke a roller coaster of emotions, will hook you from the first page.

You can find her books at all major online retailers in a variety of formats.

Jennifer started telling herself stories as a little girl when she couldn't fall asleep at night. Pretty soon, her head was filled with these stories and the characters that populated them. Even as an adult, she thinks about the characters and stories at night before she falls asleep or walking the dog. Eventually, she started writing them down. Her favorite stories to write are those with smart, sassy, independent heroines; handsome, strong and slightly vulnerable heroes; and her stories always end with happily ever after.

In the real world, she's the mother of two amazing daughters and wife of one of the smartest men she knows. She believes humor is the only way to get through the day and does not believe in sharing her chocolate.

To learn more, go to http://www.jennifer-wilck.com